IN THE SECRET STATE

ROBERT McCRUM was born in Cambridge and educated at universities in England and the United States. He has travelled widely in Europe and the Far East and now lives in London, where he works as a publisher. *In the Secret State* is his first novel.

ROBERT McCRUM

IN THE SECRET
STATE

Fontana/Collins

First published in 1980 by Hamish Hamilton Ltd
First issued in Fontana Books 1981

© 1980 by Robert McCrum

Made and printed in Great Britain by
William Collins Sons & Co Ltd Glasgow

For Olivia

'Your idea of secrecy seems to consist in keeping the chief of your department in the dark. That's stretching it perhaps a little too far, isn't it?'

Joseph Conrad, *The Secret Agent*

CHAPTER ONE

Later, when he had the loneliness to worry the events in his mind, Strange remembered the blind man rapping through the fog towards him. That was wrong. Funny that the routines should snap only at the end.

On most mornings, as he struggled up out of the yellow shadows of the Westminster Underground, the white stick was in front, tapping uncertainly towards Whitehall. But today there was fog, and the blind man lost in it, confused by an unexpected throng of commuters coming at him out of the grey weather.

As Strange strode unevenly past the news stand towards him he recognized the urgent blundering of one who has suddenly lost his bearings. For an instant he saw his father's last sightless days in the nursing home, and might have paused for a word of help, but they had never spoken before, and his curiosity sent him hurrying past into the damp blur, breathing hard.

He found himself stuck in a jostling crowd. 'They've blocked Whitehall,' someone said, helpfully. 'It's no good. Go back.' A man in a grey mackintosh said, 'There's no need to shove,' but Strange pressed forwards until, suddenly, at the corner of Parliament Square, the crowd thinned. There was a congestion of motorists thickening the early autumn air with fumes and hooting angrily at the delay. Two white police motorcycles stood propped on the pavement, but the men, sweating in black leathers, were out in the stream of traffic, diverting the flow. So Strange slipped round the corner unnoticed and disappeared into the mist.

He met nobody; nobody followed. Just past Derby Gate there were crash barriers across the road, and a policeman, whistling 'Rule Britannia', was on duty.

'Excuse me,' said Strange with a slight belligerence. 'I want to get to work.'

'Sorry, sir.' He was very young. 'Orders are to re-route unauthorized personnel.'

Strange shifted his weight and glared. 'What the hell does that mean?'

'I don't know, sir. It's orders, isn't it?'

'Whose orders?'

'The Chief's.'

'What chief? What are you talking about? What's going on?'

'No disclosure to unauthorized personnel,' he quoted. 'Are you from the press?'

'D'you see this? That's an official pass.' Strange lingered on the words. He prodded the yellow photograph. 'Look here, young man, I've had one of these since before you were born, and I've walked to work every day since I joined, and if I can't bloody well do so on my last day here then this country is worse off than I thought it was.' The policeman stared at him but said nothing. 'What's happening up there?' Strange repeated.

'Incident sir.'

'An incident! This is a bloody siege. Are you expecting the Soviet tank corps?' The man looked at the pass again, and then dragged the barrier aside without comment. The noise alerted the senior officer drinking coffee in a rearby Range-Rover. There was a loud hailer and a whistle on the seat beside him but he shouted anyway.

'Authorized personnel,' answered the duty policeman. 'Have a pleasant retirement, sir,' he added, dropping his voice. But Strange was already crossing the tarmac. He waved his pass at the Range-Rover. 'Frank Strange. Director, C Directorate.'

The officer looked up with interest. So that was Frank Strange. 'Okay, sir,' he said.

Strange walked on alone. The roadblock had silenced the usual hum of Whitehall. The imperial stone of the departments of state loomed large and dumb and, at this

8

early hour, largely unlighted, like cold cliffs at dawn. Strange strode on with purpose. He was always first at work. No sign of any incident. Jumpy lot these days. Probably a smash between a couple of lousy service drivers.

Then, very faintly, he saw a blue light flashing through the mist and caught the familiar squeak and chatter of the short-wave radio. Moving faster, he drew level with the open space at the back of the department. There was grey grass, the trunks of some trees vanishing upwards, and white tapes.

But there was no panic. The figures he could now make out passing to and fro, in and out of sight, in the enveloping obscurity, were not hurrying, but moving methodically as though they had a rehearsed part to play.

'For God's sake, Strange, what are you doing here?'

'Going to work,' he replied with forced mildness. 'I see I'm not the first.' He knew the face, he thought, but couldn't recall a name or even a committee. Another section. But the officer was annoyed. The last thing anyone wanted just now was a chap like Frank Strange involved. He'd be the first to ask a dozen awkward questions. What authority? Whose instructions? But here he was, bulky in his gabardine, a tall fellow with a friendly but angular expression that was intensified by the forward thrust of his shoulders. His lame, early-morning struggle up Whitehall had given him a slight flush – or was it a warning of anger that burnt high on the tired grey cheekbones? Strange was known to be put out by the hint of difficulty, made stubborn by it often, but he was also, to look at, a man from whose features some long-distant suffering had removed all arrogance. As always his inquisitive eye, roving the scene, seemed to miss nothing that was out of place. The blue stare could sparkle with humour, but it was also one to put people on their mettle.

'Clear out, can't you? This is our pigeon!'

Strange recognized the man's apprehension. 'I'm not interfering,' he appeased.

Not yet, thought the officer, and said, 'I thought you'd gone anyway.' Strange made a small joke against himself. 'They're teaching me to retire gracefully.'

'You're having a party?

'Afraid so.'

'Enjoy yourself – and push off, won't you?'

Strange held his ground, discreetly. The blue light was an ambulance, parked at the kerb with its doors pinched open, and the monotonous flashing fitfully illuminated the nearby statue of Sir Walter Raleigh. Men in white coats were hurrying into the cordoned area beyond the pedestal. There was a tree there, a plane. Whatever it was they had closed Whitehall for was at the foot of the tree.

It could not be a bomb. There were too many people, department personnel, fussing round the thing. Then quite suddenly four men were carrying a sheeted stretcher, running or almost running with it to the ambulance, which now, as the driver started the engine, began to wail.

Strange limped up the pavement towards the circle of sudden activity. He recognized some more faces but they were too preoccupied to notice his intrusion.

The men with the stretcher came up too fast across the grass. A tall Service doctor, backing out of the ambulance, collided with one of the front bearers in the rush. The man stumbled and cursed, the others staggered slightly, the stretcher lurched sideways and the sheet slipped. Strange took three quick steps forward involuntarily and stared. The hanging face was lifeless but so familiar, and there was pain scored across it like a scream.

CHAPTER TWO

Guy Preece was thinking that Frank Strange was the only man in the department who could start a row on his last day at work. When he was angry, Strange's genial but business-like manner became prickly and aloof. He fired questions like an examiner and with a slight tilt of that iron-grey head that suggested a profound suspicion. Now he sat at his desk, his coat shrugged off behind him, harassing his successor with objections. Room 5B was otherwise bare. The emptiness of the place gave Preece no relief from Strange's belligerent stare. The books, pamphlets, postcards, old newspapers, posters and bits of souvenir china that had accumulated to give this underground bunker in the Old War Office a famous air of clutter were now packed away in cardboard boxes behind the door.

When Strange was transferred to take over the running of C Directorate almost a decade ago and selected this gloomy basement as his HQ, his staff complained about the shabby, airless conditions. But as soon as Strange became celebrated in the department for his reforms a certain Churchillian status fastened itself to his unusual system and there was *kudos* to be had in working within earshot of his busy subterranean office. Earshot was the word. Strange hated internal telephones, preferring merely to bellow, exploiting the cavernous cellars, for secretaries, coffee, subordinates, and memoranda. But now, as he listened to Preece defend himself, he was quiet with suppressed irritation, leaning forward, drumming heavy fingers on the empty desktop, a slight frown accentuating the heavy contours of his expression.

'Frank.' Even Preece's studied reasonableness was being tested by Strange's refusal to compromise his authority. 'You must understand that it was done – or not done – in good faith. I – we – didn't want to bother you on your last day. I can only offer my apologies. If I had thought –'

'Quite apart from the security aspect,' Strange broke in crossly, 'I should have thought that it was common courtesy to let me decide how to run my own office.' He looked sharply at his wristwatch. 'When did you say you discovered the – ' he gestured helplessly, unwilling to bring himself to describe the wrecked body on the stretcher.

Preece looked across the room. He became uncharacteristically laconic. 'The police rang Michael,' he replied evasively.

'You mean Hayter?' Strange was old school about names. Preece nodded efficiently, anxious, it seemed, to avoid elaboration. 'Well,' admitted Strange, 'at least that was by the book. And then Hayter rang you?' He knew it was a pointless question. The deputy-controller had pushed hard to get Preece promoted to his job, once it was known he was going. Hayter and Preece were recognized allies in the department, while his relations with Hayter, technically senior, were always uneasy, a cold war limited by a common adherence to the rule book.

'Yes,' Preece went on, 'Michael said he knew of course that he should contact you, but that it was unfair to trouble you on the eve of retirement. He asked me to deal with the situation as director-designate.'

Strange thought, I'll bet he did, and said, 'If you'll allow me, er, Guy, that palaver out there this morning will have the whole of Fleet Street beating a path to our door by midday.'

'With respect, Frank, we made our dispositions precisely to avoid that. We didn't know what had happened to him, or what the circumstances were or anything. And the police know their instructions: they're not to interfere with Directorate personnel. I was taking precautions.'

'For a screwed-up nobody like Lister?' The sudden intrusion of the dead man's name and Strange's sarcasm silenced the discussion for a moment. That was only half true, thought Preece, flicking dust from his lapel. Dick Lister was a difficult customer, but he was a computer expert who had an awkward way of getting things right. Strange himself regretted the remark at once. He knew he couldn't write Lister off as a nonentity, but the man had got under his skin. He remembered Lister's hunted look, furtive and anaemic, the scrags of wispy hair, Lister's maddening eyes that seemed to dart everywhere at once, and the chain-smoking he detested. Never mind that people said he was a damn good software analyst, not for the first time that morning Strange told himself that Lister had got what he deserved.

Ever since Lister had arrived at the Directorate he had been a nightmare. But now he had killed himself and all the temper and self-pity and moodiness fell into place as the symptoms of a disordered life heading for oblivion. The tragedy and its very location was a bitter reproach, and Strange felt it all the more keenly for having disliked the man. Now it was up to the Directorate to hustle the body to the grave.

'Have you fixed the inquest?' he said aloud.

'This afternoon,' Preece replied quietly. 'The HQ Security people are in touch with the coroner. The usual emergency procedure. Welfare are coping with the family.'

'Good.' Strange sighed. 'Well, we'll have to risk it now, and hope that no one asks any awkward questions. Not enough clues to go on anyway – only the inquest – that'll be a straightforward "balance of mind" verdict of course – ' Strange was thinking aloud as he often did, ' – can't imagine anything – no obvious motive – harder heart would have sacked sooner – but you never can tell.' His concentration focussed. 'Since I do consider myself in charge here still, I shall handle the rest of the matter myself, please.'

Preece was glad the recriminations were giving way at last to something positive. 'I can only repeat, Frank, that we were trying – '

'Yes, yes, you've said that three times already. Very well.' He looked towards the door. 'James!' Strange's familiar shout echoed beyond the room and when James Quitman appeared his fixed stare softened. Everyone in C Directorate knew that he liked this young man, as he would say.

Quitman was tall, fair and relaxed, with an easy, slightly surprised expression, that in concentration could also suggest great seriousness. At thirty-two he looked young for his age, a fact that never bothered him, partly, perhaps, because in many respects he was mildly contemptuous of the seniority rituals of his colleagues. He was intelligent but not overbearing, resourceful but not immodest. His friendliness was not a mask of ambition; he seemed unusually detached from the work of the Directorate and in some quarters this was held to be a virtue. Others, like Preece, for whom it was a stated article of faith that their work was of national importance, could not understand such an attitude and consequently disregarded Quitman's considerable grasp of the Directorate's functions. Some knew that Quitman had once, six years ago, hankered after a university career, and it is true that he often had the uncertain manner and rumpled tidiness of a student at a tutorial sherry party. Strange trusted him completely.

'Good morning, James.'

Quitman greeted his old and new boss impartially. The voice was hesitant and refined. Strange waved him to a hard chair 'Sit down and listen.' He began to outline the Lister case, relishing, it seemed to Preece, the problems created by the suicide and the special security precautions. 'The inquest is this afternoon,' he concluded.

'Now,' he said, turning to practicalities, 'if the press discovers that Lister was a computer specialist, they'll draw the obvious conclusion from all this hullaballoo that he was involved in top secret work. Before we know where we are there'll be a dozen Big Brother editorials and every investigative reporter worth his salt on the story. So I want you to liaise with the press office boys, James, and lay a false trail. Familiarize yourself with Lister's file – you'd better get on line to Personnel straightaway – I'll give you password clearance – and prepare vague, evasive answers to any enquiries. It's not a line I like to take, but –' he paused to stress the point, 'we've no option in the circumstances.'

Quitman wondered what his new master was making of all this. It was highly embarrassing, a direct snub to Preece. He had studied him surreptitiously while Strange was speaking and he glanced at him again now before he replied. The chilly elegance of Preece's appearance – the pearl grey suit, the immaculate creases, the budding handkerchief, the grey silk tie flecked with blue, the Ferragamo shoes – was an unconscious insult to Strange's English dowdiness. But then there was always something indefinably foreign about Preece. People said that, perhaps because they distrusted his rapid, seemingly effortless, rise within the Directorate.

Preece always looked out of place in Strange's territory, but he was never ill-at-ease. His own office, on the floor above the Directorate's computer installation, was upstairs, with a view of the river, carpeted, with full-length curtains and a discreetly modern painting behind the desk. There he was in an appropriate landscape. But wherever he was, Preece commanded the verbal formulae of a career bureaucrat now in his middle forties and functioning superbly. His smooth brown features betrayed nothing.

Quitman said: 'Suicide is a notorious puzzle of course, but is it appropriate to ask if there is any indication of motive – if that's the word?' Quitman considered that Strange was perhaps the last person to be sensitive to such minute vibrations, but said it anyway for Preece's benefit.

Strange reacted with uneasy sharpness: 'None to do with the department, thank God, that we can think of.' Quitman noticed that Preece nodded in agreement. 'It's a clear case of a personal breakdown,' said Strange. 'You have to admit it was almost to be expected. I blame myself there.'

Quitman could recall Lister's controversial manner only too well. 'Yes,' he said quietly, 'it's a great shame, but an inevitable one perhaps.'

'Of course,' Strange went on, brushing past the personal issue, 'he obviously wanted to maximize our embarrassment. And succeeded.' He gave a sideways look at Preece.

The new man protested. 'Frank, it won't be *that* difficult.

It's just a case,' he went on, turning a reasonable glance to Quitman, 'of doing what we've done a thousand times –'

'Yes, yes,' Strange was impatient at this interruption, 'you know the drill, James: harmless classified stuff that won't give us away. C Directorate's never been in the news. Let's leave it that way, hm?'

'I imagine,' said Quitman, with tact, 'that you'll want a report on the case for the Directorate before you leave.' He laid stress on Directorate as a way of affirming loyalty to Preece without neglecting Strange's authority. He hoped it would soothe the embarrassment of this meeting.

Strange was unexpectedly enthusiastic at this suggestion. 'That's an excellent point, James,' he said, heaving on to his good leg with a sigh. 'Well, it will give me something to think about down in Devon when I've finished pruning the roses.' But there was none of the usual warmth in his laughter. Preece was silent. He seemed, Quitman noticed with alarm, to disapprove of the report. 'Now if you'll both excuse me I've got to start my round of farewells.'

The uneasiness lingered even when Strange had lumbered out and Preece and Quitman were left standing uncertainly in the empty office. 'He's very angry,' said Quitman, by way of explanation. 'It's a terrible blow to him on his last day, with his particular record.'

'But why?' Preece sounded cruel. 'He hated Lister.' For the first time that meeting he began to give vent to his opinions. 'Isn't it a relief to Strange that he's dead?'

'That's why he's angry. He knows people will make that sort of comment.' Quitman managed to speak without reproof. 'He's ashamed of his hostility towards the man. It made him vulnerable.'

Not for the first time Preece found himself thinking that Quitman was too subtle to be an outstanding officer. And he looked as though he had slept in that suit.

'You're being very prissy with another man's reputation, James.' He gave a placating laugh, thin and meaningless. 'It's a good thing Frank is going. You'd end up as his valet if you weren't careful.'

16

'Are there any other points *you* would like to make re Lister before I start?' said Quitman, moving towards the corridor.

Preece noted the change of conversation. Charles Neve would have wanted to gossip about all the circumstances. 'I'm sure I can trust you to use your discretion,' he said blandly.

That's enough rope to hang myself, thought Quitman. 'We must hope that no one decides to be awkward,' he said aloud.

'You can make his work sound very dull if you have to. Dwell on the personal tragedy.' Preece became animated. 'Talk about the pressures of the war against subversion and the enemies of the state. Make it sound a patriotic death. There's truth there.' They were moving towards the outer part of the bunker. The shadows lightened as they reached the foot of the stairway. Quitman stopped. 'One other thing: can I have today's incident file for background?'

Preece checked visibly. 'The incident file?'

'From this morning.'

'It's nothing to do with us. HQ Security will have it. But you won't need it. All the essentials will be on the personal file. Strange's briefing was thorough as usual.' Preece was turning to go. 'There's only one thing,' he added, staying Quitman with a light almost familiar touch. 'Frank didn't mention it. It's too obvious I suppose. You've got a privileged password, so you must keep the work confidential. You know our rule: Only what you need to know,' and he made deft emphasis with his index finger on Quitman's sleeve.

CHAPTER THREE

The computer room was at the heart of the Directorate. This was literally true, but Quitman always felt, as he passed through the double white automatic doors into the brilliant, shadowless world of the third floor, that he was entering the Directorate's mind as well.

The sense of power beyond ordinary human command was almost tangible. Grey metal racks storing tens of thousands of miles of magnetic tape stretched in long, mute rows, floor to ceiling. The tick and whine of teletype and disc-drive answered remote electrical impulses; the atmosphere was always cool and antiseptic, and the fluorescent light that glared night and day with a faint persistent hum was almost painful. Only the plastic bins of discarded computer output betrayed the presence of error and the possibility of human intervention.

Lister's file, in common with all the Directorate's records, was stored on the computer. Once Quitman's red security card had given him access to the computer room, and a special user ID had logged him on to the central databank at its secret undergound location, it was not long before the record of Lister's past, as it was known to the Directorate, was being conveyed in high-level computer language to the visual display unit in front of him. As an administrative rather than a technical officer, Quitman was not a trained programmer, but he had been given the standard course in basic computer access methods and interpretation which was indispensable to his work. A routine programme would recall all the details that he needed.

Quitman was still working at the VDU when the internal desk phone rang. Charles Neve, his colleague in their section of the Directorate, was reminding him about Strange's farewell party. Quitman looked at his watch. 'I'm up to my ears in data. Two minutes while I log off.'

Quitman released the sliding doors to the third floor access corridor and stepped back into the shabby, shadowy world of the Old War Office. 'You'll not be missing the party,' commented the security guard. 'Of course not,' he replied. The assumptions that were made about his rapport with Strange irked him sometimes. He took the lift to the basement to find his colleague.

Charles Neve threw down the newspaper as he came in. 'Where have you been?'

Neve was completely the creature of the Directorate. He had a sallow expression that was almost bloodless in the artificial brilliance of the computer room, pinched and anonymous in the ochre light of the other offices. For him the internal affairs of the building composed a self-contained world, isolated by secrecy, an absorbing drama in which the working lives of the Directorate's personnel dominated the action. To Neve, even the most trivial action on this shadowy stage was imbued with the deepest significance, and it was his invariable habit to enquire into its hidden meaning. Quitman had already caught a note of preliminary anxiety in Neve's greeting and knew that he was going to be cross-examined. Nothing for Neve could ever be taken at face value. He lived in a maze of rumour, misrepresentation and obscure motive. Unlike Quitman, he was obsessed with his promotion prospects.

'Sorry, Charles. I got rather absorbed.' Quitman liked to tantalize.

'What was so fascinating?'

There was a click and the office went dark. Neve raised his voice. 'Generator, someone?' But the surrounding offices had emptied for the party and there was only a faint echo.

'Where's the torch?' asked Quitman. Neve groped in the desk. The batteries were losing power with regular use. In a thin grey pencil of light they stepped carefully out into the main corridor, ominous with central heating, ventilation and electrical systems running along the low ceiling, and made for the main stairway. The sound of the party muttered in the distance.

'Some celebration,' Neve commented as they climbed. 'Preece in charge, Strange retiring inexplicably, Lister dead.'

'Come off it, Charles. Preece is a top man, and there's no mystery about Strange's retirement. None of us ever liked Lister.'

'Lister never liked you, you mean.' Neve was getting into his stride.

Quitman coughed diplomatically. 'Really.'

'He distrusted you because you were part of Strange's outfit. Strange had his knife into him for months.'

'That wouldn't drive him to suicide, Charles. Not even Strange on the warpath could do that to a man.'

'Though he obviously wanted to embarrass us all, if you know what I mean.'

'Not exactly.' Quitman was guarded. He recognized Neve's fishing tactics.

'You know that Lister's body was found out there in Whitehall, don't you? I know everyone's being typically cagey about the whole thing, but I thought *that* was common knowledge.'

'Oh yes. I did hear that.'

'From Strange?' There was something pathetic about his addiction to gossip. Quitman looked at him in the half light of the stairwell.

'As a matter of fact, yes.'

There was a suppressed but unmistakable note of triumph in Neve's eager supplementary: 'What did he want with you this morning? I heard him bellowing for you as usual, like the Minotaur.'

'Oh. One or two chores.' Quitman was aware that he had been bullied into betraying a minor confidence. He made a joke against himself. 'Preece says that if Strange stayed any longer I'd end up as his secretary. He's probably right.'

'When did he say that?' Quitman ignored the question. Neve turned to him bluntly. 'Why *is* Strange retiring early?'

'He won't discuss it.' Neve's disappointment suggested

disbelief. 'Scout's honour, Charles. I think he's fed up with Hayter. He doesn't believe he can achieve any more now. Anyway it's only a year or two early and the Government is trying to make the department less top heavy.'

'Nothing to do with Lister?'

Quitman stared at him. 'Good God, Charles. That is devious. No. Frank would never allow himself to get into that sort of situation. I take it you mean that Lister committed suicide to escape some threat that Strange should have known about.'

'That's one interpretation.'

'Haven't you got your timing wrong, Charles? Strange's retirement was announced weeks ago.'

'I was only speculating. Lister knew more about our secrets than most. Why did he kill himself if he wasn't vulnerable in some way?'

'Why does anyone commit suicide? I've never noticed anything dubious about Lister, though once you start thinking about it . . .' He hated the paths of Neve's mind, and counter-attacked briskly. 'For what it's worth, Strange would disagree with you. Apparently, Lister's private life is a mess. That's his explanation.'

'He told you that?'

'Yes.'

'Today?'

'That's right,' he replied with irritation. Neve would be furious if he discovered that he'd been given the Lister report and press liaison duty. 'I asked him, as a matter of fact.'

Neve's laugh was sarcastic. 'Breaking the rules on his last day at work, eh?'

'What do you mean?'

'Well, did you need to know?' Neve's question was victorious. Quitman, trapped, could only lie.

'No,' he said.

They turned the corner, and Strange's leaving party was on them in a hubbub of conversation. One or two people said, Ah there you are, have a drink, and Quitman found himself holding a warm beaker of plonk.

'You're late, James. You missed the presentation.' Rosie Walford, one of Strange's secretarial staff, came up to him with a paper plate of tired salad. To the resentment of the debs in the registry and typing pool, Rosie made up in looks and ambition what she lacked in education and background.

'There was a black-out. We were delayed.' Quitman explained.

'Here too. As he was speaking.'

'How did it go?'

'He was a bit overcome, actually.' Rosie pointed at the plate. 'Eat up. All my own work.' Quitman took a dutiful mouthful, carefully balancing the wine on a slice of beetroot. Rosie was standing so close that Quitman could not help noticing her perfume. She was shouting at him over the noise. 'Why's he going, James? We're all dying to find out. You know him better than most of us.'

Quitman swallowed furiously. 'Rubbish,' he insisted.

'Go on.'

'I'm sure he just wants to enjoy his retirement, I really do.' He looked over at his boss. Strange was at the centre of a circle of staff who were admiring the new watch and teasing him about retirement. 'You'll reform the garden, won't you, sir?' Strange shook with pleasure. 'I'll have to do a time-and-motion study of the birdbath,' he joked. Laughter. Quitman recognized the element of excitement in the happiness. No one had ribbed Strange in public for years. Strange played his part with banter and the laughter raced round the circle.

Across the crowded room, bright with tipsy office faces losing inhibitions, Preece was talking to Neve about the future. Many people suspected that the new boss had his eye on Neve. '. . . the really valuable assistance to counter-subversion that the Directorate ought to be giving is hampered by this kind of incident,' he indicated Lister's suicide with a precise gesture.

'Do I gather,' Never cut in, seizing his chance to air a suspicion nourished by his recent talk with his rival, 'that James Quitman has one or two responsibilities there?' This was also a reproach. Neve was technically senior to Quitman.

Preece was unruffled. 'Strange is using Quitman for one or two minor duties associated with the case. He relies on him, as you know. I had no say in the matter, unfortunately. Strange's great weakness is that he no longer understands the technical sophistication of the Directorate. The wonderful Strange system has been left behind by computer science. So he surrounds himself with mediocre personnel from the administrative grades like Quitman. It's time the director of this organization exploited its potential. I intend to do so, I assure you.'

Neve was delighted with this confidence. 'I suppose the security agencies will try to use Lister's death against you,' he prompted. 'I mean, it doesn't look too good, does it?'

'Exactly. Strange's inheritance, despite his reputation round here, is rather a poor one. At least Hayter knows the truth and will give us a chance to display our expertise in counter-subversion. He believes in our systems.'

'More Chateau Whitehall, gentlemen?' Rosie Walford splashed their cups full. She was doing her best on behalf of the pool to find out all about the Lister story, rumours of whose suicide ran like a sullen whisper among many conversations. Rosie stared provocatively at Neve. 'You're a friend of James, Charlie, perhaps you can tell me the full story,' she remarked with mischievous ambiguity.

Neve looked helplessly at Preece. 'My lips are sealed,' he joked.

A shadow passed across Preece's face. 'There is no full story,' he said.

'And you're not supposed to know about it,' said Neve, blundering into the ambiguity.

'But – ? Oh. You mean poor Mr Lister?'

Preece steered the conversation with skill: 'Frank Strange is retiring because he wants to. He's had a distinguished career and wants to enjoy his retirement.' Preece seemed irritated by the conversation, but before Neve could do anything about it, the director-designate had moved away.

'Such a shame that this should happen on his last day. It's a shock to us all,' Rosie persisted.

'Particularly as Strange is leaving us holding the baby,' said Neve, angrily watching Preece's retreating figure. Rosie was wondering how to tease the gossip out of Neve without the promise of intimacy. She found his pale, slightly stooping figure (as though his back was specially hunched to catch the dandruff) unattractive, and his inquisitive manner boring, which was in some ways odd because, like him, she lived for the secrets of the office.

The party was getting weary and drunk. As the musty cheap wine sank in the litre flagons the atmosphere became coarse and speculative. Lister was the topic. Nobody cared about Strange any more. Soon it was rumoured that Quitman had all the facts, but he was talking to Michael Hayter, the deputy-controller.

Hayter was much as Quitman remembered. In his club tweeds and heavy shoes, a horny hand fumbling with a briar, he wore the permanent air of the gentleman farmer up in town for the day to lunch with his stockbroker. He was in fact a brigadier, a detail that, during the recent kidnappings and bombings, was no longer advertised. Hayter, like many who served during the last war, divided the world into allies and enemies, for and against what he would call 'civilization'. He believed that most of his allies were to be found inside the department and that 'the threat' lay increasingly in Britain at large, but most especially in Eastern Europe. He was active in his efforts to find keen supporters of this view among the younger staff, which was why he favoured Preece. Hayter was well-known in Whitehall for his view, expressed in an injudicious newspaper interview, that 'democracy as we know it has reached the end of its tether in the West'. Though he would have been horrified at the suggestion, Quitman thought that he most resembled a Prussian junker in his manner, appearance and opinions. Now he wrenched Quitman's hand with native vigour and broke at once into his customary military bark.

'You've got a problem with Lister, right?' Hayter spoke

24

with such command that it was as though he not Quitman had been poring over the VDU.

'Yes, sir.'

'Right. You won't win, you never do with the press, but for God's sake don't lose. Too much at stake here to afford to allow Fleet Street to play merry hell with our outfit.'

'I quite understand, sir.'

'Sorry about Strange?' The question was shot out unexpectedly. Quitman felt the eyes, lurking beneath peppery brows, fixed on him.

'It is a blow on his last day, a real blow. He's taken it hard.'

'You know him well, I believe.'

'He's been very considerate towards me, taken an interest in my work, my career even.' Hayter said nothing. His strong blue eyes were watching Quitman. 'You see,' said Quitman filling the noisy silence, 'I have no family, no parents. I was orphaned long ago.' It sounded old-fashioned. 'Frank has been very kind to me. And I admire his work.'

'As we all do,' said Hayter with magnanimity. 'First Strange, now Lister. Sudden gaps and lots of opportunities.' He spoke like an advertisement. Then, thrusting the pipe into his jacket, he clapped his hands together, 'Well, back to work. Adapt to the new régime, Quitman. Mr Preece is a first-class administrator. To be frank with you, there has been something of a question mark hanging over your future in the Directorate. I shall be watching your work keenly. I attach a very great deal of importance to the handling of the Lister case.' Quitman watched him carve a dignified passage to the door, and then, since he had to attend the inquest shortly, went to say goodbye to Strange himself.

They were making arrangements for Quitman to send a copy of his report on the Lister case to Strange's London flat when Rosie Walford, flaunting her most winning expression with tipsy recklessness, took Quitman by the arm to interrupt the conversation. She had been having a thorough gossip with Neve.

'Come on, Jamie – sorry, Mr Strange – everyone knows

you know about poor Dick Lister. Do tell us the story.' She giggled. There was a stain of lipstick on her parted teeth; her breath was coming hot and stale with garlic and she moved in a fresh cloud of perfume.

'I – I don't know what you mean.' Quitman looked at Strange nonplussed. Strange was staring at the girl in a fury.

'Come on Jamie, Dick Lister committed suicide out there, didn't he? Everyone's saying he was being blackmailed. What *will* you say to the press?'

Strange was already turning on his good leg, thumping his stick-butt on the carpet. 'Neve!' he shouted. The conversation in the crowded room faltered. 'Neve, here! James,' he ordered, 'get this woman out of here. This is disgraceful. Get her downstairs to the lavatory.' Rosie was hustled to the door through a silent crowd. Strange, flushed with fury, turned to his staff and colleagues.

'Today has been soured by a personal tragedy that, in the interests of the department and Richard Lister's family, should receive the least publicity. I can only say that speaking for myself it has been a cruel blow that I shall never forget. Now I am going back to my office to collect my papers. There is nothing more to do – or say. You are all welcome to visit me in my retirement. Thank you. Goodbye.' He turned and limped out of the room amid complete silence.

When the long day of Frank Strange's retirement came to an end, Quitman, who had a small flat in Barons Court, left the homebound District Line tube at Gloucester Road and to clear his head, walked down the Old Brompton Road to Fulham to see Liz Sayer.

The morning fog had become low cloud, bright with the hint of sun, at midday, but now the light was fading. He hurried along the filthy streets. Decay and disinfectant was on the wind and there were rats picking at the guts of black plastic bags of rubbish piled on the pavement. He passed the hospital on the corner. Dirty lavatory paper fluttered on the cemetery railings next door and there was a mother pushing a pram between the graves.

Liz answered the door wearing his towelling bathrobe, reminding him that although he said he didn't live with her he did. Liz was demanding, uncertain, ambitious, and rather attractive. She was always experimenting with her hairstyle. Today it cascaded on her shoulders in henna-stained curls. She worked easy hours for a PR company in Covent Garden and was, apparently, very successful. Her company Cortina, still wet from the car-wash, stood parked outside. Liz's pert brown features spoke of poolside idleness in the sun. Quitman was always amazed at her burgeoning wardrobe, and on Thursdays he had to get away early to avoid a confrontation with Byron, her visiting hairdresser.

'Hi there.' There were empty glasses in the room. 'You missed Rami.'

'I'm sorry.'

'He brought that crowd from Fagin's. D'you remember? Sebastian and Amanda and Jeremy, Robin and Juliet. They're so amusing.'

'Yes,' said Quitman, without enthusiasm.

'Rami's very encouraging about the agency, and says that he knows a black American rock musician called Washington who's written this terrific novel . . . You're not listening.' He was lounging on the sofa, his feet on the table among the cocktails.

'I'm sorry. I've had rather a day, that's all.'

'You mean too much to drink at Strange's party. How did it go?'

'Fine.' He didn't want to talk about it. But Liz was always inquisitive about his work, especially when she spotted reticence.

'You're going to miss him, aren't you? Strange I mean.'

'Well, at least I knew where I stood with him.'

'Oh come on, Jamie. You told me he was fond of you.'

'Frank was an old-fashioned bachelor. He had his protégés.'

'What's his successor like?'

'I think he dislikes me.' He yawned. 'It's going to be an awkward match.'

Liz's mind was running on ambitiously. 'You could always transfer. You should think of that, you know. I met someone only the other day who said –'

She broke off when he sighed. 'I may be forced to transfer anyway,' he said, and recounted his conversation with Hayter. Liz became suddenly excited. 'But Jamie, can't you see? Gaps, opportunities, we shall be watching you closely! He must have been hinting at promotion.' She had an acute need for her lover's success. It pleased him to tease her for it. His steady grey eyes seemed very grave. 'That's not my interpretation. If you want to know I think he's greasing the skids. It's my fault. I'm too much part of Strange's reign.' He sounded almost proud. 'If I'd wanted a secret future I should have distanced myself. *Tant pis!*'

Liz was exasperated. 'Don't you care about anything?'

'What do you mean, of course I do,' he reacted with sudden vigour. 'I – I care about you, and about Frank. And I care about chivalry of course.' Not a day went by when Quitman didn't think of his study of medieval court life. 'What I don't get uptight about, thank God, is who I work for.' He sat up. 'Can't we talk about something else. I'm exhausted. Can't you save your interrogation –'

It was her turn to get angry. 'What's got into you, Jamie? Aren't I allowed to take an interest in your life?'

'All right, all right,' he said. 'Read that.' He threw the newspaper across and got up to fetch himself a drink from the table. Liz spread the page out.

'Death in Whitehall?'

'Yes. Thar was pretty fast bowling, as they say. It was quite an achievement, though I do say it, to hold the story to a single column on page five. You know how the press likes to hammer the mandarins.'

'Who was he?'

'An engineer. No one special.'

'Why did he do it?'

'No idea. Things got too much for him I suppose.'

'What things?'

'Oh – just things. We're still investigating. I see we're out of gin, shall I pop out and –'

Liz threw the paper down. 'Look, I know you've had a busy day but can't you make the effort to talk to me? You're so boring sometimes I wonder why I bother to stay with you.' She had stood up and was knotting the dressing gown coldly but, he thought, as he put his drink down and went over to soothe her, since it reached below her ankles she looked ridiculous anyway.

'I'm sorry. I'm angry too.' She gave him her familiar interrogative stare. 'You see it was so hard on Strange. On his last day. He's taken it very hard. There was a terrible row.'

'What happened?'

'One of the girls got drunk at lunchtime and started saying wild things about the suicide. It was very unprofessional but it didn't really matter as far as I could see. Of course Strange lost his temper. He's such a stickler for form, you see. If you didn't know him you'd say it was puritanical.' He shrugged sadly. 'Then he went off into a lonely retirement.'

'Won't you see him again?'

'I'll try. Of course I will. He invited us all to visit him when we're in the area but I doubt if anybody will dare. He's a difficult man, too honourable for ordinary people. He makes them feel uneasy, unworthy somehow.' Quitman paused, serious with concentration, and realized then how upset he was for his old boss. 'Lister's death stung him very deep, though to see him at lunchtime you might not have guessed it. He bottles things up.'

'Was it his fault?'

'Lister?' She nodded, serious for him. 'Well, it's easy to say it with hindsight, but he *should* have noticed something building up. For some reason in the last two or three months he's lost his grip. A year ago even Hayter – that's the deputy controller – would tread carefully dealing with Strange. He used to have the place jumping. Not any more. He lost his flair somewhere. Now he's gone – in a cloud of mystery, but gone anyway. The place will seem empty without him.' He smiled to himself. 'Of course it's typical Frank that he should leave with a bang like that.'

'Perhaps,' said Liz smiling back, happy to have broken his mood, 'You'll find that the bang has an echo.'

CHAPTER FOUR

Strange was driving west, gunning his car down the motorway, while the mad autumn wind buffeted the old Volvo and the monotonous road mesmerized his thoughts. The wild Saturday sky echoed his own mood like a polemic.

He was so angry that Rosie Walford shared his suspicions about Lister. But far more infuriating was that scene with her. It threatened everything. He found it hard enough to forgive himself for letting Lister slip through his fingers, but how stupid to give the game away with a row. Blackmail, she'd said. What did blackmail mean? Someone getting his claws into you. Why? Because you were vulnerable. How could Lister be vulnerable? Because he was corrupt. He was too insignificant for there to be any other explanation. That was his own conviction. God knows, he had cause enough to believe it. But he wanted to fathom Lister's past alone, secretly, to hug the revenge ro himself.

Yet with the nagging anger there was also the exhilaration that Lister's suicide gave him something to go on at last, and with his own retirement no distractions from it either. Like the sudden blip on the empty radar screen, the body under the trees in Whitehall had emitted a signal that wanted decoding.

He was going to do that. He was going to expose Lister's secret activities if it was the last thing he did, and he wasn't going to have any hack journalist queer his pitch for him first. All right, so he did seem to be leaving the department under a cloud with an unexplained suicide on the doorstep, but when he uncovered the true picture he reckoned the honours would be even.

Damn Rosie Walford. It had all been going so well. He'd distracted Preece nicely. He'd made it abundantly clear to his successor that a motive to Lister's suicide was the last thing on his mind. It was a good thing he'd got Quitman making the report on the Lister case. James didn't have the experience to ask really searching questions and Preece wouldn't bother to check the work. The report would give him all the details he needed to be going on with for the time being. Preece wouldn't spot the real point of the exercise and the file would be closed without much comment. They must be thankful in the Directorate that he'd gone. He hoped so. All he wanted was complete freedom and no interference.

It was annoying that Preece had got Welfare on to Mrs Lister so soon. He could have done with a good excuse to visit her, but that wasn't going to stop him calling on her anyway. It was his right as director, a duty almost, and she'd never know that he had retired. And they'd never know in Whitehall that he'd been to Cheltenham, not if he was careful. So why should there be any problem?

So Preece was okay then. What about Hayter? Hayter was senior. Hayter had been briefed about his resignation. Dangerfield must have told him. Would Hayter start an internal probe into the background to the Lister business? Strange paused in thought. Why should he? he said aloud in the manner of one accustomed to living alone. Lister's dead, he repeated. All Hayter has to do is to see that there are no loose ends and then let sleeping dogs lie. Hayter never turned over stones he didn't have to. He hated to give the Directorate a profile. He was too ambitious for its future to want publicity. Internal security would make a routine trawl through Lister's papers and a perfunctory vetting of any obvious contacts, but the point about Lister was that no one knew what he knew or whom he was talking to. God damn it, the man was a nobody. That's why they hadn't pulled him up in June. To watch him a little longer. The files weren't likely to give the game away. Lister wasn't much of a man for papers. No, Strange reckoned, the death closed the case for the Directorate.

But not for him. For Strange, Lister's suicide was the strongest confirmation of his worst suspicions about the man. Not since that shattering interview with Dangerfield in

June had he felt so optimistic. Especially, thought Strange, with the experience, better, this unique opportunity, to investigate his fears. Who else knew so much about all the administrative wrinkles in the Directorate as the man hired to reform it? And at that thought his pride and anger clashed again and, resentful at his sudden fall, he accelerated sharply.

The back of the Volvo was piled with suitcases, papers, books, a lampstand and some gardening things. Strange had decided to leave his London flat for a late holiday at his seaside bungalow. The prospect of a blustery sun, the cry of seagulls and the tang of the sea drove away the memory of Dangerfield's stone grey face behind the vast desk and the slim pink folder open beneath motionless white fingers. He turned his thoughts to Lister again. His mind ran back to the time that Hayter had asked him, over three years ago now, to take Lister in the Directorate. At first he'd been told that Lister was 'a first-class software analyst'. Then, when his transfer from Cheltenham was imminent, that he was slightly 'unsound' and needed watching. Good Lord, if he hadn't been so big-headed about running the best damn show in Whitehall he wouldn't have touched the man. But no, he'd been blind. He saw Lister as 'a challenge'. Of course he'd have him. No questions asked, or very few at any rate. And from the first Strange knew that he'd made a mistale with Lister. Within the year his main aim had become one of containment, to stop Lister jeopardizing the work of the rest of his section. The man was impossible. He was rude and difficult. Hated Preece, complained about Quitman. Alluded darkly to 'injustices' but never elaborated on them. Reported against fellow workers. Strange had a reputation for being tough with lame ducks. His firmness was almost a point of honour with him, but he was surprised to find that he didn't have the heart to get rid of a man whose private life was rumoured to be a mess. There was something maddening yet pathetic about Lister that paralysed Strange's will. Anyway, he couldn't be sacked. That was unheard of in the department. There wasn't anything to complain about in his work: it was erratic but good, often inspired. That made up for his personality. When Strange had failed to make something of this self-imposed 'challenge' he decided he'd get to the bottom of the Lister enigma, and watched for a chance to pounce.

He was too slow. Two years later, Sir Gerald Dangerfield told him that Lister's career threatened to compromise his own. It was the moment that, secretly, he had dreaded for many months but dared not face. Slowly he forced himself to agree that he was of no more use to the Directorate as its boss. His resignation, as Dangerfield had anticipated, was only a matter of time. Once he had admitted to himself and his masters that he had to go, his work lost all purpose and control slipped from his grasp. No wonder really that he didn't spot Lister's suicide in advance. But that defeat was past, and now he was on his own again, free as the wind, and with a mountain of obscurity to mine. Strange felt his old zest returning.

He concentrated on a patch of traffic. A sign flashed past. Cheltenham. It came again. The turn was half a mile off. When the old Volvo decelerated you could hear how old the engine was. The indicator glowed fitfully as Strange steered the car off the motorway.

The house was unremarkable, part of a redbrick terrace in a quiet back street. Its only feature was a stained glass porch that reminded Strange of his dentist's. He stood there now, sheltering from the rain and cold. He had rung the bell three times already; it was plain that the tragedy had driven the family away. Prying through the front window Strange could see battered furniture littered with woolly toys, books and records, but oddly arranged as though the room had been disturbed by burglars. As he turned to go, there was a click and a middle-aged woman in a plastic rainhat and coat came through the garden gate.

'Mrs Lister --?' he began.

'Who are you?' responded the woman sharply. 'Not the press I hope.' This was not Mrs Lister.

'Strange. Frank Strange.' This masterful woman was forcing him to abandon his planned discretion. 'Lister's boss. Is Mrs Lister – ?'

'Good gracious no,' said the woman, shocked. 'She is in no fit state to see anyone. It's kind of you to call, Mr Strange, but I really must ask you to go away. This whole case is trying enough as it is without other departments getting involved.'

'You're Welfare?' Strange guessed. The woman brushed the question aside. She stood in the porch shaking the rain out of her plastic hat and fluffing her hair into shape. 'I'm only here to collect one or two things for Mrs Lister.' Strange followed her closely inside and looked about him. The house was in chaos. The Welfare lady, ignoring him, bustled upstairs. Strange heard her putting things into a suitcase, exclaiming at the disorder with disapproval. The living-room was so chaotic, when seen from inside, it was as though there had been a fight. Did Lister have a study? Through the hallway he could see the kitchen, down a step; beyond, a patch of garden dripping in the rain. There were two other doors leading off the corridor. The first was a cloakroom. The adjoining door opened into a blackness. No windows. He felt for and flicked the switch. A darkroom. Strange raised his eyebrows. The chemicals stood in a neat cluster of bottles. No sign of any film. He heard the Welfare woman thumping down the staircase, turned out the light and shut the door.

'What are you doing?' she snapped.

'I'm sure Dick wouldn't have minded,' he said. 'But it's a shame it won't flush.' The woman stopped abruptly, her lip quivered and then she turned to the front door. 'I'm going now. You can't stay here you know.'

'Where's Mrs Lister?'

'Mrs Lister is in no state to see anyone. She is very severely shocked.'

'What about the kids?' Strange tried to sound casual, but he was becoming puzzled, curious. This was more than usually hostile for a government official.

'In care of course. But with respect, I don't think that's your concern.' The house seemed suddenly cold and unfriendly. They came out into the street, deserted even on this Saturday morning. Although it was only midday, the rain and cloud swung in low shadows over the town. A helicopter was throbbing somewhere overhead.

'Well, goodbye Mr Strange.' She spoke as if his name was familiar. 'I can assure you we will do our best for the family. I shouldn't worry if I was you. They're in good hands.'

'You won't mind if I send flowers to the hospital?'

'Of course not – ' she began haughtily and then, realizing what she had admitted, strutted furiously away down the street. He watched her go, roaring with laughter to himself within.

Strange felt awkward with the chrysanthemums. It was a long time since he had bought flowers for someone and he was embarrassed. When he arrived at the Royal Cheltenham Infirmary he held the dripping blooms shyly pointed down. Duffel-coated pickets, raw with autumn rain, stood outside, demanding a national strike, jeering at visitors. Once inside the flowers became a passport and he carried them proudly upright with the water running down his sleeve.

The week-end duty nurses were too busy to pay attention to an elderly visitor with a stick. Strange moved without detection on the tide of other visitors, fathers trailing small children, overworked executives and frail pensioners, in the direction of the women's wards.

Then he lost himself. In due course he found a young nurse, carrying a bundle of operating gowns. She smiled at him. 'Can I help?' Her voice had a note of pleasant concern.

'Would you?' He looked pathetic and slightly confused. 'They must have moved her. Lister's the name. Mrs Sarah Lister. Private,' he guessed.

'Just a minute, sir.' The nurse stepped into a small cubicle off the corridor and dialled on the internal telephone.

'Not far out,' she said escorting him forward. 'It's in the next wing. I'll take you.'

'Oh you are kind,' he said. 'Have you been here long?'

'Only four months, thank goodness. Look at the place, it's falling apart. It's a disgrace. In weather like this the whole building leaks. You wouldn't think it was only twenty years old, would you?'

'No,' Strange agreed.

'Every month it gets harder to get the drugs – ' she interrupted her complaint and looked at him. 'You should take your wife away from here as soon as possible – ' The swing doors stirred the stale clinical air. They passed a sister who nodded briefly. 'Here you are. Cavell Wing, Room 11. Can you find your way now? The exit's down there.'

Strange said Bless you, and limped slowly down the deserted corridor. Room 11. He knocked softly and went in.

The room was curtained, and the high hospital bed stood in deep shadow. Strange creaked slowly across the lino and sat down next to the bed still holding the flowers awkwardly in front of him.

'Mrs Lister,' he said.

The sheet was stretched over her motionless body and pulled up to the chin. Strange could see in the half-light that the face was lumpy and swollen and the dark reddish hair tangled with sweat, but she was breathing slowly and evenly and the pillow was smooth.

'Mrs Lister,' he said again.

The thin grey lips moved and she made a small noise. He was going to have to do the talking. 'I've come from London. From your husband's department,' he was bending towards her, speaking low, urgently. 'I'm very sorry about Dick. It was a terrible blow.' Looking at her now he felt for the first time that it was. 'I want to ask you one or two questions if I may.' He paused. 'If the answer's No, will you move your head. If Yes, can you make a sound. Do you understand?'

There was a murmur from the shadows.

'Good. First – '

Footsteps sounded outside at the end of the corridor. Strange stopped. The flowers rustled involuntarily in his hands. The steps drew nearer, efficient, precise, but moved on down the wing.

'Did you know that your husband worked in the Ministry of Defence?'

He heard the whisper of sound.

'Did you know that his section was involved in secret work?'

Yes.

'Did he tell you about it?'

No.

'Do you know why?'

The shadow moved again.

'Did Dick keep in touch with old colleagues?'

Yes.

Strange paused in his questions and straightened up. 'I need to talk to you about all this please. Can I come back tomorrow?'

There was a long pause, and then Strange realized that the woman was crying and her hot tears were running down on to the pillow. For the first time the shape of the body under the blanket moved slightly and Mrs Lister rolled her head to look at him.

'Please come,' she whispered faintly. 'I need to talk.'

Strange got up and limped into the empty corridor still pressing the flowers in his hand.

Strange put the chrysanthemums in the wash basin of his hotel room overnight, and in the morning, when the bells from the church next door were celebrating a late harvest festival, he wrapped them carefully in the paper he had saved from the florist. He was like that; it reassured him as well to have the flowers to hand when he returned to the hospital after Sunday lunch.

He made his way with apprehension but there was no sign of anyone from Welfare. Mrs Lister was sitting propped up in bed, the curtains were open and her exhausted features, bruised with grief, freshened slightly as he came in.

'I've brought you some flowers,' he said unnecessarily.

'Oh how lovely! I can't be lonely now.' She lowered her eyes. 'There's a vase in the cupboard.'

'Haven't you had any other visitors?' he asked, fetching it.

'Not today,' she admitted. 'The Welfare people take week-ends like everyone else. They were worried about reporters yesterday, but there hasn't been any trouble, so now I'm all alone.' She sighed. 'I'll have to go home tomorrow.'

Strange began to feel more relaxed. 'A long week-end in bed,' he joked encouragingly, 'that's not too bad, is it?'

The smudged eyes stared at him with a baleful vacancy. 'It's been terrible. The nurses treat you like a child. And the scorn is so hard to bear. I feel we've failed, Dick and I – '

Strange protested. But she responded with passion. 'Oh you don't know, Mr Strange. They come at once, the Welfare people, like sightseers at a disaster. Interfering in other people's lives. Picking up the pieces for them.' Her tears fell silently on to the sheets. Strange gripped the flowers inadequately and said nothing. At last she said, 'You see it was my fault to start with, you don't know that, do you?'

Strange looked at her, startled. What was she saying? 'No,' he admitted, 'I don't.'

'I feel guilty,' she went on, 'That's why I wanted you to come today. I need someone to talk to. And I think I trust you. You didn't have to come.'

Strange felt embarrassed.

'You see,' she continued, her eyes dull with sorrow, 'I was the one who started the affair, and that's where all the trouble began.'

Strange felt out of his depth. 'The affair – ?' he murmured, almost to himself. What was she talking about?

'Oh don't you know? With Tony – '

'Tony?'

'Tony Ellison. He's not important.' She stared out beyond the curtains. A flock of swallows twittered by, heading south. 'It seems a long time ago now,' she said inconsequentially.

'I'm sorry,' said Strange. 'Can you – ?' He wasn't enjoying this confessional, and it wasn't getting him any nearer Lister's activities.

She sighed again and began to speak in a halting monotone. 'Dick is a lot older than me. We met and fell in love and got married when I was only twenty-two. He took me away from home and brought me back here to Cheltenham. Dad never forgave him for that. But it's Dick's home town. He was born here and when he left college he got his job here. It was fine to start with, even though I didn't have many friends. Dick was very good to me. Then the children came and I was busy with them all the time, and Dick got more and more involved with his work. About four years ago – no, five – just after Clarissa was born – I'd said I didn't want any more and we had a row about that – I met Tony.'

'What does he do?' he asked the question without thinking, to show interest. He hoped he could gradually steer the conversation round in the end.

'He works with Dick.' Strange looked up with interest. 'I met him at a Christmas party. We danced together, yes, actually bopped, like teenagers. Dick hates dancing. I felt as though I was coming alive again.' She smiled wanly. 'Then Dick went away on a conference and we happened to meet at a friend's do. Then one thing led to another and the next time Dick was away we – we became lovers.' It was an old-fashioned phrase, but it conveyed the impact of the affair on her old-fashioned upbringing perfectly. Strange nodded, but it was something of which he was completely ignorant. 'Dick must have suspected something because he and Tony got across each other at work and everything was very unpleasant for a while. We talked about divorce, but there were always the children. In the end we made it up and Tony and I agreed that it had to stop.' She paused again, and Strange had the sense that the story was gathering to a climax. 'Then he moved to London – Dick I mean. That finished it. There was an idea that we would all move, but he couldn't bear to leave Cheltenham and his friends, and move the children from school. Anyway he hated London and house prices were going through the roof and we hoped that the London posting would only be temporary. So he commuted. First he went on the train every day, but that was too exhausting. Then he found a friend who had a civil service flat in Victoria where he stayed during the week. Recently he went back to commuting. I think he knew that Tony and I were starting the affair again. And on Thursday he came back unexpectedly.'

The silence that followed was eloquent with crisis. But Strange was hungry for details now. He said: 'What happened then?'

'It was all very sudden. He'd been away for two or three nights – '

'Where?'

'I don't know. He said it was work.' Strange made a mental note. 'I heard the car in the garage. It was early – about six o'clock.' Of course. Lister often left early. 'We were upstairs in bed. I'd sent the children out to a friend's. He shouted out as he always did when he came home and I went to the top of the stairs in my dressing gown. Then I realized that he was in a furious temper. I think he'd been drinking, because he came up the stairs two at a time, though he's been told by the doctor to take it easy.' She was weeping now, but forcing her story out anyway. 'He pushed past me. I couldn't stop him, he was going mad – smashing things and shouting at – at Tony.'

'What did he say?'

'I've never seen him so wild. He accused Tony of all sorts of things I can't remember. Things to do with me and the children. There was a lot I didn't understand. He said he knew they wanted to ruin him and that it was all planned.' Oh, thought Strange, that's one way of looking at it. 'There was something about knowing more than they realized. He said that when he got back to London there'd be trouble. I remembered that when – when they told me on Friday. Then he went mad and went for him.'

'What did you do?'

'I tried to stop them of course. It was no good. Dick had a piece of broken mirror and was – ' Mrs Lister gestured the rest of the sentence helplessly.

'And then?'

'I ran downstairs to call for an ambulance. He ran after me in a rage. He tried to throttle me, but I screamed I think and he ran out into the garage and drove away. I never saw him again. Now do you – see why – I – feel – guilty.' She choked and broke down. Strange felt incompetent and tried to comfort her. This wasn't his line. The emotions weren't relevant. All he wanted were the facts, new facts that he hadn't heard before. He waited, attentive, unrelenting. Sarah Lister blotched her swollen eyes with the corner of the sheet.

'So Dick had something on his mind?' he said at length.

'Yes. I used to ask him about it sometimes, but he used to get very touchy and say that I would know all about it in the end.'

'He was travelling a lot, wasn't he?' Strange hazarded.

'Yes, you're right.' Mrs Lister looked at him queerly. 'He was visiting people I think I used to get odd phone calls sometimes – '

'From who?'

'I don't know really. People who watned to speak to him. They never gave their names. And he wouldn't tell me what it was about.'

'Did you ask him?'

'I've told you already; it was something he wouldn't talk about.'

Strange changed the subject. 'Did you know about the Directorate?'

'Vaguely – I know it's computers and very secret.'

'Did you know about me?'

She paused. Her hand smoothed an invisible crease in the coverlet. 'Dick did sometimes mention you – ' she was speaking very slowly, composing her sentence carefully, 'but it was not very nice, I'm afraid. You didn't get on, did you?' She sounded quite objective about it.

'No.'

'What was the matter?'

'He seemed to be a gifted man who wasn't fulfilling his talents.'

'But I can't believe that. He was so active always, so busy. He always had work with him.'

'Perhaps that wasn't our work.' Strange caught the note of anger in his voice and checked himself. 'No,' he admitted, 'we didn't get on.'

Something of his suspicions had touched Mrs Lister, for she now turned sideways with an effort. 'Yet you visit his wife and cross-examine her. What's all this for? Why are you here?' She was clasping her hands and working herself up. 'You want to know about me and my children and my husband who is now dead. What do we do, how do we live? Yet you hated him. You're a ghoul, Mr Strange, you bureaucrats are all the same. Holy expressions, very concerned, very sorry, but give us the facts please!' Tears came again with her anger. Strange recognized that this outburst was against the Welfare people whom he had always despised.

'Please, please,' he soothed.

'I'm sorry, Mr Strange. I'm grateful to you. Not many men would do what you've done this weekend.'

'I feel responsible – like you – ' Strange admitted. 'I want to make amends.' It was a lie, but the circumstances lent it some plausibility. The conversation stalled again. Mrs Lister yawned. Her last outburst had brought the colour back to her puffy cheeks; the tilt of her small round head and the movement of her hands were less listless.

'You're tired,' said Strange, an unexpected note of tenderness creeping into his voice.

'Are you going now?' She sounded scared. 'Isn't there anything else you want to know?'

'You've been very helpful. We have to make a routine security check in these circumstances.' He wanted to ask about Ellison, but realized he would have to be more circumspect. 'Perhaps you could oblige me with the names of some of Dick's old colleagues here.'

'Dick didn't tell me much about his work at the office, and he didn't bring people home much, you see.' She seemed rather sad. Then she smiled involuntarily, and Strange saw why anyone would want to dance with her. 'Oh,' she said, almost girlishly, 'but I'm forgetting Paul. He's retired now, but that was only last year.'

'Paul – ?'

'Paul Keat. We haven't seen him for ages, but he's such a dear. He does part-time work at the boy's school now, the College. He'll be teaching tomorrow. You could see him then. Can you stay?' She seemed pathetically anxious for his company.

'How about patience?' said Strange rummaging in his jacket by way of assent. He played a lot of cards on his own and always carried a pack for odd moments. It occurred to him that Mrs Lister might like Double Demon.

CHAPTER FIVE

The College drive was wrecked with potholes. Strange noticed that although the term had already begun the grounds were ragged and unmown. There were no goal posts, none of the orderly signs of the new school year that he remembered from his grammar school days. He parked outside the main school building and walked across to the Porter's Lodge as he had been instructed on the telephone. The local sandstone was streaked with rain. There was glass underfoot and soggy paper littering the tarmac. The place seemed deserted.

The school porter, massive in a navy blue uniform, had a huge greasy head, scarred with premature wrinkles which creased when he spoke. There was a large wart on his nose. He regarded Strange with hostility.

'You're not from the press, are you?'

Strange thought it must be his old raincoat that gave him the appearance of a journalist and patiently explained that he had arranged to speak to Mr Keat. The porter consulted a well-thumbed timetable. 'He's teaching at the moment, sir. But he'll be out in ten minutes, if you'll take a seat.'

'Are you expecting journalists?' Strange asked pleasantly as he settled himself.

'We've had a lot of trouble from them recently. I expect you've read about the Cheltenham arsonist. Two houses and half a squash court burnt right out, sir,' explained the porter. 'Pure malice that's what it is, sir, and the press love it. Anything to have a swing at the public schools, isn't it, sir?'

'Yes, I suppose it is,' Strange agreed. He never cared much for the public school boys that had passed through the Directorate. Quitman was an exception of course. He settled down to wait. When the clock in the school tower chimed the hour the silence broke. At first a hum and then a rising clatter of boys and schoolmasters echoed round the small quadrangle as the school took its mid-morning break.

'This way, sir,' said the porter, locking the lodge door behind him with a 'you can't trust anyone nowadays'. Keat was alone in his classroom explaining an obscure point of Fortran to a round-faced fourteen-year-old. He stopped when Strange came into the battered schoolroom and said, in a louder voice for Strange's benefit. 'Is that clear then? Remember, the computer is a tool. It is as clever as the people who programme it.' He nodded at his pupil who, embarrassed at the stranger, hurried out with his satchel.

Where Strange expressed his commanding presence with a direct, penetrating eye which was nonetheless capable of a certain slyness, Keat was pink and gentle, a modest man who liked to please. He was nearly bald, and with an oblique, shrinking glance that was almost surreptitious. He seemed unable to restrain his smile of welcome. Strange crushed the outstretched hand in his usual way, the porter returned to the lodge and the two men strolled between the rows of desks out into a dank cloister.

'Shall we go to the common room for coffee? There's no chance of any privacy there I'm afraid, but I'm not teaching before lunch and we can go for a walk or something if the weather lifts.'

Strange said that suited him very well and was about to change the subject when Keat said: 'Poor Dick. I was quite knocked down by the news when I read about it. It was quite a shock I can tell you.'

'And the shame is that we didn't see it coming.'

'It's so hard, isn't it? One can't be expected to keep up with a large staff like yours all the time. He was very secret, was Dick. He kept things to himself.'

Strange agreed. 'How long have you – did you know him?'

'Oh. Ever since he joined the office. He was several years junior of course.'

'His wife told me you were good friends.'

'We got on. I think he liked to confide in one,' he replied modestly. 'But I haven't seen so much of him in the last three years since he went to London. When I retired last year we almost lost touch altogether. One blames oneself now, of course. Perhaps if there'd been a chance to talk . . .' he shrugged. They came into the common room. A mob of middle-aged men in shapeless tweed jackets stood drinking coffee out of sloppy cups and talking shop with the special passion of the pedantic. They took no notice of the new arrivals. Nice, gentle Keat seemed out of place in this masculine society and Strange asked him about it.

'Would you believe it, but I'm an old boy of the place. I'm from the North myself, but Dad sent me south to get educated. Reckoned it would improve my prospects. They wouldn't have taken one here otherwise. You see I'd had enough of the department. I was fed up with the routine and, I don't mind admitting it, getting a bit uneasy about some of the recent developments in the Directorate.' Strange ignored this. 'Owing to the age-structure of my section they were offering an attractive early retirement scheme. I jumped at the opportunity. The job here should tide one over to sixty. I love it.'

They chatted about this and that, drinking the milky institutional coffee, and then, buttoning raincoats, set out for a walk in the solitude of the grounds.

'The place seems in need of a face-lift,' Strange commented as they crossed the quadrangle.

'You've noticed that, have you? The fact is we're broke. No one's got any money for this sort of thing nowadays. Half the College is learning English as a Foreign Language. It wasn't like that in my day.'

'Or Lister's I imagine – he was here, wasn't he?'

'Long after my time, but he left his mark. He won the school maths cup three years running. He really was rather brilliant in his extraordinary way. As a software specialist he was streets ahead of one in all the really imaginative work one did.'

'But very difficult to work with, don't you think?'

'You only knew him in London, Mr Strange,' said Paul Keat quietly, but with a sudden firmness. 'He'd gone off the rails by then if you ask me. In the old days he was quite another sort of chap, was Dick. We had some good times together in the old days.' He looked shyly at Strange, as if wondering whether to go on, and then said, 'It comes back to me now. He used to call me Uncle – as a joke you realize . . . Oh he was very lively company, I assure you.'

'Before he was married?'

Keat seemed slightly hurt at Strange's persistent questions; he glanced away across the sodden fields. 'I know what you're saying, but it's not true. Of course he did find Sarah when he was getting on, but it was a good match despite the age gap. They were very much in love when Sarah first came here. And the business with Ellison. They could have weathered that in my belief. In fact they did weather it.' Keat was almost thinking aloud. 'They were reconciled afterwards. But by that time the damage had been done, as I'm sure you know.'

After what, Strange wondered, and casually asked about Ellison.

'I never liked him,' said Keat decisively. 'And I get along with most people you know. It's not in my nature to make enemies,' he said factually, with a half-smile at Strange. 'The truth is I hate unpleasantness of any sort.' Pausing, he stamped a wet divot with his shoe. 'But Ellison was different. How can I describe him?' he went on, anticipating Strange's question. 'Well, he was always a bit too eager to please, too clever by half I suppose you'd say. Mercurial. But when he was up the whole world knew about it and he could be very charming, if a bit flash for my taste. Sarah wasn't the first by any means. When I last saw anything of him he was still young but getting a bit frayed at the edges. Of course I'm biased. I'll never forgive the way he messed up Dick's life.'

'You mean the affair?'

'Yes – and the other business of course.'

'Yes,' replied Strange, baffled. 'What's your version of that? It would be helpful to know.'

'I was in another section,' Keat replied by way of a preface, 'so I didn't hear it all – except Dick's side of things of

48

course. I believe he told me everything, though I've forgotten some of the details. My memory's not what it was. Besides,' he looked sadly at Strange, 'it was a nasty business and I'm not the sort of chap as enjoys that sort of thing.'

'Yes,' said Strange, encouraging. Keat walked on in silence for a pace or two, marshalling his thoughts.

'It's hard to know how to express it,' he said at last. 'We bachelors, Strange, have a different view of things.' Strange began to feel impatient. Why did everyone always want to discuss the emotional issues first? 'I mean, it's hard to know whether Dick had it in for Ellison because of the affair with Sarah,' Keat paused, 'or because of the enquiry. To tell the truth, I don't even know which came first. Dick always claimed that his accusations weren't motivated by jealousy, but a lot of people in the office thought otherwise.'

'What was the atmosphere like?' asked Strange, suddenly alert and tentatively groping for a detail that he recognized.

'Poisonous.' Keat was uncharacteristically blunt. When he turned to look at Strange, his visitor could see tears drawn by the cruel wind in his eyes. 'I hated it. Of course one had to stand by Dick and that inevitably meant enemies. It got worse once your chap arrived from London and the enquiry started.'

Strange had to force himself not to break the ruminative nature of the conversation and fire off a dozen impetuous questions at this astounding piece of information. His pace quickened briefly as he wondered how to conceal his ignorance and yet sustain the flow of detail.

'Oh yes, you mean whatshisname?' he fumbled, slowing again.

'Preece – Guy Preece,' he repeated, weighing the recollection. 'A very competent young man.' There was something about the way in which Keat said this that indicated a profound distrust. Strange was not surprised, but his mind was racing wildly in many directions. He managed to say, stutter almost, in his excitement

' – despite the atmosphere?'

Keat pondered this in the manner of one wanting to be

fair. 'Well, you're right. He didn't exactly cool the temperature during the enquiry, but he did settle the issue. You chose well there if you wanted to steady the boat,' he said, and his disquiet showed through his words.

'As a matter of fact, it wasn't my choice,' Strange admitted, as much to himself.

'Please,' Keat began hastily, almost flustered, 'I didn't mean to suggest anything – ' he stopped. 'Well, well,' he went on pleasantly as though the subject had never been raised, 'I'm sure you'll find all the documents you need in the files.'

Strange could hardly keep the exasperation out of his voice. 'But don't you see that all the most revealing facts and stories lie in the memory, unrecorded? You know the rule: if it's not on the files it doesn't exist.'

'What's your problem?' Keat smoothed a few stray white hairs.

'But that's precisely where we're most vulnerable. I don't need to tell you that the department has its enemies. We at the Directorate have to be convinced that a sudden death like this leaves no cracks in our defences, if you follow me.' Keat nodded. He was familiar with the methods of his bosses. 'Tell me,' continued Strange, 'how did Lister take to Preece's handling of the – the enquiry, did you call it?'

'That's right. I know it only lasted a couple of days but it was the main topic of conversation in the office for weeks.'

'Isn't that odd,' said Strange, ruefully. 'I can't believe that it bothered more than a handful of us in London.' Hayter and Hayter and Hayter, he thought to himself bitterly. How much more was there that had been kept from him, he who prided himself on his command of the files? He became aware that Keat was talking.

' – you see it's a closed world down here, Mr Strange. We feed on each other. And it's an odd thing, but the more secret the section the more gossip there is. There were some very cruel rumours running about I can tell you. That's why it was a good thing in a way – though I know Sarah doesn't agree with me – that Dick was moved to London. He felt he'd been cheated by Preece. Ellison was still around. There would have been a crisis if he hadn't moved. He would have done something silly.'

'What sort of thing?'

'Now there you have me,' Keat twinkled at him, 'but I know he would have done *something* because he was round with me every night. He was very bitter against the Directorate after the enquiry, that's for sure. He couldn't accept that Ellison was innocent. You see it all sticks in my mind so because I retired a month or two later and had the leisure to think about it.' Keat shook his head. 'It was after that that he went off the rails. Though I doubt there was anything that any of us, even Sarah, could have done.' Keat stopped. 'I'm surprised you haven't asked me whether I believed Dick's accusations.'

Strange was infuriated to be so ignorant of the case that he couldn't make a positive reply.

'Right and wrong are hard to judge in such cases, don't you think?' he hazarded. But it was the appropriate answer for Keat because he nodded deeply three or four times. 'My view exactly. It all seemed so typical of our legitimate work, but Dick swore there was an irregularity. The evidence was controversial of course.'

'Quite,' said Strange, baffled. They walked on over the wet turf in silence for a while. Strange considered these obscure revelations. Mrs Lister had said that Ellison and Lister had got across each other at work and that everything was very unpleasant for a while. This must be what she had meant. It was not surprising she hadn't elaborated. Lister had obviously got into trouble. That wasn't new. He'd played the corruption card again in London, as Strange knew only too well. It was obvious that Lister's friendship with old Keat had become rather strained towards the end. The schoolmaster's first remarks came back to him as he pondered the story.

'You were surprised by his death, were you?'

'Yes, I was,' Keat looked at him with a sad shyness. 'He was the last man in the world to cave in, was Dick.'

'So he must have been under a hell of a lot of pressure,' deduced Strange.

'Yes . . . Or – ' Keat broke off, startled by his own thoughts.

'Or what?' Strange persisted.

'Here's an idea for you,' Keat replied, evading the issue. 'You should talk to Brian Hoskins. D'you know who I mean?' Strange thought the name rang a bell. 'He was editor of the house magazine then. I know Dick gave him a set of papers to do with the enquiry. He was relying on him to fight the good fight and publish an article about the case.' He winked at Strange. 'I'll bet you didn't know that!'

Strange agreed. 'You'd be surprised,' he added, 'how little we know about what you get up to away from the front line.'

Keat chuckled. 'I don't know if anything ever emerged from Hoskins. I fear that Dick's stuff may have been worthless, but he certainly pinned his hopes on Hoskins because he often told me that Hoskins was preparing a piece for the magazine. He's left now of course, and I've no idea where he's got to, or even if he's still alive – you know how they drink – but he'd be worth talking to if you could find him. I can see you're taking this very seriously.'

Strange protested and steered a path for the College. The bell was clanging in the damp air. 'You will stay for lunch,' asked Keat. 'It's so rare to have a distinguished outsider like yourself and anyone who's a friend of Dick's – poor fellow – is a friend of mine.' It was impossible not to like Paul Keat, so Strange stayed, chiefly in the hope of jolting some more information from the old man's memory, but the conversation turned to chess, one of Strange's bachelor hobbies. He broke away thankfully at two, in time to drown the taste of burnt cabbage and spam pie in the local bitter, having managed only to discover the additional useful fact that Ellison lived locally – 'in one of those ghastly modern housing excrescences I believe.'

So Strange came out of the pub and revved the Volvo. He was getting so used to the luggage piled in the back that it seemed he possessed nothing else in the world. Tomorrow he would pause in his quest, but for the moment the picture in his mind's eye of the hanging face on the stretcher and the dead white stare drove him forward.

He cruised past the Lister house slowly. It was still deserted. He drove to the end of the street, did a three-point-turn and cruised back again. There was a bottle green mini-van coming towards him, slowly. It didn't stop but Strange noticed that the man beside the driver was writing something on a clipboard.

He parked at the nearest phone box and stumbled to it through the rain. Anthony Ellison lived in Bunyan Close, Cheltenham, in what was undoubtedly a 'ghastly modern excrescence'. He dialled and waited. Then he dialled again just in case. But there was no answer. Back in the car he reached for his street plan of the Spa.

CHAPTER SIX

The week after Strange left the Directorate was – as everyone joked – strange. It was as though they were all working in a vacuum, without purpose or leadership, an impression that was heightened by the new offices to which Strange's old staff were transferred.

Quitman attempted to overcome his own private apprehensions by immersing himself in the Lister report, but soon discovered the unforeseen complications of his new work. Despite the 'Top Secret' security category of all aspects of the Lister business, Neve found out that his friend had a special access card to the data control room. It was one thing for Quitman to do Strange's donkey-work, as Preece had hinted on Friday, but Neve saw this privilege as a direct threat to his seniority. He had never seen Quitman as an ambitious careerist before and realized that he must have under-estimated the man. At once their easy friendship became formal with suspicion.

Quitman was dismayed by the swift change that others seemed to perceive in him. He was beginning to feel stereotyped by success, and this put him in conflict with himself. When he left Oxford six years ago, his hopes to continue his research into medieval chivalry dashed by his disgraceful Finals, he had taken the civil service examination as a desperate last measure. Passing it with ease, he had been specially drafted into the Directorate in recognition of his methodical mind, his gifts with language and his innate discretion. His new masters rightly believed that he would have no difficulty with essential computer technique. The fact that he was without connections or influence was considered especially in his favour as a recruit to the information-intelligence arm of counter-subversion.

The Directorate found him at first harmless, a source of

minor comedy with his scruffy appearance and arcane research, and later, as he mastered his job, unobtrusively gifted at the odd work in which they were all involved. The rumour that he had a stunning woman somewhere in the background lent an air of raffishness to the manner of the don *manqué*.

Quitman had kept his work at a distance, telling his friends that the Civil Service was the only institution outside prison where you could pursue a second career. His lunch-hours and many evenings when Liz was at parties were spent in the British Library or among the archives at Kew. When Strange took him up he had sustained his ambivalence towards his work in an attempt to keep his distance. Now, for the first time he felt his insouciance at risk. He was annoyed to find that he cared about his job.

When he turned to Liz for understanding, her response showed him afresh how little she fancied complications that undermined her trust in his abilities. He discovered that at times he had mistaken the vivacity of her life-style for genuine self-confidence. The truth was she had none. Her need for him was voracious, persistent and all-absorbing. To his dismay she could find no sympathy for his predicament. In fact it made her restless and argumentative.

'For as long as I've known you, Jamie, you've complained about the routine of the Directorate, now, when they promote you –'

Quitman objected.

' – well, give strong indications of promotion if you prefer it, what does it matter for God's sake – you complain.' Liz was angry. Elegant but businesslike in her Yves St Laurent suit, and made-up to kill, she glared at him across her swedish-pine breakfast table. All her ambitions for him seemed suddenly at risk.

That same morning, just before the car arrived to take her to Euston for her train to a promotional tour in the North, Quitman made an unguarded comment about literary London and they had a row about that. At times he felt as ambivalent about Liz, dear pushy, dressy Liz, as he did about his work in Whitehall. But by the time the bell rang he was telling her that he was only upset at the prospect of a week without her and how sorry he was. On this false note they parted.

Quitman worked hard all week, cross-referencing between the datadiscs of information, accumulating the necessary scraps of information with which to build his report. It was painstaking work and Dr Cornelius Mayer, the Dutch information retrieval wizard brought into the Directorate by Hayter when C Directorate acquired the new computer on which all Hayter's future hopes were pinned, noticing Quitman's scrupulous absorption, suggested they have a drink together after work.

Mayer was blond and expansive. His gold frames glinted as he outlined his plans for the linkage of the Cheltenham, Croydon and London databanks. He spoke with an Oxford accent and drank lager by the pint. 'And then I am installing the latest laser printer. Eleven thousand lines per minute.' He burped with zest. 'Nothing is secret anymore – except to us!' He pronounced 'secret' like 'sacred' and when he laughed his teeth showed gold fillings. Quitman went home, slightly drunk, flattered by the attention, but more divided than ever.

But he soon had the Lister report on his desk in triplicate: a copy for the file and a copy for Preece. The third 'your eyes only' copy was for Strange who was, he reckoned, going to be pretty irked by the fact, for instance, that Hayter had called in the security people without any of the usual consultations. Strange, who liked to swap historical references with Quitman, did not share Hayter's belief in what he referred to as 'the gathering storm', and disputed the use of troops whenever the occasion arose. 'Cut a corner once,' he was fond of saying, 'and next time it's just a bend.' The only good news for his old boss was that the report confirmed the absence of motive. He sealed Strange's copy and put it in the mail room on his way home to Barons Court that night. It's what he asked for, he said to himself.

Preece called him into his new office the next morning.

Well, Quitman thought as he stood in the lift, at least there's going to be some recognition for the work, and tried to tell himself that he didn't mind about promotion. Preece had the reports in front of him on the desk. He spoke at once.

'I take it, James, that you have the third copy in your possession?'

Quitman checked. 'Oh. I'd hoped it was all right to mail Strange's copy direct. I agree I used my discretion, but he is our retired director.'

Preece shook his head dismissively. 'That doesn't matter. Particularly – ' he stopped as though conscious of venturing too far. 'This is exactly how security leaks occur – when staff,' he stressed the menial word, 'allow their discretion to interfere with the system.' Quitman tried to protest, but Preece went on, 'The system has been refined over many years. It is the product of much careful thought and experiment. Now that I am director here I'd be grateful if you'd observe the rules.'

Quitman realized as soon as he returned to his office that Preece had been waiting for that opportunity. Analysing the pain and embarrassment of the meeting he acknowledged, too, the strength of his desire for promotion and, despite the risks of going on the record, wrote an apologetic memo. Preece had this note in his hand when he interrupted Quitman alone with a book at lunch in the canteen the following day.

'Thanks for this, James. Quite understand,' he crushed the memo in his hand and tossed it at Quitman. 'Not another word. By the way I've just had a communication from Hayter. He'd like to see you in his office at two o'clock sharp.'

Michael Hayter's room on the fourth floor of the Old War Office was more sombre than Quitman remembered. The blinds were drawn, a couple of lamps cast pools of yellow light, the air was heavy with pipe smoke. And Hayter was not alone. Preece was there, that was not unexpected. Dr Cornelius Mayer was there, that was surprising. And there, seated next to Hayter, was another silent figure whom

57

Quitman thought he recognized as a politician but couldn't place. His hopes for promotion began to rise.

Hayter rose cordially to greet him.

'Ah, Quitman. Come in, come in. May I introduce Alan Jenks?' So that was Jenks, the junior minister to the department. They shook hands. 'Have a seat,' Hayter gestured. Jenks, Preece and Mayer were already settled in armchairs. Quitman joined the circle and Hayter, who never wasted time, opened the red folder on the table at his elbow.

'Now this is an unusual meeting but I hope that when we have finished we will all agree that it was justified. Shall I lead, Minister?'

Quitman had heard of Jenks as a ministerial placeman. He had the well-scrubbed look of the trade-union official in government. A weak smile passed across his face, 'By all means, Michael.' Tyneside, Quitman thought to himself. Warships, munitions. It made sense.

'I must preface my remarks,' Hayter went on, 'by emphasizing the security of this meeting. No notes. Top secrecy.' Quitman nodded and wondered if Preece had told Hayter about the episode with Strange's copy of the Lister report. 'I'd like to bang off if you don't mind, Quitman – this is really for the benefit of Mr Jenks here – by asking you to establish one or two points for us.'

Quitman nodded expectantly and reached into his briefcase for the file copy of the Lister report. To his own surprise he found himself wanting to seem efficient.

'Now you've been in the Directorate,' Hayter consulted his notes, 'six years?'

'Yes.'

'And you worked under Frank Strange all that time?'

'Yes.'

'It was your first job after university, wasn't it?'

Assenting for the third time, Quitman wondered where all this was leading.

'You found him a good boss?'

'Strange? Yes, he was fair,' Quitman slowed to choose his

words with care, 'scrupulously fair, dedicated and hard-working. He had high standards but he was not unreasonable. He could be very generous, though not everyone realized this.'

'You liked him?'

'I owe him a lot. Yes, I liked him.'

'You owe him a lot,' Hayter quuoted, 'what do you mean by that?'

'He set a good example as an administrator and he treated subordinates with justice. I trusted his judgement.'

'That sounds like a pretty good set of references,' Hayter gave a slight laugh. 'Any faults – in your view?'

Quitman noticed Hayter's assumption of Strange's weak nesses. He paused; then he added reluctantly: 'He was perhaps too dedicated.' He began to express an opinion that he knew Preece would like to hear. 'His obsession with the re-organization of the Directorate was short-sighted. It took no account of technological progress. It took no account of technological progress. He was not a computer expert – that was not his job – and his conviction that only he could put things straight here annoyed a lot of people, I think.'

'Had he achieved all he set out to do by the time he retired, do you think?'

Quitman recognized that he had to be careful here. Strange had told him some things which, strictly speaking, were confidential. 'Nearly, I believe.' He looked at Hayter and volunteered, 'I must say that in the last few months he seemed to lose his flair.' Hayter nodded, looked at Jenks, but made no comment.

'Thank you. Does that put you in the picture, Minister?' But he didn't wait for an answer and went on, 'The reason you're here, Quitman, is because – to put it bluntly – we're getting rather worried by Frank Strange and his activities at the moment.'

Quitman looked at him in astonishment. In the Directorate, 'activities' could have only one meaning.

'Since Strange retired we have had some odd reports about his behaviour.' He opened the red folder. 'Strange's first move when he left London last week-end was to motor straight to Cheltenham which, apart from housing an important systems centre, is also,' he paused, 'or perhaps I should say was, Lister's home town.' He gave Quitman a significant look. 'There he visited Mrs Lister.'

'I know he was very shaken by the suicide,' Quitman explained. 'I'm sure he went to offer his condolences. He was like that you know.' Quitman was relieved that Strange's 'activities' were so harmless. Hayter's reaction was, of course, typical. Hayter considered this reply, looked at Preece, and went on: 'I disagree. His movements suggest that he wasn't just saying sorry. First he went to Lister's house. There, quite by chance, he was found poking about the garden by the Welfare officer who had gone to collect a few bits and pieces for Mrs Lister. According to her, he was busy rubbernecking about the house like a private detective.'

'How did she know that this man was Strange?' Quitman countered.

'He introduced himself.' Hayter was about to say more but Quitman saw the obvious objection. 'Why ever did she report his visit then?' he countered.

There was a pause. Hayter shuffled the papers at his side and said, 'Look here, Quitman, from the work you've done on the report you've got the point that the Lister business potentially poses a pretty serious threat to the Directorate. In the circumstances it's made good sense to ask the Minister to authorize the surveillance of the Lister house till the fuss blows over.' Jenks nodded in agreement. 'The Welfare girl was simply co-operating with the team who have been seconded to the case from HQ Security. Standard practice, really.'

'Oh,' said Quitman.

He picked up the transcript and began to read: ' "Mr Strange seemed very anxious to speak to Mrs Lister and tried hard to find out where she was staying." That's what the Welfare lady said.'

'Did he go to the hospital?'

'Twice.' Hayter was turning fresh pages, he almost smiled. 'A member of the surveillance team spoke with Mrs Lister. She confirms that Strange visited her on Saturday last, the day after Lister's death, when she was still under heavy sedation in a private room, and on the next day, Sunday, when they had a long conversation.'

'As I say,' Quitman repeated, 'I believe he felt it was his duty – '

Preece interrupted, 'But, James, he disliked Lister. Why should he want to go to such extraordinary lengths to commiserate with the widow of a man he – ' He shrugged, searching for the appropriate word ' – disliked,' he repeated.

'Strange had a remarkable sense of duty.'

Hayter intervened: 'Listen to this, Quitman, and then tell me if you think this has anything to do with consoling widows or any damn thing of that sort.' He picked up the transcript again, barking unevenly: ' "Then we talked about Dick and he asked me what he had been doing recently. I said I didn't really know and he asked me twice if Dick didn't tell me what he was doing. I said I didn't know and he asked me what I knew about the Directorate . . ." That doesn't sound like a remarkable sense of duty to me,' said Hayter putting the papers aside. 'D'you see what he's up to, Quitman?'

'Oh, but this is Strange all over,' he contested warmly. 'I knew he wouldn't step down gracefully. He didn't know when the job ended and retirement began. I'm afraid you'll have to put up with this for another week or two,' he said with confidence.

'Does it make any difference to your assessment of the situation,' queried Hayter, 'to know that Strange also called on one of Lister's oldest friends, a man he'd never met or seen before.'

This time Quitman said nothing, but looked at Jenks, Preece and Dr Mayer uncertainly. Hayter said: 'This is going to be a bit of a blow I'm afraid, Quitman, and I appreciate your respect for the man, but it's vital that you get the situation on board. The plain fact is that Strange is almost certainly attempting to uncover embarrassing information about Lister's suicide. We believe he wants to discredit the Directorate – possibly to the press.'

'No,' Quitman began to rise. 'I can't accept that. With respect, you don't *know* him. I explained to begin with that he was obsessive.' He leant towards Hayter. '*Why?* Why would he do such things? There's no reason for this.'

A flicker passed across Hayter's heavy face. 'Look, sit down, old boy. I fear we are shocking you too suddenly. I see that we must put a few more of the facts at your disposal.' He said this with great reasonableness and seemed almost to be enjoying the progress of the interview. Quitman felt suddenly ashamed.

'I beg your pardon, sir. It's just that I'm finding this hard to swallow. As I told you, I trust Strange implicitly.'

'Well then,' said Hayter delving into his pocket for his tobacco, 'you were close to him. What did he tell you about his retirement?'

Quitman felt his calmness going again. 'What do you mean? There's nothing – '

'You cannot fail to be aware, Quitman,' Hayter interrupted powerfully, 'that a number of people in the Directorate were surprised when Strange announced that he was retiring.'

Quitman agreed. 'Yes, I know. They wanted to know what they called the *real* reason.' He shrugged. 'There was no real reason. Frank – Mr Strange – wanted to retire early to enjoy his pension and do some gardening. As you know, I expect, he was badly wounded in the desert. He'd had to go to hospital a lot recently. In his bad moments I think he feared an early death.'

'But you have already told us that he was what I believe the Americans call a workaholic. Why didn't he want to go on to the end? Wouldn't that have been more in character?'

'I'm not saying that it wasn't a big problem with him, sir. It was. But once he'd made up his mind that it was the best thing he was quickly reconciled to the decision.' He smiled. 'I don't need to tell you he was very decisive.'

Hayter puffed his pipe and looked severely at Quitman. 'He didn't make up his mind to go, old boy. It was made up for him.' Quitman looked at Jenks, at Mayer, Preece and Hayter. They were studying him gravely from the shadows.

'You asked him to retire? For what reason?' He felt panic rising.

'We didn't ask him, Quitman. He was fired.' There was a complete silence and then Jenks added in his slow northern drawl, 'I was advised by Sir Gerald Dangerfield, Mr Quitman, that in the interests of security, Frank Strange would have to be relieved of his position without more ado and as soon as was humanly possible.' Another long silence intervened, broken only by the sound of Hayter drawing on his pipe. Quitman could think of nothing to say.

'This is the explanation,' said Hayter, 'for Strange's sudden loss of interest in the Directorate. It may also explain why he allowed Lister to go off the rails. You are right, Quitman,' he went on relentlessly, 'he does have Lister's case on his mind. There is evidence that he was willing to let it happen to embarrass the people who had fired him.'

'But it's unheard of?' Quitman was rallying. 'Why? What had he done?'

Again the Minister intervened. 'I'm afraid to say, Mr Quitman, that, for the moment, security considerations demand that the details of the Strange case remain classified. Dr Mayer has yet to produce his analysis of the available information.'

'That is so,' said Cornelius Mayer, speaking for the first time.

'We called you here, Quitman,' concluded Hayter, 'because we believe that, despite your close association with Strange, you can be trusted. Of course, it's painful. It's been a bitter blow to us all. I was one of Frank's greatest admirers. You've grasped the significance of this meeting I take it? The point is that you're now a prime target in what we suspect will be a long campaign by Strange to embarrass his colleagues. My own private nightmare is that he will try to enlist press support. He will have to be watched very carefully. At any rate he's likely to want to get in touch with you for information. If he tries anything on like that I want to make it clear to you that you give him the brush off and report at once to my office. The message is, steer clear of him at all costs.' He rose. 'I think that settles matters for the moment. We won't detain you.'

CHAPTER SEVEN

Strange realized that he was being watched just as he was beginning to enjoy his autumn holiday in Devon. There had been glimpses – shadows in the lane in the small hours, strangers in the pub – but these disturbing fragments did not compose a picture until, emerging from the village shop one morning, he was shocked to recognize unseen the driver of the green mini-van from Cheltenham cruising down to the sea-front behind the wheel of a similar vehicle.

There was a small car-park on the decaying promenade, and Strange, following urgently, saw the van pull up to face the waves, and a second man, his raincoat flapping in the sturdy wind, get up from a bollard, stride over and open the passenger door.

Strange turned away before he was spotted and climbed up the hill past the Methodist church. At the top he paused for breath and looked back over the slate roofs of the village to the tiny harbour. The van had not moved.

It was only when he was walking slowly down the lane to his cliff-top cottage, breathing heavily from his sudden burst of walking, that he began to feel afraid. You couldn't put a tail on a man without Ministerial permission, and even the Minister was supposed to consult the Home Secretary. Those were the rules, although they were broken often enough.

The sense of being watched suddenly made the landscape menacing and hostile. Helpless, vulnerable, he could be seen but could not see. All at once, for no reason, he remembered the blind man lost in the fog outside the Westminster tube station.

He reached the house and clicked open the gate. Had anyone been there while he was shopping? His property seemed no longer his own. He propped the groceries in the dry porch and walked once round the house, looking in at all the windows. The cry of the seagulls floated up from the harbour and the wind tugged at the tamarisks, but the house was still as a museum. He paced over the plot of rough sea grass to the vegetable garden and, standing at the hedge, shaded his eyes against the inland view. The van was still in the car-park. He turned to the porch, unlocked the front door and stepped inside.

The familiar cool silence reminded him of the day his mother had died. Suddenly there was a whirring. He turned sharply. When the grandfather clock at the end of the dark hallway had ceased chiming he walked slowly through to the kitchen, pausing to check all the rooms. Nothing wrong downstairs. As he turned in thought, Strange's fears became abruptly concentrated on the staircase leading to the upper floor of the cottage, the dark pine that his mother had polished almost every day that he could remember. The climb past the grandfather clock always held terrors for Strange as a lonely child, but these early fears had receded. Suddenly, the threat of surveillance made the old shadows menacing again. The steps creaked as slowly he began to go up.

The bathroom, the bedroom, the cold spare room . . . Strange tapped and prodded with his stick, looking for signs of interference. The study, which was where he kept all his documents, was the last room at the end of the short passage. He pushed open the door, his heart pounding unnaturally. The OHMS envelope with Quitman's report on the Lister case lay undisturbed on the desk. Suddenly, out of the corner of his eye, he saw someone move and lashed out wildly with his stick. The mirror on the tallboy smashed to the floor and the door swung backwards violently on its hinges. Strange stood there looking at his splintered image. You're scared, he said to himself. They're watching and you're scared. He turned over in his mind what they could know, and what they could hear, what they could see and read. Then he realized that he didn't know, that he could never know. They've got you on the run, he said aloud.

Back in the kitchen he made himself some elevenses, switched on the radio and then, feeling uneasy, switched it off again. Then he snatched the screwdriver out of the drawer and unscrewed the telephone with a shaking hand. He had the thing in pieces before he realized that if they were listening he would never know about it. He reassembled it angrily and in a hurry.

Strange sat in his favourite armchair by the cold fireplace and stared at the ceiling. They can listen to you, they can read your letters and they can watch you here, he repeated to himself. If you go on the road they can only watch you. It had been his plan to have a holiday here at home for two or three weeks and then return to the Lister case when the fuss had died down.

The prospect of getting back on the job again set his mind racing, and he was soon at his desk sorting out the essential documents he needed. When he had finished he stood up stiffly and walked to the window. The van was still in the car-park and one of the men was lolling in the sunshine, watching the high tide tossing the water against the breakwaters, while his companion tracked with his binoculars the seabirds that soared and dived around the cliffs in front of Strange's bungalow.

Quitman was scanning his section's VDU, collating some Special Branch statistics for Dr Cornelius Mayer, when the desk phone grated. 'James,' Preece's discreet purr was unmistakable. 'Would you report to Hayter's office at 1500 hours.' Quitman acknowledged the instruction and was about to put the phone down when he heard Preece add, 'I hear you've been poorly. I trust you're better now.'

'Yes, thank you. Just an autumn chill.' He felt lousy, chiefly because he was now nurturing a secret bitterness towards Strange.

After the ghastly meeting with Hayter and Jenks, he had become first of all drunk and then very sick. Liz arrived back from the North and found him retching into a bucket. Her sympathy turned to anger when she discovered the cause of his illness, and they had a bad row about his slavish attachment to Strange and his failure to merit promotion. But there was more to her temper than disappointment. Later it turned out that, not for the first time in the years that Quitman had known her, she had acquired a new lover, a minor literary man. So Quitman was left alone in Barons Court, sweating and vomiting, with a high temperature, worrying about their relationship. On Monday he reported sick and spent the day in bed, in a darkened room, listening to the radio. He slept badly that night and Tuesday was no better. On Wednesday, in the morning, knowing he could not face another day alone with his resentment and the BBC, he climbed into his chilly office suit and went painfully to work.

The Directorate under Preece was already a different place. There were new ID cards for all executive personnel, another access category for the data control room and a new security procedure. Quitman had missed the staff instruction in the new system and it was Neve, at his most patronizing, who explained the new rituals. Quitman felt the shame of the new boy who had missed the first two weeks of term through ill-health. He reflected with sadness on the shadow of rivalry that had eclipsed his friendship with Neve so rapidly, and could not help suspecting that Neve had found out about his row with Preece over the report. A number of people were commenting that Neve was doing his best to ingratiate himself with his new boss, and the new atmosphere in the Directorate – one of efficient secrecy – merely provoked this kind of speculation. The old-fashioned breeziness of the Strange régime had gone for ever.

By the time he had mastered the rules of his new environment it was lunchtime. The new offices seemed more over-heated than ever and he set out for a lonely walk along the Embankment to clear his head. He was not hungry and his body ached. A cold grey wind ruffled the river waters and struggled with the commuters hurrying across the Hungerford Bridge. A demonstration of the unemployed, placards waving, was marching slowly up the road to

Westminster. He supposed you had to be angry to march three hundred miles like that, and perhaps for the first time in his life felt he could share such anger. When he returned to the office he spent the afternoon confirming his fears that he lacked automatic access to any of the disc-packs in which he might have found clues to Strange's activities and so, still nagging in his mind at the allegations against his former boss, he left the Directorate early, mumbling about sickness. Everyone was very sympathetic but that didn't make him feel any better.

The next day, despite a brief from Mayer, his concentration was worse than ever. He sat alone with the VDU staring blankly at the truncated language. He had what Liz would have called 'one of your boring chivalry books' in his briefcase and at odd moments dipped into that to restore his sanity. No one seemed to mind. Rosie Walford told him that he looked like death warmed up, and Neve was gratuitously rude. Rosie, who overheard the exchange, buttonholed him outside the lavatory. 'He thinks he's got Preece behind him, you see,' she advised with mischief.

'You don't know who's on who's side these days,' commented Quitman bitterly. 'You can't trust anyone.' The longer he stayed in the surroundings he associated with Strange, the greater his sense of betrayal.

That night, still hoping for a call from Liz, he drank himself to sleep in front of the television and was wakened by white sound from the tube at five o'clock. His mind returned like a magnet to Strange, and he acknowledged that where he had been angry at first, then bitter, now he hated the man. When Preece rang that morning Quitman had reached his lowest.

At five to three Quitman went to take the lift and found Preece waiting as well. He nodded and said unexpectedly: 'You've had a bad time, haven't you? I know that was hard news about Strange. A shock to us all.'

Quitman was suddenly grateful for this uncharacteristic warmth. 'Thank you,' he said acknowledging the sympathy, like a mourner, with a weak smile.

Hayter was alone, fussing about among his filing cabinets, like a gardener in a potting-shed. 'Come in, come in.' He waved them to chairs. 'I'm afraid the Minister can't be with us today, so we'll get straight down to business.' He shot out a hand. 'Cigar?'

'No thank you. I've not been well.' But Quitman was already beginning to feel more relaxed.

'So I hear.' He looked keenly at Quitman across the desk. 'Has he tried anything?'

'Tried – ? No, not that I'm aware.'

'Unfortunately the situation's getting worse.'

'Where is he now?' Quitman asked.

'Exactly,' said Hayter, and took out his pipe. 'After he left Cheltenham he travelled down to Devon – '

'To his cottage?'

'Yes. Where he stayed, quite harmlessly as far as we can tell, until today. This morning he packed his bags and left.'

'Where's he going?'

'He's here. In London.' Hayter sparked his lighter. 'You see how serious this could be?'

Quitman agreed. 'You can't restrain him?'

'On suspicion? Hardly. We'd have to bring civil charges and then the fat would be in the fire. To make any other move would be to admit we know what he's up to. The fact of the matter is that at the moment surveillance is our only course of action.' He looked at Preece. 'So that's the position isn't it, Guy?'

Preece nodded. Quitman had the sense of a rehearsed exchange. He said, because he seemed trusted: 'Can I interrupt to ask one question about Frank Strange?'

'Certainly,' Hayter was almost bonhomous. 'Fire away.'

'What did he do?' he said bluntly.

By way of answer Hayter rose and walked over to the gunmetal filing cabinet behind the door, speaking slowly as he did so. 'Some months ago I received a memorandum which alleged that a senior member of the Directorate was putting the new relational data-base system and the enlargement of the data retrieval procedure to his own advantage.' And he drew out a clip of flimsy carbons, passing them to Quitman.

'But – !' he could not restrain his surprise. 'This is from Lister.'

'Absolutely,' said Hayter, nodding significantly. 'But in point of fact he doesn't name names and only refers to a certain 'senior officer'. Typical Lister of course. It was only after questioning that he agreed to reveal to me that the senior officer was Strange. He was frightened you see, and as it turned out, he was right to be. When Strange somehow got wind of what Lister was up to, he victimized him – perhaps to the point of suicide.' He looked at Quitman. 'So you see where the guilt lies when it comes to Lister,' and an odd expression passed across his face. 'You'll find the details of the case in the appendix. But they're not important. What's so interesting is the way Strange left such a trail of clues to his downfall.'

'Then why didn't you intervene sooner?'

'My dear chap,' Hayter patronized. 'You know how carefully we have to work here. We wanted to disturb Strange as little as possible. See what he was up to that way. It was a shame, a damn shame, that we were too late to save poor Lister.'

Quitman leafed slowly through the pages, but he didn't take in many details. The thing itself was the proof. There could be no more questions. He was thankful that his complete disillusion with Strange was justified before his eyes. He became aware that Hayter was speaking again.

'– you need to know that HQ Security are running a twenty-four-hour surveillance of Strange. Six men – working in pairs – on eight-hour shifts. His phone – both in Devon and London – has been intercepted and, for what it's worth, though I can't imagine he will be so clumsy, the Post Office will copy his mail. All routine stuff really.'

Quitman indicated no surprise.

'Our problem is that all the intelligence that is gathered for us about Strange's movements, conversations and plans has to be interpreted. Raw material of this kind is often very fragmentary and imprecise, full of references and allusions that only those close to the subject can understand. The key to counter-intelligence work still lies in reading the evidence correctly.'

Quitman agreed.

'Now then, Quitman, you know Strange better than anyone in the Directorate. I've cleared it with the counter-intelligence people that you should liaise between the security operation and ourselves. I'll also want you to supervise the collation and annotation of all the reports we receive about Strange.' He gave a grim smile. 'You've heard rumours about the incompetence of the internal security services. Well, I can tell you, off the record of course, that they're not exaggerated. I'm hoping that the presence of liaison-personnel from the Directorate will sharpen up their efforts.'

Hayter leaned across the desk. 'I attach the greatest significance to this programme. So, I believe, does Dangerfield, who has of course approved all these moves. A successful operation could advance your career remarkably. And I'm also hoping that you will find a real purpose in this work.' He paused again. 'Frankly, most of the battles fought against the threat to our society are mere shadow boxing. Of course we in the Directorate play our part and supply "the friends" with as much information as we can. But – what's the phrase – *sub specie* something – they're fighting the wrong battle. The real war, as I see it, the one that's going to count, is not against the traditional threat, but against ourselves, that is to say, against the buggers who want to destroy this country – and you know as well as I do how serious that threat is – from within. That is our contribution to the security of the state. In my view it's decisive.'

Quitman realized that his reactions were being carefully appraised and with typical prudence made no comment.

'You see, James,' said Preece, on cue, 'We – that's to say you and I – have to admit to ourselves that Strange is now part of this threat.' Quitman wondered momentarily if he was right to detect a note of derision in the way Preece echoed Hayter's language. 'Once we've done that, we can bring all the resources of the Directorate to bear on the matter. And I think,' Preece concluded, interrupting himself for a theatrical effect that Quitman had noticed was a mannerism with the new director, 'you'll be surprised, when we start to work together, how considerable those resources can be.'

'In an emergency, you understand,' added Hayter lamely.

'Oh, of course in an emergency,' replied Preece reassur ingly (and again it seemed to Quitman that Preece was almost mocking his colleague's concern for procedure). 'Of course,' he repeated with dramatic relish. 'But as James can now appreciate for himself, I fance, this is an emergency. In fact I'd go as far as to say that the very independence and integrity of the Directorate is at stake.' Hayter's relaxed expression hardened then, and Quitman saw that Preece's words had struck home at last.

CHAPTER EIGHT

The phone box had its glass smashed. Strange shivered in the raw cold. The press office was being difficult about Brian Hoskins. 'Who is it speaking please?' repeated the nice voice.

'I used to work with Brian before he joined you,' said Strange, dissembling. 'Way back in the Sixties. Met a mutual chum in a pub the other day and he said old Brian was with you working on the house rag.'

'He used to be the editor I think,' said the girl, 'but he left. Hold the line a moment.'

Strange held the line and pushed ten pence into the machine.

'Can I help you?' said a firmer, masculine voice.

'Yes – I'm trying to contact Brian Hoskins. An old mate of mine.'

'Can I have your name please?'

'Franks,' said Strange quietly. 'UPI.'

The man at the other end became less cagey at this revelation. 'Hoskins left some three years ago after a disagreement with his masters. I've no idea where he is now. I can transfer you to Personnel. They might have a forwarding address.' Strange said thank you very much, and waited. But Personnel were not helpful.

'I'm sorry, sir. We are not allowed to reveal names and addresses over the telephone.' Strange slammed down the receiver. There was nothing for it but to track down the back numbers of the house magazine.

The quickest, and probably the only way was a risk. He walked back to his flat, wondering where they were watching. That was an assumption now; he had given up hoping they'd go away. He changed out of his week-end clothes into his old working suit. Then, taking his briefcase and his rolled umbrella, he set out on the route that he had taken so many years in succession.

Coming up out of the Westminster tube station in the middle of the morning was an unusual experience. London seemed deserted. In place of the hurrying throngs of commuters there were only one or two conscientious MPs going to committee and a group of Japanese tourists deciphering coloured maps. He swung into Whitehall as usual and was soon at the entrance to the Old War Office. At least, he reassured himself, he could pick up his mail. The hallway was quiet. He pushed through the revolving doors apprehensively.

'Good morning, Albert.'

'Mr Strange, sir!' The doorman was genuinely pleased to see him. 'Back so soon, sir! You're looking very well if I may say – '

'Albert,' Strange cut him short. He didn't want to make a fuss. 'I've come to see Mr Preece. No, don't ring. He's expecting me. I can find my way.'

'Breaking all the rules, sir. That's not like you, Mr Strange!' Albert chuckled.

'You see what retirement does for you,' Strange joked, moving as fast as he could across the hallway. The security guard saluted in recognition. Strange got to the lift safely and was relieved to find one empty, waiting.

'Fifth floor, please.'

'Yes, sir.' The attendant smiled. 'Back so soon, sir.'

'I'm returning a couple of library books I happened to be in town.'

The half-lit, dead-cream corridor running along the top of the Old War Office was exactly as he remembered it, which only increased his uneasiness. He knew he had to hurry and pounded down the parquet, his bad leg thumping on the worn tiles. As he reached the double doors at the far end, he looked back. No one in sight. He pushed through.

The library was deserted as usual. The familiar warm bookish smell calmed him as he went over to the desk.

'Good morning, Miss Adams. I wonder – ' But he could

get no further. 'Mr Strange!' The elderly spinster in the tweed suit looked up from her catalogue, her harelip quivering with delight. 'Well, we didn't expect to see you back so soon. Now will you have a cup of tea and tell me all your news? It's no bother. Ellen has just – '

Strange interrupted her urgently. 'I'm in something of a hurry, Miss Adams. I'd love some tea, but could you put me on the right track while you're fetching it?'

'Well, of course. As busy as ever, I see. I quite understand of course. What is it you wanted?'

'I want to look at some back numbers of the house magazine.' He named the years.

'The house magazine? You mean *Print Out*.'

'That's the one.' Strange was apprehensive.

'Well, the records are rather patchy . . .' she started doubtfully. 'If we've got the one you want, it will be over there, by the encyclopaedias. D'you see, Mr Strange? There's bundles of magazines that I haven't had time to organize. You're welcome to burrow of course. Are you writing your memoirs, Mr Strange?'

'Shall I have the tea when I've finished?' asked Strange, fencing.

'Of course not. I'll bring it to you.'

There was a stack of publications in the glass cabinet in the alcove. He pulled them out on the table, spilling them this way and that, shuffling the issues like playing cards. Four years. Twelve issues a year. He worked fast. Tea arrived and he hardly looked up. Miss Adams went away. He knew she was crestfallen. He would have a chat on the way out if he had time. The muted burr of the library phone stopped his sorting. 'Library,' Miss Adams's piping tones rang clear. 'Hello, Milly.' Strange switched back to the sorting. Then he counted. Forty-eight issues, all in sequence, spanning all the possible years. That was a piece of luck. He began to read. Cover-page first, then the list of contents, then the index and then a quick glance at the letters just in case. Nothing in the first year. He finished the tea at a gulp. Nothing in the next. He looked at the clock. He'd been here half an hour already.

Hoskins's stuff was scattered throughout the following year. He checked as carefully as he dared. The phone purred again when he was on the October issue of the final year. 'Library. Speaking. Yes sir. Yes!' Miss Adams sounded so pleased. At any other time it would have been a compliment. 'Isn't that nice . . .' Her voice trailed away as the line was cut. Strange reckoned he had three minutes. Time to make one note. It wasn't the information he wanted, but it was enough to keep going on. He flicked hurriedly through the last issue and as he piled the magazines back in the cabinet, Miss Adams came across with her good news. 'I've just had Mr Preece on the telephone. He's heard you're visiting us again. So now your little secret is all over the building. Did you find what you wanted?'

'Yes, thank you.' Strange felt he was losing the art of conversation. Footsteps sounded in the corridor. He tensed himself. They had taken longer than he expected. It was not Preece but a security guard.

'Mr Strange, sir. Message from Reception. There's a taxi waiting for you outside.'

'My, but you are in a hurry,' said Miss Adams, watching the two men disappearing out of the library.

Quitman had received the phone call from Preece as he was sorting out the stationery on his new desk. He went at once. Preece looked slightly harassed. As Quitman came in he was scribbling a personal note with the dip-pen that he affected. 'Strange is here,' he said, slamming the paper on the blotter and folding fiercely.

'Good God! Where?'

'That's what I'm about to find out. Now then,' he said, calling in the group of old age pensioners who constituted the lift men, from the adjoining office. 'You all know Mr Strange. I am supposed to have a very important meeting with him at eleven-thirty but he's disappeared in this building. Which of you saw him last?'

'Yes, sir.'

'Which floor did he want?'

'Fifth, sir.'

'Did he say where he was going?'

'Oh yes, sir. He said he was going to the library to return some books, sir.'

Preece turned back to Quitman. 'Call Miss Adams, please.' He took the phone. 'Miss Adams? Is Mr Strange with you?' The liftmen shuffled back to their tea. Preece turned to Quitman. 'Get him out of here,' he said in a low voice. 'Without fuss.' Quitman had seen this coming but flinched anyway. 'I don't care how you do it,' said Preece, 'but get him out of here. I'm going to brief Hayter.' He stormed out.

The next day, reflecting on Strange's extraordinary visit, Quitman recognized in this incident the final confirmation of Hayter's account of Strange's retirement. There could be no lingering doubts now. He sat at his new desk studying the previous day's surveillance transcripts, experiencing a quiet thrill at the sense of private power. Shortly, Preece was due to cross-question Miss Adams and Albert about Strange's visit.

There was a knock on the door. It was his new secretary. 'Mr Preece says that he is with Miss Adams in his room and would you be so good as to join him.'

'Thank you.' Whatever Strange was doing in the library, he thought as he walked towards Preece's door, it wasn't changing books. He'd run that errand for his old boss during his last week.

The long day was both tiring and exhilarating. He came out into Whitehall at seven-fifteen, just as the street lamps that still survived vandalism began to glow more strongly in the dusk. He decided that he would make another attempt to see Liz.

Their last meeting had been disastrous. She ice-cool and contemptuous, he reasonable but typically indecisive. Today he resolved to be firm and winning. But a woman had thrown herself on to the District Line and the journey was prolonged and depressing. As Quitman dashed up the stairs to the flat, restoring his circulation, he felt all his apprehensions return.

But there was no answer to his ringing. He searched in his pocket for the key and tried to fit it in the door. At the third attempt he realized that she had changed the lock.

Perhaps Mrs Bennett could help. The wispy Irish landlady with the fair grey brow was down in her basement flat having a little drop of something with an old friend in the parlour, and would he be pleased to join them. But Quitman would not be entertained, despite his affection for the old lady to whom, on many occasions in the past, he had turned for help.

'There, Jamie,' said Mrs Bennett, who had a soothsayer's understanding of his relationship with Liz. 'She's running a bit wild at the moment, but never you mind, we'll be seeing some more of you, I don't doubt.' Quitman was comforted by this reassurance, and when she asked him to entrust the note he had written for Liz to her keeping, he marvelled once again at her wisdom, rifled in his briefcase for the letter he had indeed scribbled on the Tube and continued on his way to Barons Court for a lonely week-end of medieval chivalry.

CHAPTER NINE

There was a roadblock on the main road into Southampton. Strange found himself trapped in a long queue before he had time to turn. For a mad moment he feared it was for him, but relaxed when he spotted local police squad cars.

'What's all this about?' he asked when he reached the checkpoint. The lethargic police officer looked at him without interest. 'The usual. Bombers on the run. Keys to the boot, please, sir.'

'It's not locked.' Another constable pulled the catch, and rummaged about among his books, papers and clothes. 'A regular Pickfords,' Strange heard him say as he slammed the door.

Strange speeded away from the hold-up. The green mini-van was jammed several cars back and here at last was a chance to break away from the surveillance. Weaving through light traffic, he swung on to a minor road and came into the city on the west side. He ran the car to the top of a multi-storey car-park and, happy at the sudden freedom, went off to find Hoskins.

The offices of the *Southern Evening News* take their inspiration from the architecture of the inter-war dictatorships. Strange could imagine Mussolini opening the building with approval and shouting a speech from its balcony to an enthusiastic crowd in the pedestrian precinct in which it now stands. Inside, the hallway, apart from a display of press shots a few bundles of yesterday's edition, was empty. There was a spotty girl in pink at the desk. When Strange came in, she was on the phone to a friend. He stood and waited. In due course, the girl said, Bye for now, and devoted her full attention to the visitor.

'Mr Hoskins please.'

'Do you have an appointment?'

'No – but it's urgent.'

The girl made a face. 'Hold on a moment – what's the name?'

'Strange. Frank Strange.' He flashed his official pass. 'Government Service.' The girl rang through. 'They're sending someone down for you.' Strange picked up yesterday's paper and studied the account of the bomb attack on the city's shopping centre. Several dead. Millions of pounds worth of property damaged.

'Mr Strange.' It was a young man, with a stammer and a sharp suit: a cub journalist. 'It's this way.' The boy had the mild belligerence of the would-be investigative reporter.

The editor's office was a partitioned cubby-hole set apart from the newsroom. Brian Hoskins was in his shirtsleeves, a balding, swarthy journalist with strong eyebrows and a hunched stance. He was leaning forward on the desk yelling into the telephone – one of three – and correcting a set of galleys with a roving pencil.

'Murder, for God's sake,' he shouted as Strange came in. He waved him to a chair. The young reporter, cowed, withdrew. 'Yes – yes. Get in there – balls! We need it soonest.' He slammed the phone back in its cradle and dropped into his old cane chair. Then he clapped his hand to his head, stared at Strange for an instant and said: 'I know you. You're from the department. What's the name? No – don't tell me! I'm supposed to be good at this game. Strange, Frank Strange.' He extended a hand impetuously. Strange cut him short, ignoring the handshake.

'Didn't the girl tell you?' He did not conceal his irritation.

Hoskins looked at him, then threw his head back and roared with laughter. 'Don't look like that. It's not your fault, old son. I just happen to hate the department.' He seemed to be about to say more, but fell silent. Strange said nothing, but made a mental note. He observed the chaos of paper, the yellow maps on the wall, the old posters and the piles of out-of-date newsprint. Hoskins stared at the galleys with a bulging eye and made a lightning correction. 'Well,' he went on, 'what can I do for you?'

'Are you busy?'

'It never stops. As you see.' He waved expansively. 'Go on anyway.'

'I wanted to talk to you about Dick Lister.'

For the first time since Strange had arrived, Hoskins stopped performing. He looked at Strange curiously, suddenly sober. 'Poor bugger,' he said. 'I suppose you people are busy stuffing the corpse so it doesn't leak.'

'We are concerned to establish,' said Strange in his most measured tones, 'that the case is a closed one.'

'No room for blackmail, bribery or corruption, eh?' He looked at Strange curiously. 'But you're C Directorate aren't you? Lister's boss and all that. I didn't know you were into the security business. Or is Hayter getting too big for his boots again?'

'In some cases, C Directorate has to get interested in field security,' replied Strange stiffly. 'As a matter of fact,' he added, relishing the irony, 'Michael Hayter doesn't even know I'm here.'

'Typical,' said Hoskins. Then he brightened. 'Well, well,' he chuckled, 'the taxpayer should be grateful that the department is doing a worthwhile operation for a change. Lister was a leaky barrel if ever I knew one.'

'That's why I wanted to talk to you,' said Strange with emphasis.

Hoskins made another correction to the paper, and then focused carefully on his visitor. 'You know that, do you?' he said.

'I've told you, I'm following up loose ends. A close family friend of Lister's told me that Dick trusted you to put his case for him in the press.'

'I'm a journalist, Frank. Always have been. Now I'm an editor and I play editors. When I was pasting up your house rag for a living my journalist's nose smelt a lot of bad smells in the department. Wait – ' he raised a minatory finger. 'I'm not criticizing you. I remember they always said you were a good thing. You were sorting the place out, they said.' He paused to look at Strange. 'That enquiry made the nastiest of all the nasty smells I came across, but there still weren't enough hard facts for a good story. The nearest I got to backing Lister was an editorial about the risks and responsibilities of computerization within the department.'

'I missed it. Did it achieve anything?'

'It was never published. Hayter stepped in.' Hoskins made a dramatic gesture. 'Hold the front page. All that sort of nonsense. He said it would stir up needless controversy. So I resigned.' Strange remembered Hoskins's farewell letter in the November issue of *Print Out*. Some of its ringing phrases must have come from that lost editorial. Hoskins was still talking, 'Mind you, I was fed up anyway. Lister wouldn't stop pestering. I wanted to get back to real journalism. Your magazine was a stop-gap after I was made redundant. When this job came up I jumped at it. It's a hack's haven; I was glad to go, Frank. The secrecy was getting me down. God knows how you stick it.'

Strange let the ensuing silence erode some of Hoskins's self-confidence. The clatter of the newspaper office rattled through the frosted glass. Then the phone rang and Hoskins began to perform again, thumping the desk, marching up and down the office at the end of the lead, and staring malevolently at the newsroom. When he finished he stood against the door and looked at Strange.

'Most of your loose ends were with Lister – and he's dead. That's the best bit of luck you've had for a long time, isn't it?'

'Why?'

'He was an embarrassment to you, wasn't he? All those accusations.'

'Did you believe him?' Strange pursued.

'Well, if it's any indication, he thought I'd let him down. You see I just couldn't be sure that he wasn't as bent as the rest of them.'

Strange decided to risk the direct approach. 'Tell me, since Lister never told me himself, what was his version of the facts?'

'You mean about the enquiry?'

Strange nodded.

Hoskins's answer was to unlock the small wall safe behind his desk and pull out a battered envelope. 'You can't have these,' he said waving some sheets of typescript, 'because I'm not that much in love with the department, but I'll tell you what's in them. A journalist has a right to shield his sources,' he defended. 'Now I'm not a computer boffin and I may not get the jargon right, so you'll have to interrupt if I get the details messed up. Lister's story,' he went on, scanning the notes, 'was that he went into the terminal room in the Cheltenham office one evening after most people had gone home and found a chap called Ellison hard at work in front of the VDU. Okay? That was not unusual. Ellison had the right access credentials and often worked late. But what surprised Lister was Ellison's reaction to his appearance.'

'What did he do?'

Hoskins read out: 'Ellison cleared the page and logged off in a hurry.'

'That means he broke his line to the computer,' Strange interpreted.

'Then he goes on, "When Ellison had left the terminal room I went over to the VDU and rolled back the pages. Since Ellison hadn't cleared the programme I was able to run through the last two pages and make notes." Do you follow?' asked Hoskins.

Strange said yes.

'In a nutshell, Lister claimed that Ellison was getting access to an index of a library of data – I'm quoting here – and that the output was in a format that Lister, who was apparently pretty hot at that sort of thing, did not recognize. He became suspicious and made hand-written notes . . .'

'Do you have a copy of his notes?'

Hoskins shook his head. 'No – surely all the evidence went back to London?'

Strange made a non-commital reply. Then he said: 'But wasn't there more to Lister's story than that?'

'More? Certainly.' He made a clumsy gesture. 'All this, and more – much, much more – in your next instalment!' As he turned the page he became sober again. 'That was only the beginning. The next bit is more technical. Lister was determined to find out what the information was that Ellison was getting access to. He says here that on two separate occasions he arranged for the computer to "crash" while Ellison was using it.'

'Clever,' said Strange involuntarily. 'That means that the computer became overloaded. When that happens it ceases to function properly and the only way to clear it for further use is to "dump" the disc. Information on the disc-pack in use will come out as hard copy, which, presumably, Lister could then analyse. Is that what happened? What did he find?'

'It was all pretty inconclusive apparently. The Directorate's ways are so secret that it was impossible to prove that Ellison was doing something he shouldn't have been. Ellison of course denied everything. And the Directorate collects such dirty material as a matter of routine that it's impossible to prove that the stuff that appears on the screen isn't being used legitimately. I mean that's a real worry, isn't it?'

'It could be – without the safeguards,' said Strange.

'You believe in those, do you?' Hoskins sounded contemptuous.

'You obviously don't.' Strange made a guess, 'Was that what the row with Hayter was about?'

Hoskins gave him an odd look. 'It was part of it,' he admitted, 'but I'd rather not go into that, if you don't mind. It's nothing to do with Lister.'

'All right. Tell me about the enquiry.'

'Well, it was led by Preece as you know – of course you do, he was your deputy!' Hoskins laughed, 'Don't tell me – '

'He was given a pretty free hand,' Strange interrupted. 'Remember, the whole case meant a lot less to us than it did to Lister. Tell me what Lister said about Preece.'

'As you'd expect he loathed him. Preece completely discredited the notes from the VDU. There was that expert from London who explained that the index that Lister was so excited about was just part of another system.'

Once again Strange felt excitement quicken within him. Expert? It couldn't have been Mayer. Not three years ago. Hoskins was still speaking.

'So Preece got pretty angry with Lister I believe. Accused him of meddling in an area that was none of his business. You see, there were rumours.'

'What do you mean?'

'I'm surprised you haven't mentioned Aidan Cooper. As you know, Lister accused him along with Ellison.' Strange nodded, and stored the fact in his mind. 'But Cooper and Lister were friends. Dick had no reason to be fond of Ellison, but why do you put your pals in the shit except to save your skin? Do you see what I'm saying? Well, it wasn't me that was saying it, it was other colleagues. They thought that Lister was executing a clever cover-up. Retaliating first, so to speak.'

'So the London office is not alone in thinking that Lister was up to something?' asked Strange with relief. He felt his zest for the case returning.

'Well, I've no evidence either way, but there was something about Dick, wasn't there? I can't pin it down but I wouldn't have trusted him further than I could kick him.'

'I must confess,' agreed Strange, 'I never liked the man. As you say, he had such an unfortunate manner. He seemed secretive even in our secret world. I've seen his wife since – since he died. He treated her shabbily as well.'

'Ah,' said Hoskins, 'and that's another whole story, the Lister-Ellison fracas. I know there's a lot in this case, Frank. I can't say I'm sorry that he's giving you a headache though. I never much trusted the department either.'

'Your fears are groundless, I assure you. You may not like the work we do in the Directorate, but I promise you it's essential.'

'It's not the work,' said Hoskins, 'it's the people – begging your pardon. It's the people who speak another language that I don't understand. Coral. Assembler. Fortran. That's a lot of power you have at your disposal, Frank. I'm not surprised you want to know what Lister was up to. I mean I was never sure exactly where his loyalties lay.'

Strange looked at Hoskins, 'I'm glad you said that. I was beginning to wonder – ' he broke off. 'I'll be talking to friend Cooper shortly. Perhaps he can clear up one or two mysteries. He's at – ' he paused and Hoskins interrupted as he expected.

'He left Cheltenham after the Lister business. Set up on his own. Basingstoke I think Dick said. Of course they weren't speaking much after the enquiry.'

'No, I don't suppose they were.' If Hoskins was right about the enquiry Cooper ought to have a hefty grudge against Lister that would make him talk. Strange rose stiffly and stretched his leg. Hoskins came round the desk to shake hands.

'Glad of the chat, Frank. No hard feelings I hope. Don't hesitate to give us a tinkle if you want help. Can you find your way out?'

Strange slipped out of the *Southern Evening News* with the afternoon edition by the trade entrance. It was raining hard and he saw no one.

CHAPTER TEN

The Directorate did not discover that Strange had shaken off his trackers until the next day. HQ Security had hoped that surveillance would pick him up again somewhere in Southampton and were watching all the main roads out of the city, so it wasn't until the following morning that, with some embarrassment, they admitted defeat. Strange had vanished.

When Quitman took the news through to Preece, he saw that this latest shock in the Strange case had touched a raw nerve. He watched Preece across the desk and saw the crow's-feet at the corner of each cold grey eye quiver slightly. The director's immaculate professional manner was being ruffled by the strain of this operation. Anger and alarm seemed equally mixed as he spoke of the bombers, the crisis and Strange's disappearance. 'Get them to watch his London house and the cottage in Devon for a start. Ask Dr Mayer to get a print-out of all known contacts, addresses and phone numbers. Then give it to Security at once. I'd recommend that they double the detail. Where was he last seen?'

Quitman admitted that he didn't have a proper report, just a brief telephone message. Preece was very brisk. 'This loss of contact should be only temporary. There's probably a simple explanation. After all, he shouldn't know we're watching.'

As the morning progressed Quitman recognized that he still found it difficult to give orders to his new assistants. At least his new responsibilities had ceased to cause excitement. The library incident had made quite a stir, despite Preece's attempts to keep it secret. Whatever was Mr Strange up to now, people said. And when Miss Adams let slip to a friend in Data that 'nice Mr Preece' had given her an interview about it – 'quite an interrogation, you know' – she found there was a new interest in her collection of blue books and encyclopaedias. But the best bit of gossip by far was that James Quitman had been present at the meeting, 'taking notes, my dear', said Miss Adams to anyone who cared to chat for long enough.

Neve was furious. He went straight to Preece. His anger made him unusually forthright. 'What is the meaning of this? Quitman is two years junior. His attitude is a disgrace. The job wasn't even advertised. I shall take the case straight to the union. What is going on? You promised to give me a good chit with Hayter.'

Preece waited until Neve had become merely crestfallen. Then he offered him a chair, some coffee and a cigarette. Neve fussed over these minor attentions, grateful at the recognition of wounded pride.

'Now, Charles,' Preece went on, 'I am forbidden, as you know, from disclosing details, but I want you to understand that I did all that I could for you with Hayter. I am as disappointed as you are. You must understand that Quitman's new responsibilities, which do not amount to a formal promotion, are in no way a reflection against you. He has in fact been chosen for his new job not so much for his gifts as for what he is.'

Neve exhaled, calmer. 'So all this really means is an *ad hoc* secondment.'

'Precisely.'

'It is not graded.'

'No – as you rightly pointed out, it was not even advertised. Quitman was co-opted for special purposes that I am not empowered to reveal. So please don't make a fuss with the union, Charles. That *would* ruin your chances with Hayter.' Preece paused, and, sensing that Neve wanted more, added, 'The chief is only too aware of your seniority and, more importantly, your particular contribution to the work of the Directorate.' Neve began to stutter something. Preece went on: 'Now that Strange and Lister have gone it will only be a matter of time before the inevitable reshuffle gives you very considerable promotion. I shall see to that personally, I promise you.'

Neve's pride reared for a moment. 'I'm satisfied with that explanation,' he said. Then he apologized. 'That's – that's very good of you. I'm most grateful.'

Preece nodded at him with approval, betraying nothing.

'Quitman's new job is to do with the Lister business, isn't it?' Neve hazarded with fresh confidence.

'In strictest confidence,' Preece began carefully, 'it is only to do with that. Quitman had this extremely,' he was choosing his words with caution, 'good relationship with Strange. Strange trusted him. He knew a lot about the Strange régime that isn't in the files, actually.' He looked slyly at Neve. 'One of Strange's typical irregularities. The next few months are transitional. When we've used him, we shan't need him again.'

Neve smiled in triumph. Preece looked at him with gravity. 'What I say behind closed doors is of course strictly confidential,' he repeated. 'Hayter has not said as much to me, but on merit and on paper there is no comparison between you and Quitman.'

The red telephone buzzed. 'Speaking. Yes, do.' Smiling faintly, Preece looked at Neve. 'So you have nothing to worry about. As I say, this is a transitional phase.' There was a knock. 'Come in.'

Quitman came in with a sheaf of notes.

'Oh. Hello, Charles.'

''Morning, James.' Neve rose, placed his cup ostentatiously on the desk and nodded at Preece. 'Well, I must be going. Thanks for the briefing.'

Neve went out, and when the door had closed Preece smiled at Quitman. 'Poor old Charles. He's very put out at your new job. He thinks he's been passed over.'

'That was the briefing?'

'He was in a very disagreeable frame of mind when he came in at first, but I think I reassured him. He was wanting to take the case to the union, and was anxious to have your appointment rescinded.'

Quitman was shocked. 'But he couldn't do this particular job, could he? It's not his field.' He was the first to recognize why Hayter had chosen him, but was also now proud of his promotion, even though it hadn't brought Liz back.

'Of course not,' said Preece, reassuring, 'but you can't say that to someone like Neve. He's behaving like a spoilt child, and he's very imprudent. It won't do his chances any good when the next reshuffle comes up.'

'He seemed okay when I came in.' Quitman was rapidly discovering a new willingness to share his opinions with Preece. It was partly that he sympathized with the strain under which his boss was having to work.

'He came round of course. That's the absurd little man he is, you see.' He checked. 'The only serious aspect of the matter is that there must have been a leak.'

'What do you mean?'

'Neve knows that you are working on the Lister-Strange case.' Preece seemed suddenly hostile; there was a distinct note of suspicion in his voice.

Quitman was alarmed. 'I can assure you – ' he began pompously.

'James,' Preece intervened. 'I'm not suggesting anything like that. It was probably one of the girls in the office. There are some secrets one can't keep. Even here. But,' he stared at Quitman, 'you will be very scrupulous, won't you? You have to learn that power is lonely.'

As he walked back to his office, Quitman reflected on the interview and Preece's parting words. He did feel lonely now.

It was partly to do with Liz. Her silent absence was hurting. The small flat in Barons Court, the narrow cold bed and the unappetizing cycle of Vesta curries, tinned soup, and sausages and eggs was beginning to depress him. Depression was enervating. His notes on medieval chivalry gathered dust by the record-player. He was letting his work at the Directorate fill his evenings more and more. He was lonely.

Rosie Walford for whom Quitman had recently developed a particular fascination (especially when she heard on the grapevine that his woman had gone off with another man), observed this closely. She also noticed that if she stopped to pass the time of day with him, he responded with pathetic eagerness. He, for his part, considered that he was observing her quickened interest quite dispassionately. Though he was not a snob, he found it difficult in his conversations and meetings with her to forget that Rosie's pride would not let her admit that she lived with her old mother in Lewisham and had been to the local Tech. Miss Walford was on the make. In that respect she was something of a joke in the clubby, well-connected world of the department. Cases of slack security were often compared to her knicker elastic. At the same time, Rosie had a rather touching determination to acquire some *savoir faire,* if necessary at night school. She also had a definite and confident allure that she knew would overcome the deepest prejudice.

On the day that Strange vanished Quitman had a pub lunch with Rosie.

'What'll you have?'

Rosie's attempt at sophistication was to ask for vodka and lime. Quitman had a straight Schweppes and pretended it was gin-and-tonic. In her manner towards him she displayed all the frankness that he remembered at Strange's leaving party. He had thought he would never forgive her for that insult to his old mentor, and as he paid for the drinks realized how quickly his attitude had been changed by the events of the last few weeks.

They perched together in the crowded saloon bar. He had chosen a pub away from Whitehall and they recognized no one. But Rosie was worried about bombs and Quitman drew attention to himself peering under the surrounding stools. Eventually she was satisfied. They sipped their drinks.

'How's work?' he said. After so many years of easy conversation with Liz he found it difficult to chat to Rosie in the right way.

'Okay. I like Preece. He doesn't bully like Strange.'

'That's true,' he found himself agreeing, against his better judgement.

'Do you miss him – Strange?'

'I did to start with – in the first week or so. Not now. I like Preece too.' He was feeling awkward with the conversation. Out of the blue he said, 'Is he sexy, do you think?'

Rosie giggled, feigned shock, and felt a small glow of triumph. She knew she had a way with men. 'He hasn't made any advances yet, if that's what you mean.' She looked at him. Quitman noticed that her lips were wet and that there was a stain of lipstick on her left eye-tooth. Rosie giggled again. 'Not like Charles.'

'Neve!' Quitman couldn't hide his surprise. 'Sexy or advances?' He had never noticed Charles showing a special interest in Rosie.

'Oh, he's terribly suggestive. *Doubles entendres* all the way.' She looked at him again. 'But he's such a bore.' They smiled.

'Another one?'

'If you will.'

'Of course.' Quitman repeated the order. He looked at her as she bent to the second vodka. Tiny beads of sweat ran along her pale hairline and her long artificial lashes were turned down. A lot of make-up. Too much scent. Her executive women's suit, the waistcoat, the cut and colour of the cloth, was fashionable and quite expensive, though indefinably vulgar, he considered, admitting a mild prejudice of taste. You get well-paid in the Civil Service he thought. Rosie Walford was conventional and was a trifle drunk, but she had an inescapable attraction. After her third vodka she became indiscreet.

'Charles hates you, you know.'

'Has he told you?' Quitman was concerned.

'Not ex-actly,' she gave a little laugh, sensing his anxiety and loving to tease. 'But you can see he's terribly jealous.' She smiled at him. 'You're terribly successful you see, the BYM of the Directorate.'

'BYM?'

'Bright-Young-Man,' she emphasized the words carefully, looking straight at him.

'Right place at the right time,' Quitman parried.

'I'm sure Charlie doesn't think so. I'm sure he sees how clever you are and how Preece likes you.' This was too overt. Quitman felt disgusted, but there she was, flirting with him, fascinating herself with him, it seemed. She was still speaking ' – I think you're going to be very powerful one day.'

It crossed his mind then that she was about to ask him a blunt question about Lister or Strange. 'Hadn't we better be getting back to the office? I've a lot to do this afternoon.'

'Oh, yes. It is late, isn't it?' She gave a genteel burp. 'Thanks ever so for the lunch. It's a shame the time's so short.'

Quitman guessed what was expected. 'Perhaps we could meet for a drink after work one day, go and see a movie or something.' He heard himself sound diffident and began to feel embarrassed. Perhaps she wasn't interested after all.

'That would be nice,' said Rosie, overcoming his shame. They came out into the November weather, an ambulance was racing down the wrong side of the road towards them. 'I won't let you forget that,' she shouted against the siren. Quitman felt a surge of pride. Rosie added, 'That gives me a lovely excuse to keep Charles at bay. He's such a drag.'

Soon they were back at the office. The latest reports on Quitman's desk indicated that Strange was not to be found in London or in Devon.

It was extraordinary to watch the effect of Strange's disappearance. When Lister died Quitman's section had crowded round the corpse like parasites. In a week they had picked it clean. HQ Security had been doing the same to Strange. But suddenly their victim had vanished. The Directorate was buzzing in confusion.

By the following morning Preece had surrendered any pretence at disinterest. He summoned Quitman early. The department's security unit's abbreviated admission of failure the previous day lay on the desk before him. Quitman had never seen him so animated.

'Hayter's right. They're incompetent. I mean, Strange isn't even aware of the surveillance. It would be different if he was trying to evade – '

94

Quitman cut in tactfully, 'That's not so certain now. The operators I spoke to yesterday suspect that Strange knows what he is doing.'

Preece took note. 'It's possible, I suppose. A man with a guilty conscience . . . it's not as if he doesn't know what we get up to here. He'll have seen it done dozens of times in the past.' Quitman cut in. 'It's almost a certainty that he knows what's happening. For instance it appears that Strange has managed to deactivate the radio bleeper they fitted to his car.'

Preece looked serious. 'I see,' he said, then became optimistic. 'Even so, Southampton's not London. They say they're watching all the roads.' He slapped the transcripts petulantly. 'What are they doing, for god's sake?' He pushed the papers away. 'But we mustn't pre-judge. Perhaps they've tracked him down overnight.'

But they hadn't. By mid-morning there was still no sign of Strange. Preece began to interfere more and more in Quitman's liaison work with HQ Security. Dr Mayer was told that the secrecy of the Strange operation necessitated disguising the applications programmes. Delays occurred. By lunchtime Preece was in a state of rage against the information flow.

'Memo. to Michael Hayter, copy Cornelius Mayer,' he dictated crisply into the desk recorder. 'The current data-flow arrangements are abysmal. I recommend that we originate a speed-up of the data-merge programme soonest.'

Quitman, who was in the office, knew that was exactly what Dr Mayer was after. And Hayter would back it if he thought he could carry the Service chiefs, who were suspicious of the Directorate's independent computer system, with him. It would depend on Dangerfield. Remote, but all-seeing, Dangerfield's view was always decisive. Quitman knew very well that the Directorate's modernization programme was probably the most controversial development within the department.

'You see the seriousness of the situation,' said Preece, switching off the tape-recorder. 'One man can move twenty times as fast as a bureaucracy, especially when he knows what he's after. We're slower – we can't help that – and we have to react to his movements. There's only one comforting aspect to this silence. It means he can't have gone to the press with his story yet. If he had all the evidence he needed to make a plausible case to Fleet Street – though I can't imagine what it could be – we'd have heard about it by now. That's why we've got to find him. To see who he's visiting. Who he's talking to. We can intuit a lot from the people he talks to.'

It was late afternoon when Quitman got an urgent call on the internal tannoy – 'Mr Quitman, please report at once to Room 10B. Mr Quitman, please report at once to Room 10B.'

Preece was jubilant. 'I've just heard that Strange visited the *Southern Evening News* at their main Southampton office yesterday afternoon. I've just spoken to the editor.'

'One of Strange's contacts?' Quitman queried.

Preece seemed defensive about the tip-off. 'A man named Brian Hoskins. Quite amiable as journalists go. You may remember him. He used to work on the house magazine.'

Quitman did not enquire how Preece had discovered this contact. He said: 'Where is Strange now?'

Preece checked. 'Unfortunately Hoskins didn't have a clue.'

'What was he after?'

Preece looked at him. He sounded offhand. 'Oh, as you might expect, information about Lister's past.' He seemed rather evasive. 'All our assumptions are right. Strange is still on the Lister trail.'

CHAPTER ELEVEN

The grey city concrete of Basingstoke had merged into the
weather that was spread like a dark bruise above it. Strange
drove over the railway bridge away from the city centre.
Accutron Systems Ltd occupied a brand-new building in the
industrial estate. But he avoided the glassy reception office
and found the trade door at the side.

'Is Mr Cooper in today?'

'Would you hold on a moment, sir. I'll find him for you.'
The flashy young executive disappeared into an office behind
the counter, and then bobbed back in confusion for
Strange's name.

Through an open door Strange could see a small
warehouse in which he recognized standard personal
computers. The office door banged open and another, older
salesman came out. 'Mr Strange?'

'Yes,' said Strange with expectation.

'I'm afraid Mr Cooper is very busy in a meeting at the
moment.'

'Will he be in this afternoon?'

'I regret he'll be away this afternoon.'

'I have a very important matter I want to discuss with
him.' But the man was not going to give an inch. 'I suggest
that you get in touch with Mr Cooper in writing, outlining
your proposals in a letter. Mr Cooper is a very busy man. If
you go out and turn left you will get back on to the main
road.' The man was escorting him to the door. There was no
point resisting.

The day before, on leaving Hoskins, Strange had gone
straight to Avis cars down at the docks and hired a smart red
Ford. Now he sat in it, listening to the radio, watching the
Accutron offices. At one-thirty, the young man in the
maroon suit came out of the front door, looked up and down

the street and then disappeared inside again. Shortly afterwards, he came out in the company of the older salesman and a small, overweight businessman in a rumpled dark suit, heavy executive spectacles and a small military moustache.

Strange gave them a hundred yards and then switched on the engine. They left the industrial zone, passed two pubs and turned down into a back street. No Entry. Strange parked in a hurry and, following on foot, saw the three men queuing into an Indian restaurant. As he followed them inside the sound of the raga jangled with the bells on the door. Cooper and his men, the only other diners, were settling themselves in a corner. The manager hurried forward to greet him, and he was ushered to an empty table.

Cooper was two away with his back to him. His young assistant and the older salesman were facing. They ignored Strange, speaking in an undertone to Cooper. Strange ordered and sat sipping a warm lager. Suddenly Cooper and his men got up in the middle of their meal, placed fifteen pounds on the table and moved towards the coat rack.

'Aidan Cooper?' said Strange, also rising. 'Could I have a word with you in – '

'I beg your pardon. I don't know who the hell you are,' said Cooper. 'I've never seen you before in my life. I'm a busy man. Excuse me.'

The bells on the door clashed and the manager, ascending from the basement kitchen with Strange's curry, found three customers leaving in a hurry and a fourth, glass in hand, standing in the middle of the restaurant. He broke into Bengali and had an argument with the waiter. Strange returned to his seat. The food was tepid, but he ate it stolidly out of habit, drained the lager, paid and left.

This time he went straight to the reception desk.

'Mr Cooper, please.'

'Mr Cooper is – ' But at that moment Cooper, in the middle of an already-formed sentence to the telephonist, burst in. 'By the way, Sue – ' He stopped. 'Now look here, Mr Strange, I'm very busy this afternoon – '

'You're going out, aren't you?' said Strange pleasantly.

'Who told you that?' he snapped.

'You ought to be more careful how you choose your staff, Mr Cooper.'

'How dare you. Now kindly leave my premises before I lose my temper and call the police.'

'Is this how you usually treat your customers?'

'You know very well –' Cooper stopped and looked at the girl. 'Please go away, Mr Strange. I'm very busy just now. By all means write me a letter, but I can't talk at present. Show Mr Strange out, will you Sue. Good afternoon.' He slammed the door and went back inside.

Strange, to the receptionist's relief, turned and walked out into the street crowded with housewives queuing for bread. He bought some Queen's Velvet and also a cheap blue biro at the nearest W. H. Smith. Back in the car he set about accepting Cooper's invitation. Once the letter was delivered all he had to do was wait.

The Basingstoke Post House is no place to pass the time, but when the office day was over Strange knew he had to be available, just in case. If nothing happened, he would try again tomorrow. He enjoyed the anonymity. It meant freedom. He sat in his ground floor room, with the Avis car parked outside, making endless cups of tea at the self-catering unit and watching television. The gaudy images from all over the world danced across the screen and he reflected that, even when so much could be seen and so much known, he could still sit quite alone in old-fashioned obscurity. The fear would come later.

At ten o'clock there was a knock. Strange pulled on his shoes and went over to the narrow hallway. There was another. Strange tensed himself.

'Who is it?'

'Room service, sir.'

Strange unlocked the door. The black maid was holding a pile of trays of pre-packaged breakfasts. There were ugly lacerations down the side of her face. She seemed exhausted.

'Breakfast, sir? There's no restaurant in the early morning, sir,' she explained. The tears in her eyes must be pain, thought Strange.

'Yes, thank you very much.' He hesitated. 'I've got a kettle on now, actually, if you'd care for a cup, It'll be fresh,' he added.

'Oh, thank you, sir,' said the girl and burst into tears. Strange was embarrassed. He shut the door quickly, hoping that the corridor was clear. 'Now don't cry,' a sense of inadequacy rose within him. 'Drink this and you'll feel better.' He sat her down. 'Don't you think you should see a doctor?'

'There ain't no doctor.' There was anger and frustration in her voice. 'They've closed the surgery. My mother done her best. She was a nurse in Birmingham, see.'

'What happened to you?'

The girl cupped her hands round the hot white rim. 'My boy-friend crashed his bike. Now – ' she choked and the tea spilt.

'Don't worry – '

'Now he's – dead.' Strange let her cry then, and the tragedy removed his embarrassment at her tears that ran into the tea. At length he said, 'You were lucky.'

The girl turned on him with a rustle of her nylon costume. 'No, I ain't sir. Not in this country. He was the lucky one.' A bitter laugh drove the tears freshly down her face, 'I'd rather be dead.'

'Oh, it's not as bad as all that. You'll get over it. The cuts will heal,' Strange repeated the old formulae.

'I'm sorry sir. You're a very nice man, but you don't understand. If you're black, you're nobody. I'd rather be dead.' The girl got up. 'Ta for the tea, sir. Have a nice breakfast.' And she walked straight out not looking back. Strange didn't move for a while. Later he locked the door and waited.

At midnight there was laughter in the next room, but by one o'clock the Post House was quiet. At two there was only a grey glow like moonlight through the curtains, and the occasional sound of a car revving into the night. At three he dozed. At four there was only night sound. At five, headlights searched past his window in a sweeping arc, and a car stopped at the front entrance. He had an urge to go and see who it was but stayed staring into the milky darkness listening attentively. Then the car started again and the sound receded. The door in the next room clicked. There was some low conversation and he heard footsteps thumping down the corridor. At six o'clock the commercial travellers began to wake up. He could hear the early morning jingles and news bulletins bickering on the radio. He dozed again and woke to find that it was eight o'clock. He had his breakfast and went along to the foyer.

'Message for you, sir.'

The light was going when Strange coasted the Avis car into the car-park. The rough gravel was scarred with waterlogged potholes. The attendant, a school-leaver in a dirty white coat, came out of his hut to divert him. Strange lowered his window.

'I'll park over there, by the toilets.'

The boy shrugged and gave him a ticket. You got all sorts of perverts in this job. Strange locked the car and went into the Gents. Coming out slowly he scanned the other cars. The white Rover was over in the corner. Cooper seemed to like corners. Strange limped across and opened the passenger door. Cooper was waiting.

'I don't know whether I should kick you or shake your hand,' he said, 'but hello anyway.' He had a peremptory way of speaking, but the sparkle in his eye betrayed the possibility of a sense of humour. Strange noticed that Cooper's moustache twitched nervously as he spoke.

'You're scared,' said Strange, with his usual tact. 'Forget it. I'm alone. No one saw me.'

'You're sure? I don't think you realize the risk I'm taking.'

'As sure as I can be. What are the risks?' Cooper's anxiety was perplexing. He should be only too glad to tell all he knew about Lister.

101

'I'll come to that later perhaps. First, I want to know what you want to know.' The cold eyes were animated. A man with a lot at stake, thought Strange. Perhaps that explained the anxiety. He decided to counter with another question.

'What do you know about me?'

'You're Frank Strange. I recognized the name at once. From the Directorate. You were very well known in Cheltenham.'

'Why – for the sake of interest?'

'Come on, Mr Strange. I'm not here to boost your ego. We feared you. You were the hammer of the department. You were streamlining the system, making everyone work harder. We knew it wouldn't be very long before you reached us. I'm glad I left before that happened.'

'So you got a kick out of hiding things from me.'

'Hiding what?' Cooper was agitated. 'What are you accusing me of? I didn't come here to be accused of things. I'm a private citizen. I only agreed to come and talk.'

'Does it come as a surprise to you that Cheltenham never told me about the enquiry into Dick Lister's accusations against you and Tony Ellison?'

Oddly, Cooper seemed to take heart at these words. He said: 'I don't need to tell you that there are some very secret operators in the Directorate, Strange. Besides, Cheltenham wouldn't want to give you an excuse for a purge, would they?'

Strange acknowledged that.

'What surprises me, Strange,' said Cooper, with more confidence now, 'is to find that this is why you want to talk to me.'

'What is?'

'The Lister case.'

'Why?'

'Oh, because I'd heard that you'd retired from the Directorate. What's it to do with you now?'

Strange turned sharply. Cooper was better informed than he expected. He looked at him now with candour. 'Lister ruined my life in the Directorate,' he said simply. 'I left because I'd had enough. I wanted to enjoy my retirement.'

'Are you enjoying your retirement now?' Cooper did have a sense of humour. Strange gave a grim smile. 'What would you do if the man who'd made your life a misery was found dead on your last day at work?' He didn't want an answer, but pressed on, 'I want to find out what Lister's game was. Then I'll enjoy my retirement.' Cooper wrestled with this information. At length he said, 'There was no game.'

Strange was angered by this deception. He became suddenly relentless. 'It's going to make things a lot easier if you co-operate, Mr Cooper. We can't go on lying to each other all evening. Bear in mind that Lister killed himself because something was getting too much for him. You are linked with him and there are plenty of people who know that.'

Cooper was panicking. 'But I left three years ago. I – I haven't seen him since. We're not friends any more. I don't know what you're talking about.'

But Strange knew he feared something and went on implacably. 'Do I have to spell it out to you, Mr Cooper? I don't care whether you're friends or not. If it's a working assumption that Lister accused you and Ellison in order to cover up his own activities, whoever he was dealing with knows that and probably still knows how much power you have over them. Now that Lister's dead, that would scare me.'

Obviously that was it. Cooper's small mouth was working beneath his moustache. He seemed to speak with reluctance. 'I'd rather drive somewhere else first. I don't like to stay put any more. You never know, do you. I'll bring you back. Here.'

'You're not expected anywhere?'

'My wife knows I may be late.' Cooper reversed the car and, crunching across the gravel, swung on to the main road. 'Where do you want to go? Any ideas?'

'This is your territory,' said Strange. 'Go where you like.'

They drove in silence for a while. Cooper was accelerating down a lonely heath road with not a light in sight when he braked sharply and pulled into a rough lay-by.

'This is nowhere in particular. It'll do.' He switched off the lights. For a moment Strange feared violence, but when he heard Cooper speak again he realized this was not a man to risk that.

'Who told you that Lister was covering-up his own trail?'

'Hoskins.' Strange couldn't resist adding 'And he's a journalist. You're very lucky that more of this story hasn't been published already.'

Cooper was angry. 'Stop this attitude, Strange. Let's get on with what you want out of me.'

'Well, for a start, how well did you know Tony Ellison?'

'Hardly at all. You're labouring under a misapprehension by the way if you think Lister accused both of us. Dick wouldn't wreck a friendship that easily. What happened was that he accused Tony, and Tony, who was a nasty piece of work all right, implicated me as well. I was his senior in the section you see. Then Lister claimed to have an audit trail which proved Tony and I were doing unauthorized work. Preece exploded that fast enough: it was just a suite of programmes that wasn't in Lister's index. The fact is he couldn't prove his accusations so he tried to back them with some wild arguments. That was one of them. Lister liked to think he knew everything, but he didn't. He wasn't top dog by any means.'

Strange knew that was true. He said, 'Ellison implicated you, you say. Does that mean he accepted the accusation?'

Cooper reacted sharply, 'Of course not. Don't be absurd. Let me explain. Lister filed his "complaint", right? Tony was sent a copy for comment. I think he was scared that even when it was proved to be nonsense it would be a black mark against his name. So he insisted that it should be a section matter. So I got lumbered.'

'When Preece had resolved the question with the enquiry, why wasn't Lister sacked?'

'I've already explained, Mr Strange, that the last thing that we in Cheltenham wanted to do was to attract anyone's attention, especially – if I may put it this way – if it was going to be a red rag to a bull.'

Strange chuckled and Cooper, pleased at the metaphor and the relaxation in the atmosphere, laughed with him.

'In fact,' said Strange, 'you thought you'd go one better. You wouldn't cause a fuss on your own doorstep, but you'd export it to London.'

Cooper protested. 'It was nothing to do with me. I admit I kept quiet, but I didn't wish him on to you. Frankly, all I wanted was a quiet life. The Lister business opened a door on to a nasty world – '

'How nasty?' Strange interrupted.

'What? What are you saying?'

'I'll put it another way if you like, Who was Lister working for?'

Cooper seemed surprised by this line. 'I don't know. Himself, I suppose. You don't think – ?' he broke off.

'Well, you've said it,' said Strange in some triumph.

'Honestly, I don't know about that. I was frightened by the whole business. I wanted to get as far away from it as possible. You've already told me yourself how much at risk I am.'

'That's presumably why you didn't bring counter charges yourself?'

'We ran for our lives, Mr Strange. At least I did. Tony, who's a much cooler customer, sat tight. He may have been behind the move to shift Lister. I don't know.' And later Lister went for him, Strange thought. That works.

'It's not a pretty picture,' he said aloud. 'Moral cowardice,' he added, almost thinking aloud.

Cooper riposted with fury. 'I assure you, Mr Strange, if your life was in danger in the way mine is, you'd be a moral coward. I don't know who's behind Lister and I don't want to know. I don't owe the department my life.'

'What about the country?'

'Bugger the country.' Strange bowed his head sadly. 'It's

105

worth nothing, certainly not an ignoble death like Lister's.'
He looked at him, 'It's odd, Strange. Because we feared you
so much, you're the one man I can think of who isn't
implicated in that Lister business, yet you seem to want to get
in on the act. It's not natural.'

Strange reacted. 'Are you suggesting something?'

'Maybe.' Cooper looked at him through the darkness.
'I've told you what I know this evening out of self-interest,
that's to say I wanted to know what's going on in the
Directorate. I can't believe you aren't acting out of self-
interest too.'

Something in the conversation died at that point.
Cooper's sudden accusation damned the flow of the
interview. Strange became restive. Time was running out. He
couldn't trust Cooper to keep his mouth shut for long. There
was a risk he had to take now. They drove back to
Basingstoke in desultory conversation. The mood lifted only
when Cooper stopped the car two streets from the car-
park.

'I'd rather you walked the rest. Here's my card. If you find
anything more, let me know. What's your number?'

Strange invented a number on a scrap of paper and was
about to get out. The silence between them was loaded with
unspoken thoughts. Suddenly Cooper said: 'Were you
surprised by his death?'

Strange was about to admit that he shouldn't have
been but said, on impulse, 'Yes. We all were. It was very
sudden.'

'He gave no indication?'

'None at all.' For a moment Strange remembered
something Paul Keat had said to him. He looked at Cooper.
'You were quite a close friend, weren't you? Would you say it
was like him?'

'He was the last person – ' Cooper began and then
stopped. 'Well, I suppose it was possible.' He said it
unconvincingly. In a flash, Strange saw why Cooper was so
frightened. 'You can't believe the suicide, can you? You

think – ' and the idea frightened him as well, 'you think he was murdered?'

'No I don't – ' he started. But this time his eyes betrayed him and he panicked. 'Get out! Get out!' He was almost shrieking. Strange had hardly heaved himself clear of the seat before the white Rover roared off into the darkness.

CHAPTER TWELVE

'The squyer ought to knele to fore thaulter, & lefte up to god his eyen corporal and spyritual, & his hondes to heuen, & the knyghte ought to gyrde hym in sygne of Chastite, Iustyce, & of charyte with his sword . . .'

Quitman was in his dressing gown, wrestling with medieval chivalry. The failure to find Strange distracted his attention from the courtly rituals of the fourteenth century. Where was Strange? What would happen next? Had he failed? Preece was getting angry. He was to review the situation tomorrow. Would he take control of the liaison with the security section? He missed Liz. He sprawled back in his armchair and listened to the music on the tape, Britten's *Serenade*. The mournful horn solo from the Elegy that had filled the shadows while he thought about Liz faded. The Dirge reached its frenzied crescendo. 'This ae nyghte, this ae nyghte, every nyghte and all . . .'

The door bell rang.

He looked at the alarm clock on the bedside table. It was after midnight. Was she back at last? He shuffled to the door in his slippers.

'Who is it?'

There was no answer. The bell rang again.

'Who is it?' Then his curiosity and his desire to find Liz there got the better of his doubts and he pulled the door open. Strange rammed a foot in the doorway and said: 'James. I've got to talk to you.'

Quitman stared at him in horror. This was the situation that Hayter had warned about. Strange, his good foot in the door, was leaning on his stick, breathing hard from the stairs. Despite the cold, beads of sweat stood on his forehead and a thin film of perspiration accentuated the hard lines of his face. He looked tired. He was wearing casual clothes beneath his open sheepskin donkey jacket, but the shirt was grubby and the trousers badly creased.

'You can't come here, Mr Strange. It's impossible.'

'No one saw me. I've shaken them off. Let me in – just for half an hour. I'll explain everything.'

Quitman stood aside, and then slammed the door behind him.

'Are you bugged?' asked Strange in a low voice, taking off his coat, his big frame filling the little hallway.

'I've no idea. I don't think so.' Once Strange came into the living-room Quitman's hostility towards his old boss expressed itself as formal politeness. 'Would you care for some tea?' he asked.

'Thank you, James.' Strange was drawing deep breaths, relaxing in the only comfortable armchair, shedding his anxiety like a sleeper waking from a nightmare. He was brushing aside Quitman's coldness without difficulty. 'It's good to feel safe at last,' he said as the tea arrived.

'Safe?'

'They've followed me ever since I left the Directorate, James. Don't you know about it?'

Quitman hesitated. He was too tired to dissemble. 'I –'

Strange knew him too well: 'Of course you do. What are they saying?' He thrust his head forward, emphasizing the question in his familiar way.

'I'm sorry, Frank, I can't tell you. I'm risking my neck having you here now as it is.'

'Don't worry. I told you I shook them off in Southampton. A stroke of luck. I've been free for nearly three days. It's a good feeling, but it can't last.'

Quitman said nothing.

'Well, there's one comfort.' Strange gave a rare but characteristic chuckle. 'You won't give me away. You wouldn't dare, would you?'

Quitman was feeling torn by old loyalties and new affiliations. But he managed to say, 'You can't stay here, Frank. I'm sorry but you'll have to go.'

'So you're in this too, James.' Strange looked sternly at him with a remembered expression. Quitman did not answer. 'You must be.'

Quitman admitted that this was so.

'Loyalty comes cheap these days, James. I came here tonight because I thought I could trust you.'

'I thought I could trust *you*.' Quitman retorted. 'I know all about you now. Do you blame me?'

'How can I if I don't know what they're saying about me?' Strange sounded aggrieved.

Quitman stood up angrily. 'Frank, for God's sake, why can't you admit it?'

'Admit what?' He looked puzzled.

Quitman sighed. 'You're only human, Frank. You did many superb things for the Directorate. It would have been too good to be true if there'd been no flaw in your achievement. With all that power and influence at your disposal, and almost no accountability, it's not surprising that you let your standards slip at the end.' Somehow Quitman could not bring himself to make the blunt accusation of corruption.

'Is that what they're saying?' Strange looked silently into his tea. 'So I had my hand in the till at the end, did I? Is that it?'

'Well, you were sacked, weren't you?'

'I was forced to resign.'

'That comes to the same thing.'

'No, it doesn't. Not when the man who forced you to resign was Lister.'

'Lister's behaviour was perfectly honourable. He was entitled to bring his allegations if they were justified.'

'Justified!' Strange was really angry. 'You don't know about Lister, do you? You don't know about who he was working for, do you? You don't know that he was probably murdered, do you?' Quitman stared at him. 'They didn't tell you that, did they? They didn't tell you that because through my own arrogance – I'll admit that – I had allowed Lister to

110

get out of hand. I resigned rather than let the Directorate become compromised?'

Quitman was confused. 'What happened? What's your version?'

Strange let that pass. 'Dangerfield came to me and showed me Lister's memorandum. You know about that I gather?'

'Yes. I've seen it.'

Strange raised his eyebrows, but went straight on. 'Well, it may interest you to know that Dangerfield accepted that I was not the "senior officer" refrred to.'

'But –' Quitman began.

Strange looked at him. 'Yes?'

'Oh. Nothing, Go on.'

'All right. You don't believe me. Not yet. You will when you've read Dangerfield's letter.'

'What letter?'

'Wait. I'll come to that. To go back to the memorandum for a moment, the plain fact was that Lister had damaging information about some unspecified person in the Directorate. He wouldn't or couldn't say who they were. No one knew whose side he was on. There were plenty of suspicions but no proof. He may have been *bona fide*. I didn't think so, but if he was, his secretive manner was against him. And there was no way of finding out without getting him alarmed, so that if he was working against us would run for it. Do you follow me?'

'Perfectly.'

'All we could do was watch, and hope that we could get at the truth that way. Nonetheless, Dangerfield made it quite clear that it was important that I retire to diminish the security risk. You can't have a director as badly compromised as I seemed to be. In theory they should have purged the whole Directorate and started again, but that's not feasible apparently, so they cut out the most vulnerable part of it – and that happened to be me.'

'But – but you said there was no motive for Lister's death

the day it happened. Now you say he was murdered. What –?'

'It's silly, but I wanted revenge. Against Lister. Against Hayter too, for his hostility. Actually I thought it was suicide then.'

'Is this what you've been discovering from all these meetings you've been having?'

'So you know about those do you?'

'I'm working with Preece's team,' he admitted.

'Are you? Liaison officer I suppose. The man who knows Strange best can interpret his movements best. Good thinking, Hayter. And to get you on their minds, they've told you lies about my professional integrity. It's not nice work, is it?'

'If you're telling the truth, Frank, no.'

Strange was hurt, indignant. 'Look here, James, don't talk to me like a church elder! When have I bloody well not told you the truth?'

'I don't know now. Honestly, Frank, I'm confused.'

'You should be more than confused, James. You should be scared. That's why I'm letting go of the Lister business, and that's why they, that's Hayter and Preece, are not letting go of me.'

'What do you mean?'

'Lister was mixed up in one hell of a big racket. I'm convinced of that now. He may have allies in the department that we don't know about. It's possible he was pointing the finger of suspicion in order to stir up confusion in the Directorate. If its data-corroborating powers are as important in the war against subversion as we all believe, then any action like that is going to be welcome to our enemies. Then there is also the possible commercial exploitation of some of our secrets. That's been on the cards a long time. I guess that Hayter suspects that both these things may be true, but he'd rather not know about it. The implications are too frightening, and it would ruin his plans for the Directorate's new role in the department as a whole.' He paused. 'That's typical Hayter. The puzzle is

Dangerfield. I know he believed that Hayter would behave like this. But he promised he would take precautions. He also promised that he would do something about Lister after I'd retired. Is there any sign of that happening?'

'None at all.'

'Well, we may not know about it.' He frowned. 'So I'll have to press on alone.'

'Then you're not working against the Directorate?'

Strange looked surprised. 'Is that what they've told you?'

'I was briefed by Hayter that you're so angry at being sacked – his word – that you're going to do all you can to discredit it, preferably to the press.'

Strange did not seem shocked at this. He nodded carefully. 'Plausible but untrue. I'm only working against the Directorate in the sense that when I get to the bottom of the Lister story, Hayter will have to resign.'

'Why?'

'Negligence. Or at any rate admit that I was right. Knowing how the Directorate operates it will all be kept pretty dark.' Strange's voice became harsh. 'I was the first casualty of the Lister business. There are going to be others for sure. If I have my way, they'll have to reconstitute the Directorate in the end.'

'More tea?' Quitman was feeling overwhelmed by Strange's revelations. He ran the water, warmed the pot again, measured the tea, infused and served with calming deliberation. 'As a matter of interest, who were you visiting today?'

Strange shook his head. 'Whose side are you on, James?'

'Is it a question of sides?'

'It shouldn't be, but it is. Hayter is basically trying to cover-up the Lister case. Of course I know that Hayter and his colleagues are all honourable men with fine records, but they're moral cowards. It's not in the national interest that the secrets of the Directorate should be available for exploitation by non-government personnel.'

'Presumably Hayter has weighed the evidence and decided that not enough is at risk. He's a true professional.'

'He may be. On the other hand, his professionalism may lie in his desire for a quiet life. The department puts a high price on steady ships in calm seas. If you take on the Lister case you're steering into rough water.'

'You'd trust Preece, wouldn't you?'

'Not out of my sight, no.'

'Oh come on, Frank. I've worked with him closely for some weeks now. I don't like him but he's very efficient.'

'But he's covering-up. Don't forget that James. His efficiency, like Hayter's professionalism, lies in a course of action which may be disastrous.'

'That's your opinion.'

Strange looked at Quitman with exasperation. 'Look here, I worked in the government service for thirty-five years. Ten of those years were spent in the Directorate. I've watched it grow from three floors in the Old War Office, to a vast network of data-bases with major offices in Cheltenham and Croydon. Don't tell me what is or not disastrous. I know.' He moderated his tone and repeated, 'Whose side are you on, James?'

Quitman stared at the single lamp casting its sick yellow glow across the small sitting-room, and was momentarily reminded of the naked bulbs that burn all night in the underground rooms of the Directorate. 'If I have to choose between betraying my friend and betraying my country,' he said slowly, 'I hope I shall have the guts to betray my country.'

Strange recognized the academic's fondness for quotations. 'Who's that?'

'E. M. Forster.'

'Oh. You're dramatizing, James. There is no conflict, believe me. I have what civil servants like to call the national interest as much at heart as you do. No, it's not that,' he added perceptively. 'You're worried about your career, aren't you? That's an unusual thing for you to bother with, James. What's happened to your knights?'

Quitman waved a dismissive arm in the direction of his cluttered desk. 'They seem irrelevant. In the last few weeks

114

I've tasted power in a way I never did with you, Frank.'

'So you like the games we play. The watching, the listening, the manipulating.'

'Yes,' he admitted, 'I do.'

'But they're not games,' Strange responded with spirit. 'They are to you. They hold a fascination for intellectuals. People like you are too easily seduced by power. That's why the Directorate likes clever people, people who are too clever for their own good – it can use people like you. You're naïve, James. You're being used. Yet you prefer it. Under me, you were never used. But we didn't play games, did we?'

'No.' He stared into the shadows reflectively. 'No, we didn't.'

'That sounds like a reproach. I see that Preece has got his claws into you.' Again he asked, 'Where do you stand now, James?'

'Why are you so anxious for my vote?'

'I need your help, but if I can't trust you I'm not going to tell you what I want you to do. It'll become part of the cover-up otherwise. How much control do you have over that, out of interest?'

'Not much. You're right. I'm the liaison officer between the Directorate and HQ Security. My job is to tell Preece who you've seen, where you've gone and what you say on the telephone, which, as you know, has been almost nothing.'

'You don't spend ten years in the Directorate and not learn to steer clear of telephone wires.' Strange chuckled. 'Your problem, James, is that I know all the tricks – all your tricks.' Then he roared with laughter, and his sudden merriment echoed round and round the small room. Quitman smiled.

'You wouldn't try to use me if you had all the aces.'

'That's true. But if I'd known how much they were using you, I'd have tried someone else. You'll make a poor double agent.'

'Is that what you want me to do.'

'Yes. I need information, but I don't want Hayter or Preece to know I've got it.'

'So you won't try Miss Adams again?'

'That was a mistake. No, I need a better source than the library. I need someone who has access to the computer room and some of the office files. You, in fact.'

Quitman hesitated; the little room seemed cold and menacing.

'You don't trust me.' Strange's tone was almost mocking.

Quitman protested. 'It's not – ' he began. 'I'm confused. Don't you see that my loyalties have been shaken up recently.' An idea came to him. 'What about this letter from Dangerfield. If I can see that I'll believe you.'

Strange reached for his bulging briefcase. Clothes and papers spilled across the floor. 'Damn, I can't find it at the moment. Save it up for tomorrow. I'm exhausted. It corroborates what I've told you. Let's play it by the book. If you're satisfied with it, will you work for me?'

Quitman did not hesitate. 'Yes,' he said.

A sudden calmness came over Strange. 'That's what I wanted to hear,' he said with warmth. 'I'll stay here tomorrow. Don't worry, I shan't go out. Come back in the evening. I'll have the letter. Then we can get to work.'

Quitman left the flat at seven. Strange was lying, still in his clothes, on his back, on cushions on the floor, snoring. The London winter dawn was breaking over Earls Court, grey slabs of cloud and an early airliner turning against the wind towards Heathrow. But as he hurried towards the underground station, Quitman was oblivious of his surroundings. His mind was preoccupied with the watchers from his own department. Strange claimed to have shaken them off. But what if they'd picked him up on the road? He was anxious to get to yesterday's surveillance reports as soon as possible. He sat in the empty train imagining the worst.

'Good morning, sir.' Albert nodded as he pressed his ID card into the slot. Quitman gave an anxious smile. The office was nearly deserted. The skeleton night staff at the Directorate was just coming off duty, high with tiredness, chattering brightly in the cloakrooms.

Quitman obtained personal identity clearance to go forward to his floor, unlocked the door to his section, and threw his briefcase down on the table. In a moment he was dialling through for the latest surveillance reports. As the door closed behind the departing executive security officer, Quitman picked up the familiar folder. It has the usual secrecy coding. He spilled the few pages of the report on to the desk apprehensively. The surveillance team was still in Southampton. They had found Strange's car in a multi-storey car-park, but of the man himself there was still no sign. They were watching the vehicle.

The sense of relief that followed this disclosure was short-lived. At nine-thirty Hayter was on the line in a temper. Preece had already delayed the news of Strange's disappearance for forty-eight hours. Finally he had sent up an edited version of the surveillance reports to the deputy-controller who spotted the deception at once and, guided by Preece, accused Quitman. The storm that followed raged all morning.

Neve as usual attempted to interpret the situation. 'He's very pleased with himself, isn't he?' he said to Rosie Walford as they watched Quitman almost running down the corridor towards the typing pool with a sheaf of classified instructions. 'And it's not as if he's out in the field. Most of the credit belongs to HQ Security, though I doubt if Preece will hear about that from James.'

'You're very mean about him, Charlie –' Rosie began.

'So I should be with three years' seniority.'

'You shouldn't be so jealous. Preece knows that, I'm sure. Your turn will come.'

'That's what he keeps telling me. He says I'm next for promotion. If I'm not, the staff association will want to know why.'

But Rosie Walford wasn't listening anymore. She had caught the sound of Quitman's returning footsteps. If he saw her with Neve that would ruin her chances.

She need not have worried. Quitman was finding Rosie open and attractive and provocative. Her company was a welcome contrast to the long hours of secret briefings. Later that day she engineered a chance rendezvous in the lift. They were alone. He stared at the indicator. First floor – second floor – third floor . . .

'Are you doing anything on Friday evening?' he asked.

Rosie was rather amused at his shyness. 'Oh. Nothing as it happens.' She made a joke, 'Nobody loves me!'

'Then I can take you to the theatre, can't I?' Quitman teased with some nervousness. They came out into the corridor.

'That would be terrific. You choose.'

'A surprise?'

'Mm.' Quitman felt a sudden intimacy between them; it embarrassed him. He realized suddenly that he was standing awkwardly outside the lift. He looked at his watch. 'Must fly. Meeting with Preece.'

Preece had already forgotten the row with Hayter and was optimistic again. He had just received a call from a man called Aidan Cooper, a former employee of the Directorate now living in Basingstoke, who had been approached by Strange. Quitman knew that he had to get Strange out of London by the morning.

When he got home, Strange was waiting with a copy of his letter from Dangerfield. 'Here you are, Jamie,' were his first words as Quitman came in, 'proof positive. As soon as you've read – '

Quitman slammed the door.

'For God's sake, Frank, can't you let up for a moment. I've had an awful day. They know you were in Basingstoke yesterday,' he added, taking the letter. 'Your time's running out.'

'That's Cooper.'

He made some tea and slumped in the decent armchair. The letter, in Dangerfield's royal-blue hand on the controller's notepaper, was short and personal.

'My dear Frank, I'm sorry you're going, but this is the only honourable way. It will be a cruel blow to the whole department. I know there's nothing you could have done about this situation, and vastly appreciate your contribution here. There will be a thorough investigation as soon as possible after you've gone – how much more rigorous it would have been if you had been here to conduct it! With best wishes, Yours, Gerald.'

'Nice,' said Quitman. 'Very confidential. He'd be pleased if he knew you were making the investigation.'

'Dangerfield appointed me, you understand. I believe my retirement was as much a blow to him. He's having a sub-zero feud with Hayter. He doesn't trust him not to turn a blind eye to a serious threat to the Directorate. The more central the Directorate becomes to the running of the department as a whole, the greater any threat will be.'

'Why doesn't he act decisively, if that's his fear?' Quitman queried, as he and Strange sat enlarging the discussion later that evening. The remains of the Chinese takeaway lay spread across the table. Strange, with a mug of beer, lounged in the armchair.

'Dangerfield's cunning. He sits at the top of a huge pyramid of secret power watching us all teem beneath him. Occasionally the routine flow of paper and hum of committees is disrupted and a confidential memorandum or phone call reaches him. He studies this discreet signal, evaluates its significance and plots a subtle response. Like this, for instance.' He waved the letter. 'He knows very well what's going on. He'll act decisively when he has to.'

Strange scooped the papers together.

'And now you've seen this letter, will you accept that I have the confidence of your controller. I want to get on with this briefing.'

'But if you've got Dangerfield's confidence, why is Hayter against you?' Quitman had worried this question from several angles all evening.

'Perhaps he knows more about Lister than we think. He may know that whatever Lister was up to threatens the security of his little world.'

'And Preece?'

'Preece is like all ambitious subordinates. He can't see why he should be more royalist than the king.'

'I'm not sure,' said Quitman reflectively, 'that I like the idea of playing a double game inside the Directorate, but . . .' he paused to hitch himself up in the chair, '. . . but I'll do it.'

Strange looked across the half-lighted room and clapped his hands together. 'That's more like the James Quitman I used to know,' he said triumphantly, fumbling for his briefcase.

CHAPTER THIRTEEN

Strange left the flat at dawn with his things in two plastic carrier bags. The question-and-answer briefing had lasted until two-thirty. Quitman now knew as much as Strange about the Lister case including the suspicion of murder. Strange had given him a list of subjects to check. Together they had planned an ingenious way for him to gain access to the Directorate's files on the subject. Quitman distracted his anticipation that first anxious morning in the office with furious hard work.

'He's got his tongue so far up Preece's bum,' the technicians commented among themselves, 'that all you can see is the soles of his feet.' The technicians were like that: vulgar but to the point. It was lucky for Quitman's reputation that the news came through to him at the end of the morning that Strange had been found, returning to the multi-storey in Southampton. He yawned when he heard the news and thought, that was slow. Now, relaxing slightly, he brought the good news to Preece. 'They've found him,' he said laconically. 'In Southampton. Reports will be in this evening.'

Preece half-rose from his desk, and began to smile. 'Well done,' he said with emphatic approval. 'Well done, James.' He noticed that Quitman was wearing a fresh suit and that his tie, with a club motif, was knotted with uncharacteristic firmness. His manner seemed brisker, more efficient. This one is turning into a first-class officer, he thought to himself.

A sheaf of handwritten notes that Quitman recognized from Strange's cunning scribbling the night before lay on Preece's desk. The antiseptic modern luxury of the office emphasized the roughly torn paper and the raggedness of Strange's strong black hand-writing.

'I have something here,' said Preece, waving Quitman to a

chair, 'that is almost more important than finding Strange. You'll be interested to know that Security have intercepted an envelope, posted in London early this morning, addressed by Strange to his home in Devon. Perhaps, after all, he is not aware of the surveillance.'

'Why?'

'Because these pages prove something that I have suspected for a long time. Strange has discovered, it seems, that the Directorate was aware of irregularities in Lister's own past career. This is going to strengthen his grudge against us, Hayter in particular.'

'These irregularities you're referring to,' Quitman began cautiously, 'do they fall within the ambit of our operations?'

Preece studied the notes in silence, composing his thoughts. For a moment Quitman thought he'd missed the question, but then, having apparently settled something in his mind, he looked up, taking off, as he did so, the pair of half-tinted glasses that he affected for desk-work, and toying with them in his mobile fingers.

'Shortly before Lister came to London – this is in confidence, but you need to know it for background – he was at the centre of a row in Cheltenham about the misuse of database information. I was sent down there by Hayter to hold a confidential enquiry. Strange was not told – deliberately – because there were already some doubts about his reliability.'

Quitman registered no surprise at his claim. He asked:

'What did you find?'

'Nothing was proved. My job was to lower the temperature. There was a suspicion that Lister made the fuss to cover his tracks, but there was not enough hard evidence to support this rumour. Lister was, of course, subsequently given a fresh positive vetting by the security services before he came to London.'

'There were no links with Strange?' Quitman was rather proud of that one.

'No.'

'Is there a file on this enquiry?' he asked casually. Preece looked at him, weighing the question. 'Yes,' he said, 'there is. It is, of course, highly classified. One doesn't like to admit any wrinkles in the Directorate. I suppose you're going to say you'd like to read it?'

'Well, it would provide useful background.'

'It will provide a lot more than background. You will see at once why Strange's movements have been so alarming to the Directorate recently.'

'Of course,' he said, 'if the material is too sensitive – '

'No.' Preece cut him short. 'You should see it. I have to admit that we have been less than frank with you over some of the details up to now. I am concerned that the failure to track Strange efficiently stems from the fact that you didn't have all the information at your disposal. I'll tell Hayter you're having access to the file on the usual "need to know" basis.' Preece reached into his desk for a requisition slip, consulted the codebook and filled in the form, signing it with his fine italic signature. 'Read it carefully, and when you've finished come back here for a de-briefing.'

After he had given the requisition form to the duty officer, Quitman sat at his desk staring at the internal phone, paralysed with apprehension. He had to be quick. He had to do it before his nerve failed, before the clerk arrived with the file. He was astonished how easily Strange's ruse with the letter had worked. Then, with a decisive movement, he lifted the phone, dialled the library and asked Miss Adams to look out two books for him.

'I'll come and collect them in a minute.'

There was a knock. He slammed the phone down. The man from Data (Personnel) came in. 'Here you are, sir. Sign please. This has a special security rating. Four hours limit and documents not to leave possession. Okay, sir?'

Quitman acknowledged the rule. As the man withdrew Quitman piked up the bulky folder. Never, in all his years of research, had he experienced such an excitement with documents. He began to turn over the pages quickly. There were depositions from all the parties involved. Strange had most of that information. There was a summary by Preece, minuted 'your eyes only' to Hayter. There was a transcript of the enquiry. Then there was a large brown envelope marked 'Documents relating'. He tipped it up. He recognized at once Lister's rough pencil notes of what he had seen on the VDU the evening he had found Ellison alone at work. There were three sheets of pencil scribble, quickly jotted. The symbols made no sense. That was not to be expected. Strange was making his own arrangements to decode the documents. He stared at the notes almost mesmerized and then thrust them into his jacket pocket. There was no going back now.

'Just running out to pick up a couple of books from the library. Miss Adams always goes early on a Friday,' he explained to his secretary.

Miss Adams was packing her knitting into her battered carpet bag. The books were waiting on the table.

'But you should have seen the dust,' she remarked as Quitman admired the bindings. 'Now what are you up to?'

'I won't be a minute,' he said. The light on the library xerox machine glowed intensely. He dropped another coin into the slot and slapped the record sheet on to the glass, praying that the pencil wasn't too faint. 'It's just some stuff for my chivalry research.'

Miss Adams knew all about Quitman's historical interests. Once or twice she had borrowed books for him on her London Library ticket. 'I should have asked,' she said. 'How are they – the knights? It is knights, isn't it?'

'Yes – knights. There we are. All done.' He scooped the pages together and sandwiched the original between the copies, pressing all the paper against the library books. 'Sorry to have kept you. I promise you an acknowledgement in the preface.'

Miss Adams thought he was a dear boy. A footnote in history, she said to herself as she rode down in the lift and out into the busy afternoon in Whitehall.

Quitman hurried back to his desk with the books, hid the xerox among a tatty file of chivalry notes, and in due course, at about the hour when they serve tea and two biscuits in Whitehall, joined Preece to hear, officially, what Strange had

124

already told him about the enquiry. He found it hard to pay attention to Preece's confidential words. It was not only that he knew it all anyway; as the briefing dragged on, he began to worry about the time. Tonight was his evening out with Rosie Walford. He felt excited at the prospect. But when he met her, by arrangement, at the pub next door to the theatre, and complimented her on her tasteless get-up, he knew himself to be moving into a rhythm which, if neither broke the rules, would carry them through at least another twelve hours.

There were the drinks to start with of course, then the slow shuffle into the theatre, some shallow nonsense with the programme, the curtain rising, bright lights and dialogue, an interval, drinks, more bright lights and laughter, drinks again, but now succeeded by dinner with an Italian menu that Rosie couldn't understand, then coats, and freezing in the rain for the taxi, an almost silent ride to Barons Court, and, at the end, as a beginning, a kiss.

It was not until morning that it dawned on Quitman that Rosie had probably slept with most of the other men in the department. At first, as they struggled together in the darkness, Quitman blamed himself. Later, when they talked, he realized from her gossip that she'd done this with other colleagues. No wonder it bored her. He began to feel like a statistic. Rosie wanted to weave him into a sad emotional tapestry of divorce and lovers, affairs and separations. She also wanted confidences and secrets. But he resisted, fearing the accuracy of some of her suspicions, and gracefully refused to be drawn about either Lister or Strange.

Now, the light was sharpening the contours of the little bedroom and he was dozing fitfully in bed. Rosie was standing barefoot in his shirt at the stove making coffee. She seemed very confident with the flat's equipment. The phone rang.

'I'll take it,' he said in a hurry, alert only to its third ring. 'Hello,' he said. But it was Liz. She sounded distant. Then he realized that she was crying.

'I'm sorry. I've got to see you. Please, darling. Please

forgive me.' Rosie was bending over him from behind playfully. He felt her breasts pressing on his back. She was kissing the nape of his neck. She put the coffee beside him on the table. He swathed a sheet round himself and waved her away with a forced smile. She seemed offended. He pressed the receiver closer to his ear. Liz was repeating herself at the other end.

'Don't worry,' he heard himself say, trying to check the tenderness in his voice. 'I'll come round as soon as possible. Stay where you are. I'll be round right away.' He cut her off, and turned, with an apology, to Rosie, who was now wearing his sweater as well and sitting cross-legged in the armchair combing her tangled yellow hair in a tiny vanity mirror.

'Who was that?'

'An old friend. They've just been burgled.' He found the lie easy, almost satisfying.

'Oh dear, what a shame. Can I come with you for moral support? I've nothing else on today except – '

'I'd rather – ' he broke in. 'If you don't mind Rosie, I'd rather you didn't – '

'Why not?' She put the mirror down. 'What's the matter, Jamie? Why can't I?'

'It's not – '

'So I'm the girl from the office you can screw in private but leave at home when you're with friends who matter?'

'What are you saying, Rosie? Are you crazy?' He felt suddenly aggrieved. 'This was your idea,' he gestured at the tousled sheets, and then realized what he'd said. 'I mean, you were happy – '

'Are you accusing me of being an easy lay?' She swung her legs in front of her and marched across the room.

'Of course not – ' he began.

'Oh, don't bother to deny it.' He stood staring at her, ridiculous in his sheet like a Roman. She was dressing quickly, speaking as she did so. 'I thought you were sweet, you know. You didn't seem hung up on the job like the others. Now I see that you're no different really.' She sounded upset. 'I thought I could love you, James, I really did.' Her wounded pride was turning to indignation, 'But for Christ's sake you've treated me like – like – ' She thrust her feet into her best evening shoes, defeated by her own fury. 'No wonder your girlfriend walked out on you.' She was standing at the door. 'Have a nice day with your friends, whoever they are, but don't ever do this to me again.' The door slammed and she was gone. Quitman shrugged. It was pique, he told himself, frustration that she hadn't wormed any secrets out of him. Strange's question came back to him as he stood there. 'Whose side are you on, James? Everyone's on sides in this game.' He wondered vaguely whose side Rosie was on now.

Liz knew that he had been sleeping with another woman the moment she kissed him, and his shy admission sent her into a fit of weeping. He knew he should be hard and distant after all her cruelty towards him, but he took her in his arms and cradled her pathetic figure.

'He's left me, James. You've got to come back. I need you.' She held him fiercely. His head was throbbing with lack of sleep and the pain of reconciliation. Gradually Liz calmed down and explained that her last lover – the one she'd started in the North – had left her. With him, apparently, went all her hopes for her literary agency. She had nothing left, she said. Her friends pitied her; her work was drudgery; she felt exhausted and suicidal. He had to help her. He was all she had in the world. She would devote herself to his success. Quitman urged her to have a bath while he made coffee. It was nearly lunchtime. He had to make a journey with the xerox before nightfall, according to his arrangement with Strange.

They tried to drive out for a late lunch at a favourite pub down on the river, but a football crowd was rioting in the Fulham Road, overturning cars and smashing shop windows. Riot police had cordoned off the district. Liz, red-eyed and curious, questioned him about the state of security.

'At least the trouble is only to do with football. There are no broken wondows in Whitehall yet.'

'Do they – does Whitehall fear that?' she asked with mouse-like apprehension.

'Things can only get worse,' he said.

So they had a junk-food hamburger instead and then went for a walk on Hampstead Heath. The clouds were racing and one or two families were tugging kites into the wind. Back in her cosy little flat they made tea together and Quitman sat comforting her on the soft carpet, feeding her with toast and biscuits. It was very warm, and when he left her with the promise that he would be back for a late dinner *à deux* she started to cry again.

'It's my new job, darling' – he'd told her all about it, with a finger on her lips, to please her – 'new responsibilities. There's a lot of personnel to deal with. It never stops.' She smiled fiercely with pride through her tears. It was marvellous to see him so ambitious and successful.

Quitman took the Piccadilly line to Heathrow. The anonymous form of transport suited him. He stared out of the window as the train rattled out of the tunnel towards Hammersmith. Part of West London was blacked-out with a power cut. Candles glimmered in dozens of trackside kitchens and the winter rain fell black and heavy past the window. Soon he was standing on the travolator, riding up towards Terminal Three. He looked around with some apprehension. But there were few other passengers at this late time on a Saturday evening, and he was fairly certain no one was following. The bulky brown envelope crushed into his inside pocket pressed against his ribcage like a threat.

The concourse was vast and empty, the check-in desks darkened. A dozen barefoot Indians sat in a circle by the souvenir shop staring blankly at the other late travellers. They sagged with exhaustion. The mother had a baby on her lap, but like the rest of the family, it was silent and still. Quitman looked at his watch. He had to hurry. There, as Strange had said, was the sign pointing to the car-park. Quitman climbed to a mezzanine floor and passed through two sets of automatic doors into an empty corridor, glassed in, bright with neon, bridging concourse and car-park. An airport truck passed below, its yellow light flashing slowly. Quitman crossed over and went into the echoing shadows.

He was on the second level. Fifty yards in front there was a dimly lit arrow pointing upwards. He began to walk fast towards it. At the corner, the silence was suddenly broken by a car starting and revving its motors. Quitman froze. It shrieked at a corner on the level below and then cruised away down. He continued to climb upwards. As he reached the open roof a jumbo jet thundered down the runway and lifted into the sky. The roar was deafening. He watched the lights winking out of sight. Then he took his bearings.

The exit sign was where he expected. Next to it was the trash can. He couldn't believe that such a primitive system would work, but knew there was nothing else to trust. He walked slowly round the perimeter of the roof, marvelling at the city lights laid out in all directions before him. But there was no one in the shadows. He walked quickly across towards the exit, skirting huge black puddles, and then dropped the envelope into the bin with a thump.

There was a dark stairway at hand and he went down several steps at a time. He reached the bottom suddenly frightened and out of breath. He looked at his watch again. Nine-fifty. Strange would be here in ten minutes and with him the surveillance team. He had to move out of the way fast. the travolator seemed incredibly slow, but he dared not run. He watched the frieze of foreign capitals flow past: Zagreb, Paris, New York, Helsinki, Berlin . . . His claustrophobia lifted temporarily as he reflected on these names. The Tube back to London was crowded with a delayed flight of American students enthusing about Yurrup: Quitman felt old and cynical, and when the doors rumbled together, at ease once more.

CHAPTER FOURTEEN

Davenport was mad. Strange remembered that. Davenport was the talk of the Croydon section of which he was boss. He was famous as the only software programmer in the Directorate – apart from Dick Lister perhaps – who could make the computer work almost faster than it could think. Davenport was a man of inventions, a five-star boffin who had more or less invented the Croydon database. Strange remembered the eccentric scientist with some misgivings, but Quitman had given him something good to go on and he knew that he was the only computer expert who could possibly decode Lister's notes. He hoped he could trust him. Davenport, for all his dottiness, knew that Strange had retired and had sent him a farewell card designed by his wife. Mrs Davenport was, if anything, madder than her husband.

The Davenports lived on a decayed housing estate in a bad part of Croydon. Council budget restrictions and urban crime gave the suburb a wrecked, beleaguered air. One or two of the houses lay empty, with broken wondows, and trailing wires and wallpaper. Others were occupied by squatters. The Davenports stayed on, oblivious to the decay and danger. Their garden, or more properly the rough ground in which their house stood, was littered with old iron, the discarded inventions of many years. The remains of a week-end bonfire smouldered there as Strange picked his way over the broken concrete to the front door. But that had been nailed up years ago. There was a smudged notice in biro, tacked with a rusty pin to the lintel: 'Try back door.'

Strange tried the back door. It seemed to be in use for there was a bell-push. Footsteps sounded on the lino inside. A voice said, very faintly, 'Who is it?'

'Frank Strange, a friend of John's. Is he at home?'

'He's in the darkroom,' said the voice. 'I'll get him.' The footsteps receded and Strange waited. After a long delay the shuffling resumed. 'He's just coming,' said the voice, stronger now, and reedy. 'He won't be a moment.'

Strange stood waiting among the piled bottles and the dustbins. A thin grey cat, crouched in the shadows, was licking itself. Suddenly the door scraped back and Davenport, wearing a brown lab. coat, poked out. His face was pinched and beaky. His eyes darted beneath spectacular foxy eyebrows. He was wearing Wellington boots, and responded at once to Strange's curious stare.

'You can't get a plumber out here to save your life,' were his first words. 'The darkroom's a swamp, and so cold in this weather. Awful, isn't it? Add to that a shortage of hypo – did you know that? A national shortage would you believe it – and you see the difficulties one faces nowadays. But do come in Frank, come in and enjoy the fire. What brings you here. This *is* a surprise. Mind that wire. It's usually live in this damp weather. Come on in and take your coat off and tell me all about your retirement. Ivy, Mr Strange is here. Will you bring us some poison in the lounge?'

Strange recalled that it was Davenport's talk that had prevented him from rising higher within the Directorate. But his eager flow of pleasantry and the sound of his wife crashing about in the kitchen lent an odd warmth to the bleak surroundings, the squalor and the uncertainty.

'It's the only room we can afford to heat these days. Heat properly, that is. We live in it, don't we, darling?' He looked up at his wife with pathetic tenderness as she came in, bent carefully over a tin tray of glasses and bottles in her flowered apron. 'Ivy. This is Mr Strange,' repeated Davenport.

Mrs Davenport bobbed a welcome. Strange said hello.

'I'm sorry we couldn't come to your party, but I was installing some new hardware that day, and you can't trust the engineers with anything in this day and age.'

Strange remembered to mention the card.

'Oh, you did get that. We did wonder. I am pleased. It was Ivy's invention. Mr Strange did get your nice card, darling,'

131

said Davenport, addressing his wife. 'Now you will have some of this won't you? Ivy makes it. It's cheaper than gin and really very tasty. She's experimenting with a new brew at the moment, aren't you darling? But it's not quite ready yet. This is last year's.'

Mrs Davenport, who was perched unobtrusively on the arm of a sofa, cleaning her spectacles on her apron, nodded.

'She's very shy,' explained Davenport, 'but she knows about gin, don't you, darling?' He smiled his toothy smile and toasted Strange with clumsy gusto.

'Cheers,' said Strange, and sipped gingerly.

'But, oh dear, I'm forgetting the sad news about Dick. That was a blow and no mistake. D'you know something though, Frank? I wasn't surprised.'

'No.'

'I sometimes get a hunch about people. To me, Dick was always doomed. Ever since . . . since I first knew him, he seemed fated in a sort of way. You get the same feeling with experiments, you know. I had a plan to invent a folding bicycle – yes, even the wheels – but I knew from the first that it wasn't going to work. But I pressed on, and in the end I had to scrap it. Lister was like that. He wouldn't let go, but I believe in his heart he knew he was doomed.' Davenport shook his head sadly. 'That must have been a blow to you, Frank, that death. A suicide is not a nice thing to have to deal with when you're retiring.'

'It's not,' Strange agreed.

'Do you know, I'm quite glad we didn't come to your party on that account. A suicide disturbs people. And Ivy and I, we're very sensitive to vibrations.' He looked into his glass. 'Dick was a good programmer, too. He really understood computers.'

Strange said nothing.

'But here I am chatting on about poor Lister. What brings you to Croydon, Frank? Aren't you supposed to be pruning the roses in Devon. Which reminds me. Before you go you must have some of my latest fertilizer. A scientific mixture of my own devising. The neighbours swear by it, don't they darling?'

This time Strange did not wait for Mrs Davenport. 'As a matter of fact,' he said, breaking in, 'it's about Lister that I've come to talk to you.'

'Oh.' Davenport looked up nervously. 'Oh. The plot thickens. How can I help?'

Strange put his glass down and leant forward. 'After I left the Directorate I tried to visit Lister's family in Cheltenham. As Lister's old boss it seemed the least I could do. They're in a very bad way, John. The children are in care. The house is mortaged to the hilt, and Mrs Lister is probably having a nervous breakdown.'

This recital had the desired effect on Davenport. He ran his hands across his head in some distraction. 'Oh dear, oh dear – ' he repeated.

'Since when,' Strange continued, 'I've been trying to get to the bottom of Lister's death.

'Do you suspect something?' Davenport asked, twisting a loose button on his coat.

'I'll come to that.'

Davenport interrupted in a fright. 'Look, Frank, I only said I thought he seemed doomed. I didn't imply anything else. I don't know anything. I'd rather you didn't – I mean I haven't seen him, Dick I mean, for ages.'

'When was that?' Strange pursued.

'Oh. About four years ago.'

'In Cheltenham?'

'No. I mean yes. I was there on business,' he added quickly.

'You were with Preece at the enquiry, weren't you?'

Davenport looked shocked. 'How did you know that? It's supposed to be secret.'

'It still is. But it's on the files in London. Nothing on the files is a total secret.'

'But Preece promised – ' he began.

'What did he promise?'

'That I could stay anonymous.'

'Why?'

'Well – no, it's not important.' Davenport was very agitated.

'Really?' There was a threatening sarcasm in Strange's voice. Davenport was fiddling nervously with his hands. Then he came out with: 'Keep this to yourself, Frank, but I was used against Lister.'

'You were given a brief?'

Davenport nodded miserably.

'Why did you accept it?'

'I was told that it was in the national interest to calm everyone's nerves there. They said it was lying in a good cause.'

'Who said?'

'Hayter.'

'What did you have to say?'

'I had to testify that the information on which Lister based his allegations referred to a secret suite of non-standard programmes originating here in Croydon. That explained why he had never seen the index before.'

'Did they show you his evidence?'

'No.'

'So you didn't know what Lister was up to?'

'No. I didn't want to get involved. They didn't want me to either.'

It was infuriating, thought Strange, how nobody seemed to want to bother with the details. He said: 'You just said what they told you to say?'

Davenport nodded wearily. 'Of course it was a tussle. I didn't sleep for days. But I was being hard pressed to do it.'

'What sort of pressure?'

'They promised that my stock would rise. I was in a very weak position. I was badly in debt at the time. I'd just invested too much money in the folding bicycle. Not a soul would back it. I needed the extra. Telling lies for the state is what we do all the time, isn't it, Frank? This was just a bit more dramatic.'

134

'What did Lister say about it?'

'He didn't.'

'What do you mean?'

'He refused to speak to me. I never saw him again.' Davenport's beady eyes were large and honest with sorrow. He seemed upset. Strange noticed that Mrs Davenport had disappeared. 'D'you know I've never talked about this with anyone. I'm ashamed really. But I believed that the whole thing would be kept secret and I trusted them that I was fighting for a just cause.'

'But was it a just cause?' Strange looked hard at Davenport. 'What would you say if I told you that Lister was a real threat, but that Hayter was trying to pretend he didn't exist?' Davenport was about to speak, but Strange brushed him aside. 'The rumours were right. It was Lister who was covering up his own trail by going on to the attack. Hayter was embarrassed. He didn't want to know.'

'I –'

Strange was implacable. 'I know you think you killed Lister, John. But you didn't. Somebody else did.'

'What – what are you saying?' Davenport was stuttering with fear.

'Lister was working for someone who thought he was getting untrustworthy. So they got rid of him.'

'You mean he was an agent?'

'You've said it, John,' said Strange. He was glad of the corroboration.

Davenport stared reflectively into his glass. 'We've got so much at stake in the Directorate now, haven't we? So much information, so much power. Fifteen years ago the office didn't matter to anyone. Now it's at the heart of things. I suppose they thought it was worth planting someone inside it then. Well, they were right. It's odd to think of Lister like that, but I'm not surprised.' Davenport was speaking slowly, seriously. 'You know Frank, I'm getting frightened by the state we all live in now. Power means security. No one knows what anyone else is up to. You know the faces but not the names, some of the names but not the numbers. The numbers hold the key to everything in the Directorate. It's all on tape. That's beginning to frighten me.'

'Why?'

'Every day they add some more. You know Dr Mayer – the Dutchman – he's behind all that. Accumulating details, information, lists. Census records, school records, health records, social security records, insurance and credit records, political records: I don't think most people realize how much personal information is collected by the department in the counter-subversion sections. The power we have over people, that's what's frightening, Frank.'

'Don't you believe in the safeguards?'

'I wish I could. But the security forces we serve are beyond Parliament. Their existence is not recognized in law. There's no accountability worth speaking of – '

Strange interrupted, 'But what about the good faith of the people who – '

Davenport waved the objection aside. 'I know, I know, that's what they always say. Perhaps they were right – once. Not any more. The department's too obsessed with crisis for the old informal safeguards to work. Take our data-gathering programme. There's no stopping it. Each scrap of data leads to another piece of data. It gathers momentum of its own accord.'

'So you'll agree,' said Strange, steering the conversation back on course, 'that if Lister was betraying the Directorate, he should have been exposed?'

'Of course. Why wasn't he?'

'As I've explained, Hayter wanted to contain it. You know how ambitious he is for the Directorate. If Hayter admitted the truth about Lister, that would have discredited the Directorate with the other security agencies.'

'So that's why I was sworn to secrecy.'

'It was more secret than you realize, John. Not even I was told.' Davenport looked at him in amazement. 'That's why I'm here. To find out why,' added Strange, gambling.

'Oh, now really – that's – how very interesting – oh I see,' Davenport digested this revelation with much agitation. 'But

Lister's dead,' he countered. 'So you'll never know what he was up to.'

Strange looked quizzical. 'Why's that?'

'Oh, isn't it obvious? Lister's notes obviously contain all the clues. But they'll be buried in the department somewhere – if they haven't been destroyed. There's no way you can find them now you've left, especially if Hayter – '

Strange broke in to reprimand him with good humour. 'You haven't been paying attention, John. I told you I've been investigating the Lister case since I retired. I haven't drawn a complete blank you know.' He laid his briefcase across his knees. 'I have here,' he said with a flourish, 'the document that will reveal all, a xerox copy of Lister's original notes, made minutes after Ellison had left the terminal room.'

Davenport was astonished. 'When – ?' he faltered. 'How – ?' he began.

'Don't ask any awkward questions,' Strange commanded. 'I want to know what these notes mean – in confidence, mind.'

The little scientist studied the pages in a fluster, making little squeaking sounds as his eye ran over the faint jottings. 'Oh gosh, oh my goodness,' he said after a moment. 'This is interesting. You see I recognize some of this, but – no, wait.' His sparrow eye darted back and forth. 'Yes, this is most int – ' he stopped. 'Won't you have another dose of poison. I'll be a minute or two, I'm afraid. Will you read the newspaper while I fiddle?'

'Thanks.' Strange took up the *Daily Telegraph* and began the crossword. Davenport was a distracting worker. He whistled and tapped his pencil. Every now and then he cursed freely and hurried over to an overflowing desk for more scrap paper. After about half an hour he looked up. His former jauntiness had gone.

'You see I recognized some of this data at once,' he began. He spoke quietly and with seriousness, as though there was something on his mind. 'It's a low level programme, designed to process an input file to produce hard copy. But the thing about it that's really odd is that it's unsorted data. And you know that an applications programmer like Ellison is only cleared to use specific data extraction routines and not the algorithms manipulating the database itself.'

'But that's incredible,' said Strange. It was standard practice within all sections of the Directorate to keep the routine programming and key access functions separate. 'You're saying that Ellison was both on line to the database and in possession of the key fields for accessing the secret files.'

'There's no other way of looking at it.'

'Then why didn't Lister point this out?'

'That's where the other odd part of this document comes in. I told you I recognized some of the data and the programme that was being used at once. That's true, but only for the first few lines of output. After that it suddenly becomes a lot more complex. That suggests only one thing.'

'What's that?' asked Strange, wishing that he had a better knowledge of computer science.

'Ellison must have set up his own files of information which only his UIC could access. These files would be read using existing key fields on the database. What he did was take an existing data extraction programme and edit it to read his own files.'

'I didn't know that Ellison was that clever.'

'More than that he was clever enough to devise the programme to run in two parallel versions. With the standard sequence of commands the existing routine would run as expected. Ellison's version was initiated by running the programme in conjunction with a system debugging aid. After the first few lines of output he could stop the run and amend the programme to call special procedures which aren't normally accessed.'

'But that breaks all the rules . . .' Strange began.

'These procedures,' Davenport went on, ignoring him, 'were the ones that read the files that Ellison had installed in the database. If you run the programme in the standard way, which Preece, anxious to calm everyone's nerves, undoubtedly did, the complex secret material won't show up.'

Strange listened in amazement. 'You're saying that it was Ellison who had access to this secret information.'

'I'm afraid so. There is no way Lister could have invented that data, still less have a motive for doing so.' Davenport was hushed. 'So Lister was right. He found something, perhaps by mistake, but was determined that it should be known. And I helped to stifle his enquiry. I shall never forgive myself.' He shook his head slowly.

'Then what do the notes consist of?'

'It's a secret index.' Davenport was speaking in a low monotone, barely sharing his thoughts. 'It's all becoming clear at last. That's why he got the system to crash.'

'You mean the memory dump?'

'Yes, yes. It's all quite clear. He was trying to correlate index and data. It was clumsy but it was all he could do.'

'Have you any idea what the index refers to?' Strange said impetuously.

Davenport lowered his voice. 'Do you remember David Fenton?'

'It's a name that rings a bell – I forget why – what's he got to do with all this . . .?'

But for the moment Davenport wasn't listening. He was speaking low, almost thinking aloud. 'You're right. It can't have been suicide. He must have been murdered. But he can't be an agent. They killed him because he knew too much.' Suddenly he got up and went to the curtained window and looked out. It was quite dark. One or two of the street lights were working and further up the estate a squatter's fire flickered. For a moment Davenport thought he saw movement in the empty house opposite, but when he looked again whatever it was that had moved had gone.

'The index has all the clues. I can give you those. If you follow them carefully you'll find out where the threat was really coming from. Who it was. D'you know something, Frank, I'd rather we finished this conversation in the darkroom. It happens to be soundproof.'

CHAPTER FIFTEEN

Dangerfield's club was broke and, to the intense annoyance of its members, in the process of amalgamating with its rival down Pall Mall. He and Jenks sat over a tepid English dinner in the almost empty dining-room watched by four Spanish waiters. He reflected that there was nothing like a deserted club dining-room for privacy. They did not speak much anyway. Jenks, concentrating on his food, had no breath for conversation; Dangerfield, grave with good manners, was more at home withdrawn in silence. Only the clatter of cutlery disturbed the desolate stillness of the icy room.

Dangerfield marshalled his thoughts with each deliberate mouthful. This meeting was a formality, but an important one. No one was ever going to accuse him of not playing the game by the book. The Minister had to know. The only problem was Jenks's inexperience and what he feared was a dangerous naïvety. He couldn't be trusted to be discreet with Hayter. On the other hand the book said he must be consulted. The cheeseboard arrived. Jenks chose cheddar. Dangerfield signalled for coffee, and sat back in his chair.

'The Strange case seems to be running smoothly,' he opened.

'Can you tell me, Sir Gerald,' queried Jenks with deference, 'what's there to stop us pulling him in now? It strikes me that we're all trying to be a bit too clever with this fellow. Wouldn't it save us a lot of trouble in the long term?'

Dangerfield seemed to consider this suggestion with great seriousness. 'You see, Minister,' he said at length, 'the advantage of a surveillance operation of this kind is that this is precisely what one can do if the subject shows any sign of becoming an embarrassment. For instance, if, as I believe Michael Hayter is arguing, Strange tries to take his story, whatever it is, to the press, we can stop him dead in his tracks. But only if we watch him night and day.'

'Speaking man to man,' said Jenks, 'what's he up to?'

'We have to assume,' Dangerfield replied, 'that whatever it is, the interests of the Directorate and therefore of the department as a whole, lie in letting him carry on undisturbed. In that way he may lead us in some rather interesting directions. Strange is making connections that we can't see. He's discovering secrets on his own that a bureaucracy by its very nature cannot see. Strange is like a computer programmer who has been given unlimited access to a secret database. He's navigating uncharted territory. He's good at that. He's done it for years. I want to see where he ends up. As I see it, we're exploiting his, how shall I say, malevolence against us for our own ends. It's a slow process: you can't expect instant results.'

'That's just the point I wanted to make,' said Jenks. 'I mean it's all very well him navigating, as you put it, but how long's this navigating going on for. We mustn't lose sight of the fact that he's bent. Mind if I smoke?' He pulled out a plastic tobacco pouch.

'By all means.' Dangerfield did not demur as his taste might have dictated.

'You're running a risk, Sir Gerald,' repeated Jenks. 'That's all I'm saying. I know you're a cunning lot of buggers in the Ministry, if you'll pardon my French, but when you're taking on one of your own kind, is it wise? That's what I'm saying.'

'My feeling exactly,' said Dangerfield with practised urbanity. He studied Jenks closely. 'You'd like to see the investigation accelerated?' he said.

'Oh. No doubt about it.'

'Then you must leave the matter to me,' said Dangerfield with satisfaction. 'Will you allow me to act according to my discretion?'

'Grand,' said Jenks, nodding assent.

'Excellent,' said Dangerfield. He had gained one point.

'It won't be a moment too soon, Sir Gerald. I had Hayter

on the blower only today. He's very worried about Strange's latest movements.'

'So he should be. I don't have all the details at my command – that's for Michael Hayter's office – but to my mind there's only one explanation, especially for the Heathrow business.' He looked at Jenks. 'The obvious explanation of course,' he added.

'Oh yes, of course,' said Jenks, quite baffled.

'But there too,' Dangerfield continued with confidence, 'a number of customary remedies suggest themselves. I take it I have your approval.'

'Oh yes, of course,' replied Jenks. He was always very impressed by Dangerfield's calm sense of control. He was lucky, he told himself, to have such an efficient controller. Dangerfield for his part was pleased to be getting his way so easily. He'd known Ministers want to vet every detail. He took a sip of cold coffee. A couple of younger members who had been dining away by the window passed their table with civil nods. 'Have you come across this young man, James Quitman? But of course you have. You gave a briefing –'

'A young fellow. A bright lad as I remember.' Jenks couldn't see the connection.

'As you know, he's been working on the Strange case for some weeks now. Michael Hayter and Guy Preece speak highly of him. That can be dangerous of course,' he reflected, 'when he knows the ropes and has the confidence of his seniors.'

'It sounds as though he's doing well. I must say I liked the look of him, Sir Gerald.'

'He was a close colleague of Strange's. It might be as well to take one or two precautions, don't you think?' he went on obscurely. 'It would be a shame if we allowed him to blot his copybook so early in his career. And one doesn't want to take any risks where the Directorate is concerned.'

'Oh no. I quite agree with you there,' said Jenks.

'Well, that's settled then,' said Dangerfield, having clinched his final point. 'I'll send you a memorandum in due course for the usual clearance with the Home Secretary and now if you'll excuse me Alan, the third act of *Siegfried* will be starting in – ' he looked at his watch, 'ten minutes. If I dash I can join my friends. Can you find your way out? Splendid. I do beg your pardon.'

Charles Neve climbed the steps to the house in which Liz Sayer had her flat in a state of breathless expectation. And it was decent of Quitman to invite him, even if there was some motive to it. He pressed the bell.

'Hello! Come in.' Quitman was very informal in jeans and an old sweater. 'How nice to see you; you found it all right.'

'No trouble. I took a cab from the club as a matter of fact.' Neve hurried through the door, took his host by the arm and steered him to one side, ignoring the sound of festivity within. 'James, I must tell you the most extraordinary thing. I've just been having the usual stodge dinner at the club – '

'Oh, but you should have said. You could have joined us for supper beforehand – '

'Wait. The place was practically deserted of course. But guess who was there?'

Quitman was about to say Strange, but checked himself. 'The Prime minister,' he joked.

'Dangerfield.' Neve looked very impressed. 'With Jenks.' Quitman stared. 'And as I walked out past them you'll never guess what they were talking about?'

'Oh. I don't know.' Although he was host, Quitman was getting irritated by Neve's inquisitorial manner. 'You, I imagine. You're very much the coming man in the department.'

Neve was grateful for that, but shook his head decisively. 'Wrong.' He paused dramatically. 'You.'

'Dangerfield was talking about me? I don't believe it. What did he say?'

'I was dying to hear. But I just caught your name.'

Quitman was so taken aback by this that all he could say was, 'Come in and have some mulled wine.'

'Splendid. I haven't had mulled wine for ages. Oranges are such a terrible price these days. Mind you I expect you can afford it with your new – ' he paused momentarily, ' – elevation.' Quitman ignored the hint of favouritism and Neve pressed on busily, 'Let's take our glasses over here out of the crush – lovely place you have – I want to have a good gossip about all this. I'm relying on you to tell me what it really means.'

It was Liz's party. The small pink sitting-room was crowded with freelance journalists, advertisers, literary people, and actresses, all Liz's friends and members, Quitman supposed, of what she was occasionally pleased to call the 'artygentsia'. He had invited Neve along for company and in the hope that in this festive atmosphere he might be able to do something about moderating the temperature of the cold war that Neve and Rosie (who was not invited) were waging against him in the office. Well, at least the man had accepted. He had not confided all the details of this piece of tactical hostmanship to Liz. It would only have provoked a diatribe against the twisted *mores* of the Directorate, although, in truth, most of the guests now gobbling mince-pies had been invited out of similarly tactical considerations.

The Christmas party was Quitman's idea. Liz had been reluctant. Her confidence, after the departure of her last lover, was at rock bottom. The plans for the literary agency seemed once more as far from fruition as ever. Slowly, Quitman was rebuilding her social courage and her self-respect. It provided a deeply satisfying contrast to the deception he now practised every day at the Directorate.

Liz came over to them now, glowing with success and alcohol.

'Jamie, darling, you can't hide away in a corner talking shop.' She was shepherding a smart young man in a white suit. 'This is Daniel. He's coming in to the agency as business manager.' She stranded them together and disappeared. Daniel looked at the two civil servants with a slightly quizzical insolence. He cocked his head at Quitman. 'You live with Liz, right? I've heard a lot about you. You work at the Ministry of – '

'That's right,' said Quitman, cutting in. 'This is my colleague and friend, Charles Neve.'

'Colleague and friend,' repeated Daniel with irony, 'how do you do.' They shook hands with an uneasy flutter of laughter. Then Daniel said: 'I wanted to join the civil service once. But they wouldn't let me.'

'Why not?' asked Charles.

'My grandfather was Czech. The family's Jewish. I was born in Israel. So I'm bad security,' he laughed, 'but they didn't find that out until I'd passed all the exams and come through most of the interviews with flying colours.'

'What happened then?'

'They were reluctant to lose me. But there were the regulations, and you're a wonderful race for the rule book, you people. So I got a final interview. I think they were curious. The chairman leant across the table and said, "Tell me, Mr Goldman, do you think of yourself as more British than Jewish?" ' Quitman and Neve joined in his immoderate laughter. 'It was incredible. I freaked them out. Later they wrote a charming letter apologizing for the cock-up but explaining that for reasons of state security, etc., etc. Are they as strict as that when you get inside?'

Quitman looked at Neve. 'I'd say so.'

'The security's obsessive,' said Neve with unusual force. 'Everything, even the smallest detail, is secret. And the reasons for the security are secret. Secrecy is the lowest common denominator in our work.'

'It's like a pair of mirrors repeating against each other,' said Quitman. 'There's an infinite regression.'

'And these secrets,' asked Goldman, 'do they need to be secret?'

'I've just said,' Neve replied with a short laugh, 'I can't say – because it's secret!'

Quitman explained reasonably. 'Secrecy's a habit. We're trained to think of everything as a matter of national security. In theory no one knows what his colleagues are up to. The organization's broken down into non-communicating units.'

Goldman narrowed his eyes. 'And who's the boss of this secret world?' he asked, off-hand.

Neve was almost euphoric with indiscretion. 'Well, it's breaking all the rules to mention his name, but since you can find it in Whitaker's if you know where to look . . . he's called Dangerfield, Sir Gerald Dangerfield. I've never met him. Have you, James?' Neve had failed in his private attempts to get Quitman to decode the meaning of Dangerfield's conversation.

'No.'

'This isn't the secret service you're talking about?'

'Certainly not. They're quite different. Everyone knows about them of course. Nobody knows what we get up to. Of course we help them, but we're much more secret than the security services, aren't we James?' Quitman's reserve induced a sudden caution in Neve. 'And what do you do, Daniel?'

'I'm a journalist,' he replied with a faint smile.

Neve checked, and turned to Quitman in some panic. 'But Liz said he was a business executive.'

'You should listen more carefully,' Goldman said, rather nastily. 'I'm going to be her manager when she gets started. For the moment I make my living as a freelance.' He gave another immodest cackle and made an excuse about looking for some more to drink. Neve lost his temper with Quitman then.

'That was pretty bloody embarrassing. I do think you might have taken the trouble to warn me.'

'I'm frightfully sorry, Charles. I had no idea.'

Neve was getting pompous with too much alcohol. 'Well I think it's very irresponsible of you not to find out beforehand. I don't think I really want to stay here any more. I'd be grateful if you'd call a cab.'

Quitman took a long time to get through to the local taxi-rank, but eventually the doorbell rang and he escorted Neve down to the street. They didn't speak.

'Clapham, please, driver,' said Neve.

'Sorry, mate. I don't go south of the river.'

'Oh my God,' said Neve as though this was Quitman's fault. 'Take me to the bridge. I'll walk it.'

'Rather you than me, mate.'

'Goodnight,' said Quitman but got no reply. He watched the car bounce and rattle over the rutted tarmac, and wondered about the repercussions of this unfortunate incident. Liz met him coming back.

'So you're the draught. Your friend left early.'

'Charles? He had a row with Daniel whatshisname.'

'Danny Goldman? He's a dear. What happened?'

'Charles had too much to drink and started telling Goldman about the Ministry. I must say I do wish you'd said he was a journalist. One has to be discreet.'

'James! Can't you even relax at a party,' Liz flared up and then regretted it. 'I'm sorry, darling. I didn't mean it. Daniel's ratlike cunning is rather insufferable at times. He'll be a good business manager, don't you think?'

'Now who's talking shop?' They smiled at each other and kissed. Their lips, sticky with wine, clung briefly. The floor next door was shaking with dancing. Liz went through to mix more wine. Quitman found himself with Goldman again. Goldman smirked knowingly. 'How long have you lived here, James?' Quitman sensed that his relationship with Liz was being challenged and wondered if Goldman fancied her.

'Oh – on and off – for quite a while.'

'That sounds terribly British,' Goldman replied.

Quitman could not think of anything to say in reply so he said: 'It was lucky about the oranges and lemons. You can't begin to make mulled wine without oranges and lemons. They're terribly scarce you see. It's the strike of course. They're probably rotting in the docks. So there'll be a British marmalade shortage I shouldn't wonder.'

The music was running slower, couples were necking in the middle of the floor, swaying in slow circles like dolls on a string. A bearded guest in a tee-shirt who had been hovering on the edge of the conversation joined in: 'I had to advertise oranges once you know. It was too boring for words and when my staff found out that oranges can come from South Africa, why then the whole account became a perfect nightmare.'

The telephone rang, sounding faintly from the hall. 'I'll go,' said Quitman to no one in particular. But one of the guests, standing by the receiver, had already picked it up.

'Wrong number,' she said as Quitman came into the hall.

'What did he want?' asked Quitman.

'Male chauvinist pig,' she said.

'What d'you mean? What did he say?' he repeated.

'How d'you know it wasn't a woman?'

'But it was, wasn't it? A man, I mean.' He laughed to conceal his nervousness.

'Well, as a matter of fact –'

'What did he say?' he interrupted, almost furious.

The girl was annoyed too. 'Well, I don't know for God's sake. It was from a phone box and he rang off as soon as I spoke.'

CHAPTER SIXTEEN

Quitman knew that Strange had been frightened off using the telephone again when the postcard reproduction of the London underground arrived two days later. It was sealed in an envelope, but Quitman recognized the uneven typewriter at once. How often, in the days when Strange was still boss, had he come into the office in the morning to find a sheaf of notes from Strange's old Remington, roughly typed on the clean backs of envelopes or circulars, waiting on his desk. 'J.Q. Please draft brief for tomorrow's PQ meeting. F.S.T.' Strange was always known as F.S.T. in the office. The extra initial dated from the time when another colleague whose name no one could recall, shared the initials F.S. Quitman broke the seal impatiently.

On the back of the card Strange had written 'Albinoni', the agreed code, and holding the card carefully to the light, Quitman found a faint pin-prick in the High Street Kensington stop on the District and Circle line.

'I'm going shopping this evening, love,' said Quitman as he kissed Liz goodbye. 'Can I get you anything?'

'Where?'

'High Street Ken.'

'Can't you wait till Saturday. We could do our Christmas shopping together then.'

'We'll do that too. I want to pick up one or two things at Smith's.'

'I'm out at a launching party tonight, so get yourself some supper while you're there.'

'Well, I hope you find the novelist of your dreams. Bye.'

The day was unmemorable except that there was no escaping Neve's bitter hostility. Added to Rosie's vicious campaign against him, Quitman found it depressing. He was glad to leave the office early on a pretext, arousing no suspicion.

Rush-hour Kensington was sullen with office-workers in heavy coats jostling along darkened pavements. The crisis had not stifled Christmas shopping, but there was little festivity in it. There seemed to be a lot of money about. Taxis were queuing up, spilling passengers with fists of ten and twenty pound notes into all the main stores. Quitman made his way towards W. H. Smith's. It was five o'clock. The arrangement was that he should always arrive early at the chosen location to avoid surveillance.

He established that Records and Tapes were downstairs in the basement and then walked to the back of the main floor of the shop and began browsing through the Travel section. But nervousness ruined his concentration and he moved quickly from Patagonia to the table of dog-eared best-sellers. By five twenty-five the suspense was unbearable. Then above the eager chatter of the shoppers he heard the familiar thump-thump of Strange's stick on the stairway, going down. He must not look round. There would be surveillance on the door, probably a man reading the *Evening Standard*. Quitman turned the page, straining to catch the sound of Strange's returning footfall. A shop assistant, a young man with a ragged orange beard, interrupted: 'Can I help you, sir?'

'Oh,' Quitman spoke in a low voice. 'No thank you. I'm just browsing.'

He put the book back on the pile and fingered another. He looked at his watch again. Five thirty-five. He hadn't heard Strange come back but with all these shoppers he couldn't risk a delay. Turning slowly, looking about warily, he walked towards the stair head. There was no one in the crowd that he recognized. He hurried down the stairs. There was Classical, Opera, Concerto and Sonata. Where were the tapes? Then he saw the revolving stand with the cassettes in racks. There were two music lovers in the way. Quitman elbowed his way alongside and began a determined search for the Albinoni. The music lovers, affronted at his rudeness, moved away. There it was. He detached the cassette from the rack and opened it carefully. The BSA tape he'd given Strange from his own collection was inside. He closed the plastic with a snap and substituted an identical cassette from his coat pocket on the rack. Then to mask the exchange he selected some Chopin and some Messiaen which he paid for at the counter. That would make a nice present for Liz.

Strange's voice, which was usually dignified and controlled, sounded urgent in Liz's empty flat. The sturdy clarity of Strange's accent was always made oddly fascinating by the occasional note of his native Devonshire, and it provoked in Quitman a surge of private affection for the elderly battler to whose cause he was now so deeply pledged. He turned the volume low and sat forward in his chair to listen. 'Today's message is simple, James. I've got it wrong, so incredibly wrong that you'll find it hard to believe. But when I give you the details you'll see that there's no other interpretation possible.' A siren sounded in the distance and for a moment Quitman didn't realize it was on the tape. Then he imagined Strange sitting alone in his car, in the dark perhaps, bowed in secrecy over the microphone. 'You know,' the familiar voice went on, 'it's a curious game of self-humiliation I'm having to play. Towards the end of my time in Whitehall – before Lister of course – I thought I knew everything about everyone. I thought I was in command. I spoke the right language, had all the right contacts I thought, and had all the information at my fingertips. Information is power they say. Well, now I'm having to admit that I didn't know everything. It's odd what an illusion of power secrecy can give you. In fact the more I can admit that there are secrets I never dreamed of, the clearer the picture becomes. Then I start to see things without prejudice.' It sounded like a confession.

'Take my judgement of Lister for instance. That's turned out to be a complete prejudice. You won't believe it – I didn't to start with. But he was right about Ellison and Cooper. They're the guilty ones. Lister, for all his shiftiness, was in the right. Davenport's proved that beyond question. That was a good tip-off, James. Well-spotted. You didn't know it, but he's an old friend I can trust. Of course I never suspected – the humiliation principle again – that he had anything to do with the case. When I showed him your xerox of the VDU material he was thrilled. He'd been feeling bad about his part in the enquiry ever since it ended. And when he managed to puzzle it out – he's not a chap to stay baffled for long – he was amazed. He explained that Lister couldn't possibly have invented it or planted it on Ellison or any of the things that were rumoured. The plain fact is that Lister did uncover a scandal and the Directorate, for reasons I'll come to in a minute, covered it up. What's so maddening is that if I hadn't had such a bad relationship with him, he might have trusted me to take up his case for him. As it was, it seems he kept it to himself, poor fellow.'

Quitman stopped the tape for a moment. Strange had always prided himself on his ability to upset received opinions. He wondered how many more revelations this relentless quest would yield. He poured himself some of Liz's whisky and pressed the button again. The voice went on without a break. 'Davenport had no trouble decoding Lister's notes. Now I've got to find out what they mean. There are several clues, names, figures and so on, but because I'm getting superstitious about false speculation, all I'm going to tell you for the moment is that Lister was on our side and he was on to something that the Directorate didn't want him on to. I guess that Aidan Cooper knows a lot more than he's told. No wonder he was scared. So I want a full report on his past, please James, if you can manage it. I'll pick up Sibelius from Holborn next. Davenport tells me that Cooper has a Polish wife and that they used to have their summer holidays near Warsaw. He was vetted many years ago I know, but that was in the early days when they were hard up for technicians and didn't ask too many questions.'

'But I'm running ahead.' There was a rumble on the tape as Strange cleared his throat. 'You see what all this points to. Someone outside must have cottoned on to the potential of the Directorate years ago, almost, you could say, before we did ourselves. That's no surprise. The obvious thing then was to put someone in it, fairly low down, who could gradually build up a power base. I'm convinced that's Cooper. What's the betting he did it to get his sweetheart out of Poland? It's likely that he recruited Ellison and paid him off without Ellison ever being aware what he was doing. But Cooper can't be alone. There must be others, not necessarily in the Directorate. How else did Lister find similar evidence in London? I must have another careful look at his memo. All this supports my theory that when Lister first made his allegations Hayter realized what the implications were and tried to pretend that nothing was wrong. That's why he used a man like Preece who could be trusted to be discreet in exchange for promotion. You must admit that he was lucky to get my job so young. Hayter daren't tell Dangerfield the true story because that's exactly the excuse Dangerfield needs to bring the Directorate under his immediate executive control. Hayter's been resisting that move for years like the typical empire-builder that he is. So now he's trying to suppress the scandal. My guess is that he's got Preece to help him.'

'Lister's murder now fits into place as well. You see when Cooper's masters discovered that Lister was up to his old tricks in London they got rid of him rather than risk another Cheltenham. It takes professionals to arrange a good "suicide". Meanwhile Hayter, who must have thought I'd interpret the memo. business correctly, and start asking awkward questions, had got Dangerfield to push me out.' Strange's voice had a laugh in it. 'If he'd realized how little yours truly realized what was going on he needn't have bothered. As it happens he's made more work for himself. And if he'd realized that I was only after Lister he would have been better advised to keep the bloodhounds – two of whom are catching their deaths just down the road now – on the leash. As you'd say, James, how ironical it all is.'

'One last point before the cold gets unbearable, the further I go down this trail it's going to cross Hayter's mind that there's a leak. If it has, then the first thing he will do is to check all the possible outlets from the Directorate. It's worth bearing in mind that even though you're working with them, you're not above suspicion. In some ways, because you have privileged access you're a more likely target for this kind of vetting. And you may not know it's happening. Now, erase this and carry on the good work.'

There was a faint click. Quitman ran the tape forward for a few seconds and then played it again, the sound of Albinoni's *Adagio* soothed the darkened room.

Quitman got up and put on the kettle. He was, oddly, not as preoccupied with Strange's revelations about Lister as with the threat of being discovered unawares. Suddenly, quite a normal encounter the day before yesterday became charged with significance.

He had thought nothing of the request from HQ Security to go and discuss developments in the surveillance operation at their central office. It was the first time it had happened, but there was nothing odd about that. Quitman was quite glad to enlarge his experience.

HQ Security occupied a basement in an anonymous building in Northumberland Avenue. Turner, the operation's commander, was a bulky sedentary man with an easy manner and a friendly illuminating smile. He and Quitman had spoken often on the telephone and were getting to know each other quite well. When Quitman arrived in the over-heated ops. room, Turner was talking to a thin man with pebble glasses and a lugubrious expression that Quitman recognized but couldn't identify.

'James,' said Turner, breaking off briefly from his conversation, 'I don't think you know Alec Reeve.'

'How do you do,' he said, shaking hands. Reeve's pink-rimmed eyes quivered slightly in greeting. The two men returned to their discussion of their work, their families and an analysis of the season's racing.

'. . . badly astray at Doncaster. The horse never flattered.'

'Do you go racing?' asked Turner, drawing Quitman back into the conversation.

154

'I – ' he began.

'You don't look the racing sort,' said Reeve. 'God, if I didn't have the horses, I'd go mad in this job.'

'That's true,' said Turner. And Quitman had a momentary flash of colour and cheering, flying turf and the thunder of hooves, and thought he could understand why men who spent their days underground or watching from the shadows in the backs of parked cars, should need the open excitement of the flat.

'You know something, Horace,' Reeve resumed, 'we haven't had a good gallop ourselves since Lister.'

'And even then they wouldn't let us go the full course.'

Quitman broke in, 'You watched Lister?' He was amazed. Neither Hayter nor Preece had ever admitted that.

Reeve looked at him. 'As I'm standing here.'

'Richard Lister?' Quitman repeated idiotically.

'He was the devil.'

'Knew all the tricks,' added Turner.

'What was he up to?' Quitman enquired.

'What wasn't he up to? Every day, after work, off he'd go, folded umbrella, briefcase and *Daily Telegraph*. The model civil servant. But as soon as he got to Paddington he became a different chap, didn't he, Horace?'

Turner nodded.

'What did he do?'

'Well he didn't go home I can tell you. It's no wonder his wife had that affair. And then we lost him.'

'What do you mean?'

'They took him away from us as soon as the case got interesting. Handed it over to the boys in Army Intelligence. God knows why. They screwed up all right. They should never have let him do away with himself.'

'You see, James,' said Turner, 'what wicked work we get up to.'

Quitman said Yes he did. This was baffling information.

Reeve looked pensive. 'If this Strange business gets any hotter, it might turn interesting.'

'So long as they don't hand it over to Army Intelligence,' said Turner.

'That's not part of the London security service network, is it?' enquired Quitman interested.

'No,' Reeve intervened quickly, 'it's based on Aldershot.'

'That's right,' said Turner chiming in. 'It's run by a fellow called Matthews.' He looked at Reeve. 'It is Matthews, isn't it?'

'Oh yes. Colonel Matthews,' Reeve was smiling slightly as he repeated the name.

Now he visualized that queer smile, Quitman realized where he'd seen Alec Reeve, the thin man, before. It was only weeks after he'd joined Whitehall. Reeve was with Dangerfield in the corridor. Dangerfield had been pointed out to him by a colleague. But Reeve's face had stuck. Again he saw the smile exchanged with Turner yesterday when they talked of Colonel Matthews. All that information about Lister and Army Intelligence had gone into the tape that Strange had just collected. Strange was probably already on his way to Aldershot. Yes, Reeve had smiled. That didn't seem in character. And it was a smile of satisfaction, of having achieved something. Quitman panicked. Of course, Reeve had passed him a marked card and he hadn't spotted it. He wondered wildly what he could do.

There was the scrape of the door opening. It was Liz. Quitman got up hurriedly and switched on the light. He had been sitting in the dark in the sitting-room staring at the light on the tape-recorder. In the kitchen the kettle was boiling its heart out.

He kissed her as she came in. Her lips were cold but alive. He forced his concentration in her direction.

'Good party?'

'So-so. The usual crowd. And I didn't meet the world's greatest novelist.'

'Who's he?'

'Oh, come on, James! What's the matter with you? You said to me this morning, as you left, that you hoped I met the novelist of the century.'

'Oh yes. So I did. Sorry. I forgot. It's been a long day.' Was there any point in trying to get to Aldershot now? He wouldn't know where to go.

'So I see. Good shopping?'

'Yes,' he said absently. Then he remembered. 'I've got a Christmas present for you.'

'A presie! How lovely. What is it?'

'Wait and see.' He took the small paper bag out of his coat pocket. 'You'll never guess.'

'Oh, Chopin, oh darling, Messiaen. How wonderful! We must play them at once. What's this you've been listening to?'

'Just some odd notes from the office.' She knew about taped memos. He could always cruise round Aldershot in the early hours and hope to catch Strange that way.

'Let's hear.' Liz was tipsy, he thought. 'Your secret life!'

'No!' He was ashamed at his violent reaction. He stabbed the reject button with his finger. Strange's tape flew into the air with a clatter.

'Don't you trust me?'

'Of course I do. It's just that – well, it's very boring anyway.' He took the Chopin gently out of her hands and switched it on. The music stilled the beginnings of a row about secrecy.

'Coffee?'

'Please.' He knew from her tone that she was biding her time. Well, he thought, perhaps Reeve's smile meant nothing. If they're going to find out they probably will. He could always edit the surveillance report.

Later, when they were in bed, Liz's last cigarette glowing in the darkness beside him, he said: 'Do you ever worry about the ethics of your job?'

'I don't think so. There's nothing wicked about PR.'

'Except the shallow smile. There is no art to read the mind's construction in the face, and all that.'

'That's not ethics, that's relationships, surely?' She turned towards him. 'You're worried darling. What is it? Is it the tape?' It was his own fault that he hadn't avoided the question.

'No, the tape was nothing. It's all part of something larger – the way we all behave. In the office I mean,' he replied. 'It's not merely that one cannot read the mind's construction, it's the construction itself that is so often dangerous and obscure.' He saw Strange driving past rows of barracks.

'You've been telling noble lies again, haven't you darling?' That was a joke between them, but Quitman did not laugh.

'No. It's much worse than lies.'

'Corruption?'

'Worse than that.'

She hushed her voice in mock-horror. 'Buggery?' This time he smiled to himself in the darkness.

'You're smiling, aren't you?'

'Yes, but it's worse than that.' He wanted to feel safer by telling her but couldn't.

'Assassination? You don't do that, do you?'

'Not exactly. But someone in the Directorate committed suicide, at least we say it was suicide, but Strange has proved – ' He was about to say 'murder' but Liz interrupted 'I thought Strange had retired.'

'He has. But he still keeps an interest in things.' Quitman was becoming vague again, scared at what he was now saying, but scared also to keep his thoughts to himself.

Liz kissed him and then they made love. For a few minutes Quitman forgot his fears. When he woke later it was very still and, climbing uneasily out of bed into the cold, he went and sat in the lavatory and played Strange's tape to himself once again while the cistern muttered reproachfully overhead.

CHAPTER SEVENTEEN

You wouldn't choose to live in Aldershot, Strange thought as he drove in past rows of pre-fabricated service maisonettes, not even if you were in the Army. The main barracks, already ringed with barbed wire, was now guarded by tanks as well, a shadow of snow on their barrels. There was a checkpoint at many access roads, and in the interests of security other entrances to the compound had been blocked off with concrete. But despite all these measures the base seemed curiously vulnerable in the early morning winter stillness.

Strange, who knew the place well from the war and from frequent visits during his time at the Directorate, was confused. But after a couple of false starts he found the Intelligence Corps HQ he was looking for not far from the officers' quarters. There were Christmas streamers in the gatehouse, but the duty officer looked at the battered Volvo with suspicion.

'Park that over there, chief, if you wouldn't mind. And stay with the motor please. I'll send one of my men over in a minute.'

Strange complied without dispute and spread his newspaper across the steering wheel. Bombing in London again. A young soldier with a clipboard bent down to the window.

'Good morning sir. Would you state the nature of your business?'

'It's personal. Look, all I want to do is see Colonel Matthews, Barnaby Matthews you know. Can you call him up and tell him Frank Strange is here?'

The private looked at his clipboard. 'There's a lot of questions you're supposed to answer, but if you just want to leave a message I suppose – '

'That's the boy,' said Strange and gave a wink. He turned

159

another page of the paper. The soldier crunched back to the checkpoint. When Colonel Matthews came hurrying across the square behind the wire his men couldn't believe it. 'Frank,' he said ducking under the guard rail.

'Breaks every security regulation in the book,' commented the sergeant on duty. 'I ask you.'

Rather pink and jolly, Matthews had the air of a responsible schoolboy, though his short figure was the worse for regimental dinners, while his voice, noisy and commanding, had a clean-shaven, parade-ground ring that carried well. In another age he would have joined Gibbon as a captain of the militia and drunk plenty of port in good company.

Strange pushed his newspaper on to the passenger seat and got out stiffly. 'Hello, Barnaby,' he said, with less enthusiasm. He liked Matthews a great deal but he always had difficulty with his Christian name. They shook hands.

'Well, what brings you to this neck of the woods? They told me you'd retired. Barbara said I should write, but we'd lost your Christmas card. Cornwall, isn't it?'

'Devon.'

'Lucky fellow. How's retirement? Vegetable marrows and a deckchair in the garden with a good book. D'you know I'm re-reading Carlyle at the moment. Marvellous stuff.'

Strange thought that with some people friendship takes up again as though it has never stopped. He and Matthews had long ago discovered a shared love of history.

'I haven't got time for the past at the moment. I'm too busy with current affairs. And that's why I'm here. I need some help. Is there somewhere we can talk – privately.'

Matthews gave him an odd look. His bonhomie vanished as fast as it had come.

'I thought you were looking tired, Frank. You've got something on your mind, eh? Look, old boy, I've got a lot on my plate thanks to this latest round of unpleasantness, but I'll give Barbara a ring and you can come and have dinner with us tonight and have a natter round the ancestral hearth. How's that?'

'Thank you very much. What time?'

'Any time after eight. If I'm not back help yourself to a drink and have a round of snooker.'

'Barnaby,' said Strange, arresting his attention. 'I think it would be a good idea if you didn't mention our meeting tonight – to anyone here – it's rather delicate actually.'

'Sounds very mysterious. Terrific! See you this evening. You know where to go, eh?'

'Don't worry. I'll get directions from your batman.'

Matthews gave a broad strong wave and, shouting his congratulations to the guard for breaking all the rules, hurried back across the compound, his open battledress flapping like a sports jacket.

After a few words with the duty officer, Strange turned the car and rolled slowly away from the depot towards the town. He would need to buy some chocolates and flowers for Matthews's wife.

Lady Barbara's family stretched back through several centuries of family and national vicissitude to the early years of the reign of Elizabeth I. Barnaby Matthews was her second husband. They had been married in 1946, four years after her first had been executed by the Gestapo in occupied France. Barnaby was also in military intelligence, but unlike most of his colleagues remained in the Army after the war. He liked the club atmosphere and, as people often remarked, it was so convenient for home.

Home was Lady Barbara's family estate. Her only brother had died in Spain and the cadet branch of the family were not pressing to administer the cockroaches and woodworm of the old house. After more than thirty years of peace and inflation the place was decaying fast. Strange steered the Volvo up the pot-holed driveway, manoeuvring into a squall of hail that rolled down the avenue of monarch oaks baffling the beam of the headlights. As the car bumped and splashed slowly through the darkness, he wondered if the watchers would follow him down or wait under the dripping trees at the head of the drive.

A single light was shining over the front door. The rest of

the building, which towered and rambled above him, was darkened. There was no bell that he could see, so he pushed the door ajar, stepped inside into the damp stone hallway and gave a friendly shout. He was glad to be expected.

After a long pause and the sound of distant barking and the slamming of a door, he heard footsteps tapping along a stone corridor. 'Hello,' he gave another shout, apprehensive slightly that his call was not answered.

But it was Matthews. 'Frank – welcome. I must ask you to keep the decibels down, old chap. Barbara's not well, so it's scrambled eggs in the kitchen I'm afraid tonight. You got here all right?

'It's quite a mansion,' Strange admired.

'A millstone, Frank, a terrible millstone. I'd show you round, only we've disconnected most of the electricity to save money, when the unions aren't doing it for us of course! To be very honest with you it's bankrupted us near enough. You're one of the last to see it as a private citizen. I'm giving it, I should say Barbara's giving it, to the National Trust – if they can afford to run it – next summer. Barbara and I will move to a semi in Aldershot and eke out a meagre existence on our dibs.'

The kitchen was stone flagged. There was an artificial Christmas tree on the television. A casserole was steaming on the Aga.

'Soup?' said Matthews, handing him a bowl. 'Tuck in. I'll just take this up to Barbara. Won't be a minute.'

Strange sat at the kitchen table and watched the steam rise into the shadows of the ceiling.

'Now then,' said Matthews clattering back into the kitchen down a narrow flight of cipboard stairs. 'We can relax. Beer?'

'Please.'

'Home brew I'm afraid. At ten pence a pint you can't complain.' He put two pewter mugs on the table. 'What a day! This unpleasantness is very trying. Random violence you know. Wears you down. Fortunately the terrorists seem to be pretty unsophisticated intelligence-wise.'

162

'You're winning?'

'I hope so. We've drawn, as it were, the map of their organization now. All we have to do is to fill in the names.'

Strange reflected that his own problem was not dissimilar. 'Is that going to be easy?'

'It's never easy. There's the usual revolutionary business of closed cells. Everyone has an alias. No one knows who controls whom. We hope to pick up one of the high command and do a spot of mind reading. I've got my eye on a very promising house in Fulham.'

'Is this in association with the Directorate?'

'Oh, it's the usual co-operative effort: everyone at each other's throats.' Matthews laughed and pushed his soup bowl away. 'How do you like your eggs scrambled?'

'As they come.'

'Good. You know the only time I've ever worked happily with the department was when you and I did that operation together back in '68.' Strange smiled at the compliment. 'Yes, that was a success.'

'It was fun,' insisted Matthews. 'It's never been the same since.'

'Who do you deal with now?'

'Somehow the command structure seems more confused now you're not there any more. I never hear much from Hayter. Your successor – whatshisname?'

'Guy Preece.'

'That's it – he's cagey too. I suppose Dangerfield is the only one I know at all well. And he's an enigma.'

Strange decided that it was time to focus the conversation slightly. 'What did you make of the Lister business then?' he hazarded. He hoped Quitman had got it right.

'Oh. He told you, did he?'

For a moment, misunderstanding, he panicked. 'What d'you mean?' he said quickly.

'My instructions from Dangerfield were that it was Top Secret. Not even Hayter knew about it.'

Strange was shocked. He stared at Matthews inanely. So Dangerfield had been investigating Lister, perhaps he still was . . . Typical that no one should know about it. He took a deep breath. He had to relax if he wasn't to give all his hand away at once. It would have to be another calculated risk. 'As a matter of fact, Barnaby, he didn't tell me. That's why I'm here.' Matthews, who was fussing over the bowl with a whisk, turned round. 'Are you ready for your egg?' he said.

'Thanks.'

Matthews put the plate on the table and offered pepper and salt with exaggerated courtesy.

He looked at him directly. 'What the hell's going on, Frank?'

How much do I have to tell him to get him to talk, Strange wondered. His quest for information was doing odd things to his friendships.

'What would you say if I told you that my retirement was premature?' he countered.

Matthews looked puzzled. 'I'd say that's what we all think, Frank. Nobody can understand why you of all people wanted to give up.'

'You're not getting my point, Barnaby. I didn't retire exactly. I resigned under pressure.'

'Sacked!' exclaimed Matthews. 'I don't believe you. No one's been sacked from the department since – since God knows when.'

'So nothing must ever be done for the first time? That sounds like the department. Well, I'm the exception. I went – it wasn't exactly the sack – because of Lister. To phrase that delicately, I resigned because it was made clear to me by Dangerfield that my position within the Directorate as its boss had become compromised by Lister. It was the only honourable course.'

'No wonder Dangerfield didn't want London to handle the surveillance.'

'Now you can see why I'm rather interested in what Lister had discovered.'

'Don't you trust the department to act in your best interests?'

Strange laughed for the first time that evening, his old laugh. The bare kitchen responded to it. 'The department acts in its own interests. What it calls the national interest.'

'That's too cynical for me, Frank. I won't go with you that far. I sometimes think that the department is run by some crazy lunatics but it *does* work for what it believes to be the national good. They're a dedicated lot, you know.'

'So do I, Barnaby. But this time I happen to know that it is betraying itself on behalf of those ideals.'

'You're speaking in riddles, Frank. We intelligence chaps need to have it a good deal more obvious than that.'

Strange's tone indicated that he was starting from first principles. 'Lister died on the day I retired. Never mind what Dangerfield was up to, I believed, rightly as it turned out, that the Directorate would do nothing. Hayter would close both the files with a sigh of relief and send them off to the central office to await the attentions of the historians.'

'Yes.'

'That's how Hayter acts in the national interest,' Strange wished he could keep the bitterness out of his voice.

'I'm sorry, Frank.' Matthews looked serious. 'I can't agree with you there.'

'Leave aside whether you will or will not accept that judgement,' said Strange, a shade peremptorily, 'what would you have done in those circumstances?'

'I,' said Matthews with emphasis, 'I would have selected half-a-dozen March browns and gone fishing.' He smiled and went on. 'But you, being the awkward bugger you are, said to yourself, "I want to know what Lister was up to." ' He raised a friendly hand. 'Don't get me wrong, Frank. I mean you make us all look pretty feeble.'

'Your mind-reading is improving,' said Strange. 'And so far my investigations show that what Lister was up to was highly embarrassing to the Directorate – '

'I should have thought – ' Matthews began.

'Because contrary to my firm expectation, it turns out that Lister was on the side of the angels.'

Matthews shook his head. 'I'm sorry, Frank. I don't know

165

where you've been sleuthing, but I'm glad you've come to me. Lister was up to no good I can assure you.'

'What was he up to then?' Strange sounded irritated.

'We only had him for a few weeks – on daylight surveillance only, that was good enough even in September – but in that time he behaved very strangely. He used to put on disguise in the gents at Paddington station if you'll believe it, and he visited some pretty shady types.'

'Oh – who?'

'Well, there was that TV chap. The fellow who was in that scandal. You know who I mean. Tall and willowy and rather good-looking actually.'

'I don't have a television. What did he do?'

'He was an interviewer – oh, terribly well known, you know the one.'

'Roland Selzer?'

'That's it. The Selzer Interview. The man we all loved to hate.'

'Lister visited Roland Selzer?'

'Suspicious, isn't it? Selzer's a well-known rotter politically.'

Strange said nothing.

'Who else? Oh yes, that Tribunite MP Fenton. He had a long talk with him.'

'Did you listen?'

'No. I told you it was a low key operation.'

'That doesn't look too suspicious to me.'

'Come, come, Frank. Fenton's a long way under the bed.' So, Strange noted, Matthews believed in hammers and sickles too, like everyone else. For some reason it irritated him, but he suppressed the feeling and asked mildly: 'What else did Lister do?'

'I forget the names but he was visiting left-wing trade unionists, shady import-export types, an arms dealer in Birmingham, a couple of bent computer consultants. Good God! He even called on the permanent Soviet trade delegation. And when he wasn't talking to every subversive on the Directorate's files, he was at home with his wife.'

'Happy situation?'

'Hardly, with the other chap in between the sheets as well.'

'What happened on the night before he died?'

Matthews was lighting his pipe, packing the tobacco, fiddling with matches. He spoke out of the corner of his mouth.

'That *was* embarrassing. He went back to Cheltenham. We thought we'd pick him up again in the morning. Next thing we heard was that he'd done himself in outside the office.'

'You believe it was suicide?'

'Quite honestly, Frank,' Matthews took a long pull at his pipe, 'I don't care. I don't think it matters either way. He had plenty of reasons to commit suicide it seems; but on the other hand he was mixed up with the kind of people who would get rid of him if it suited them. They must have found out he was rumbled.'

'What do you think they wanted?'

'Don't kid yourself, Frank. Lister was one of the backroom systems boys. He had access to all the databases. Isn't it obvious?'

'I suppose it is.' Strange looked doubtful. 'Then why isn't Dangerfield reorganizing the Directorate now that I've gone?'

'You don't know that he isn't. Dangerfield's cunning.' Matthews put his mug down. 'I'm sorry, Frank. You were caught on the bridge when the ship went down. You have to take the rap. It's a hard old rule, but I hope you'll get over it and enjoy your extra retirement. They won't stop your pension. I'd give anything to be in your shoes.'

The silence of the great house crowded round them, affirming Matthews's commonsense formulae. The colonel scraped his hair back.

'I must go and look at Barbara. Help yourself to beer. At ten pence a pint it's not bad, is it, though I do say so?'

Strange stretched and refilled his tankard. Matthews had no difficulty making an identification between Lister's behaviour and his true loyalties. But it was only a prejudice.

There was no proof. Davenport, for instance, would disagree with Matthews, and Davenport had seen the facts. There was something about Matthews's glib answers that was annoying him. He'd forgotten how establishment some of these military men could be.

Matthews came back, smiling this time. 'Sound asleep,' he said. 'I hope she'll be better in the morning. She was very disappointed to miss you.'

Strange moved his mug on the table like a chess piece. 'One thing,' he said, 'you'll keep this conversation to yourself, won't you?'

'Why should anyone know?' asked Matthews.

'Because they might ask you.'

'Who might?'

'Hayter.'

'Why?' Matthews looked worried. 'He's not following you, is he?'

'You said it,' said Strange quietly.

'Good God, Frank. I had no idea. You must go, at once, if you don't mind. It could be very awkward.'

'Yes, couldn't it,' he said coldly, looking at Matthews with calculation. 'I'm sorry, Barnaby. I came to Aldershot because I thought there was still one man in the government service who could see his way past a lot of outmoded prejudice.'

'Thank you very much.'

'Instead, I find that you're obsessed like all the others with things that don't matter any more.'

'What the hell do you mean?' Matthews turned a surprisingly piercing eye on his guest.

'I mean that if you were the man I thought you were, you wouldn't give a damn who you talked to, if you thought it was the right thing to do. And by that I mean if it was in the defence of this country's real interests. After all that's what you're paid to do.'

'Are you suggesting that I'm incompetent?'

'That's not the word I'd have chosen. Out of touch might put it better.'

'How dare you!' Matthews, Strange thought, was conventional in his anger as in everything else.

'Before I go,' he continued, 'let me explain what exactly I mean by that. The fact is that you're so mesmerized by the apparent threat, the one you talk about in the mess every night of the week, that you can't see what's in front of your nose. And when someone like Lister comes along and points it out, you refuse to believe him. I'm partly accusing myself here. It was not until our conversation tonight that I began to see clearly the causes of Lister's failure.'

'What in God's name are you talking about?'

'I mean that there's no necessary reason why Cooper and Ellison and, as you insist, Lister should be controlled from beyond the Iron Curtain,' Strange continued steadily. 'The external threat that you and I and everyone else in Whitehall have been brought up to believe in at the peril of our administrative souls is far less real than the enemies we nurture here ourselves. If I may use the sort of historical metaphor that we used to enjoy together, you and I, and thousands like us, believe that Boney will get us, don't we? But Boney is always red, and always over there, even when he seems to be in our midst. We're a lot of natural chauvinists, you know, Barnaby.'

Matthews was slightly softened by the appeal to their friendship. 'I always thought you were a patriot, Strange.'

'I hope I am. But not when it comes to defending, as you do, men like Hayter who'll do anything to conceal what's really going on here. You're just the same, Barnaby. You'll try to save your reputation rather than face up to the situation as it really is. And you'll fight battles that are irrelevant just to prove that you can still fight them. That's partly why you tracked Lister – '

'I beg your pardon, Strange, I was ordered to do that.'

'Of course you were. Lister's blown the gaff and no one wants to know about it. Least of all you and Hayter. Lister's a threat to the bosses you serve and admire. His big mistake was to indicate that he suspected a "senior officer". The bosses can't be wrong. So Lister's hounded. That's not how I work, I'm afraid. That's why I'm here. I became a boss, but I wasn't born one. Not like you. I didn't marry one either.' Matthews's look of amazement had changed to fury, but Strange wasn't going to stop now. 'I went to a grammar school because I was bright enough. I worked my way up. I lived in rented accommodation. And for thirty years I went along with the class arrogance that will not trust ordinary people with the facts of government because they're considered too stupid.'

'If I may say so, Strange, you're the arrogant one.'

'No. I'm just angry. The arrogance I'm talking about has deeper social roots. And nowadays it's mixed up with class fear.'

'What the hell are you getting at, Strange?'

'It's like this. Hayter is just an old soldier, like yourself, who is beginning to resent the catastrophic loss of power we've suffered as a country lately. It takes a while for the facts of national decline to sink into the thicker military skulls,' he went on, noting with approval Matthews's startled expression, 'but when it happens they get very agitated. It's a sort of retrospective fear they get. Suddenly they find they'll contemplate any steps to preserve what's left, even though it's long since eroded. What I'm talking about, Barnaby, is a loss of ideals among the people who run this country. Hayter, and there are many like him in the department, no longer cares how he behaves in power, so long as he can prop up what's left of the society that gives him the most of what he calls freedom. He's as unscrupulous in the defence of these ruins as, in his opinion, are the people who threaten to take them over. And now all he cares about in practical terms is that his little empire – that's the Directorate – can play a star role in this last battle. That's why I was pushed out, because I threatened to mess up his crusade. Hayter knew very well that if I had an inkling of the truth of the Lister memorandum there'd be no end to the investigation till I found that "senior officer". Oddly it's not until I get inside this decaying pile here that I see the real reason for my disgrace. Yes, say it, I'm bitter. I want revenge.

I don't disguise that. But I think I'm entitled to it, because I know I'm going to be proved right in the end.'

'If you want my opinion,' said Matthews icily. 'I think you're drunk.'

Strange banged his tankard on the table. 'On this!'

Matthews jumped up then. 'Clear out! You're mad! You're sick! Get out!'

Strange was very dignified as he got to his feet. He had never felt more sober. He limped slowly down the corridor. Matthews followed in silence. Strange fumbled with the latch without help. It had been snowing and the sky was clear and crystal with wintry stars. Matthews slammed the door behind him. When the welcome light was switched off, Strange looked up into the deep blue emptiness and laughed aloud.

CHAPTER EIGHTEEN

Selzer was high. He waved Strange into the living-room of the spacious ground-floor flat with an incoherent gesture of welcome and then fell asleep on the floor without further comment. The place was like a hothouse and it was in chaos. Bottles and plates and mugs were spread across the carpet. Sour milk stood in warm cartons on the table in the bay window and there were the remains of a shrivelled pizza on top of the television. The only light in the gloomy winter's afternoon came from an electric fire, blazing on all bars in the fireplace.

Strange took the opportunity to explore the rest of the flat. There was a kitchen (more squalid if possible than the living-room) and a large bedroom with a tousled double bed. The garden beyond the high windows there had the anonymous look of shared territory. In summer it would be green and formless, with a few random flowers, a place for the occupants of the other flats to sunbathe and read the Sunday papers. In winter it was grey and ragged. A branch had fallen off the elm by the wall at the end, perhaps during the recent gale. Strange was distressed to see that no one had bothered to chop it loose and cut it into logs.

He went back into the main room, feeling like a burglar. Selzer was snoring now, sprawled in his jeans and his tracksuit top with his left arm resting on the white telephone. Strange hoped that it wouldn't ring. He could use Selzer's snooze to get up to date on his career.

The debris in the room concealed quite a bit of auto-biography. Stacks of paperbacks by prison governors, radical unionists, whistle-blowing civil servants, bisexual film stars and corrupt MPs spanned many of the subjects of his famous interviews. Some of the editions were carelessly signed in biro. A pile of framed photographs in the corner behind the television revealed celebrity galas, a meeting with the Queen, the opening of charity fêtes and several first nights.

He made himself some tea in the kitchen, found some Marvel and settled down on the sofa to leaf through a couple of cuttings albums from the bookcase. He had just reached the point in Selzer's career when the star was jetting to and fro across the Atlantic, conducting weekly interviews in London and New York, when Selzer stirred.

'Hi,' he said, not moving much.

Strange stood up incongruously. 'How do you do,' he said to the prostrate Selzer, 'My name is Frank Strange. I'm a friend of – '

'Hey,' Selzer cut in. There was still a professional edge to his voice, but in his appearance he was almost unrecognizable from the dashing whizz-kid of the press photos. The tight brown curls were wild and long and streaked with grey. Selzer was unshaven and his eyes seemed heavy with exhaustion. He propped himself up against the wall with a defeated lethargy. And when he spoke, the mouth that once had playfully hinted at irony and sarcasm and wit and disdain and irritation in as many successive moments was now lifeless and sullen. There was a sore at the corner of his upper lip –

'Hey – ' he repeated. 'Slow down. Aren't you the guy that came in?'

'Am I?' Strange joked, as much to himself.

'You didn't see a chick go out, did you? Blonde, hm?'

'No, I didn't. The flat is empty I believe.'

'She must have gone before.' He fumbled in the slit-pocket of his jump suit and took out some cigarette papers and a bag of tobacco. 'Smoke?'

'No thank you.'

'And don't drink either from the look of you.' Selzer focused unsteadily, rolling the tobacco in his fingers, 'You're not BBC are you? If you are you can clear out now. I've had enough of that shit house.' Selzer's voice had an intermittent mid-Atlantic drawl, as though he was conscious of a need to play a part but uncertain of his location.

'I had a friend called Richard Lister,' said Strange. 'I believe he visited you some months ago.'

Selzer was scattering marijuana into the tobacco. Eventually he broke his concentration and said, 'You believe right Mr –'

'Strange. Frank Strange.'

'That sounds kind of familiar.'

'Perhaps he talked about me. We were in the same –'

'Who did?'

'Richard Lister. The man who visited you. He was a friend.'

'No friend of mine.' Selzer licked the cigarette paper and rolled an unwieldy joint. 'Perhaps he did,' he added, picking up the echo of the conversation. The star took a suck and passed the joint automatically to Strange.

'No thank you,' said Strange, waving it away coldly.

'Yeah,' said Selzer, exhaling. 'Lister. He was a kind of scary guy.'

'Why was that?' Strange fell into his familiar mode of questioning.

'He knew so much. He had all this information.'

'About you?' Strange guessed.

'Yeah. It was kind of weird. Like reading your own obituary. He'd come out with comments like "And then you went to New York and interviewed X, Y and Z".' Selzer pronounced the last letter in the American manner, 'zee'.

'What did he want to know?'

'He said he was doing a piece on my career for some magazine –' He broke off. 'Hey! Come ro think of it he said there'd be a photographer round the week after. And I've never seen the piece. He was probably a nutcase. I've had plenty of those in my time.'

'What would you say if I told you he was involved in counter-subversion.'

Selzer jerked up sharply. 'Hey! You are trying to freak me out! Who are you anyway?'

174

'I told you. Frank Strange. The Government Service.'

'What's that mean for God's sake?' Selzer's voice was slightly slurred. Strange passed over his defunct pass.

Selzer looked at it curiously. Then he asked, 'Do you know a guy called Cornelius?'

'Mr Cornelius?'

'Hell, I don't know. He just called himself Cornelius.'

'What is he like?'

'A big blond guy with a lot of gold on his mouth. Dutch. D'you know him?'

'He must be in another section,' said Strange with caution.

Selzer seemed to be wandering. 'God knows why I'm talking to you,' he said, almost privately. Strange ignored this for the moment and pursued his first question. 'How many times did you talk to Lister?'

'More than once. Man, those sessions. He never stopped. I'd say twice – it seemed a lot more.'

'What happened?'

'He came round the first tome, like I said. He wanted to know all about me. He looked at all my cuttings and watched a few of the shows on the video. And asked questions. Always questions, questions, questions.'

'What sort of questions?'

'Shit. I don't know. The whole bit. Was I married? Who were my friends? What were my politics? Did I travel? Where to? Who with? He was cheeky too. He wanted to know what I earned. Whether I had any investments.' Selzer laughed. 'I told him to go see my accountant.' He paused. 'He'd got some odd shit about me too.'

'What?'

'For instance that I once planned to become an underwriter with Lloyds. We nearly had a row about that. He was a proper little Boswell.'

'Then he came a second time?'

'Yeah.'

'What did he want then?'

'He was more specific that time. He claimed he'd been

doing some research. He was very interested in the Fenton interview.'

'What was that?'

'Now you're getting like him.' Selzer pointed the joint at him accusingly, but relented. 'The Fenton interview was what caused yours truly to bomb out.'

'I'm sorry. I don't watch television.' Strange was determined to hear all the details.

'You're the lucky one. When I think how – ' He stopped and changed tack. 'Okay, so I used to do those interviews with famous people.' He waved his hand. 'Top people and rich people and beautiful people. I was famous for interviewing the famous. An odd sort of fame you may think, hm?' He became animated. 'Hey, d'you want to see my video of me quizzing the Archbishop? Gee, I forget what it was about now, the three in one I guess.' He laughed. 'That was a gas.'

'No thanks,' said Strange with distaste.

'Okay. But the reason I always got away with it was because I had my facts right. I was rude, I was brash, I was vulgar – but I was always right. My God, you should have seen the research that went into some of the shows.'

'Yes,' agreed Strange, 'It must have been remarkable.'

'Okay,' Selzer sounded almost defensive, 'so it was just showbiz, but I was born into showbiz, wasn't I, even if I did go to Oxford. I used to interview stars of stage and screen for a late-night current affairs programme on ITV. I was known in the trade as "Horlicks". Horlicks Selzer. But I got pissed off with that. They were all the same, the stars, ignorant as swans, vain, and idle often. All they wanted to do was gossip in make-up in front of the camera. I soon got tired of that even when I was showing them up for what they really were. So then they put me on to top people. Bishops, judges, MPs, civil servants, minor bosses, policemen, generals if we could get them. God knows they're vain and stupid too, a lot of them, but at least they had ideas, even if they'd been ripped off from the latest book the day before yesterday. And anyway in those days I played it straight and was good at my job and all that.' Selzer sucked on his joint and stared unblinking into the smoke. 'You want to know what happened then I suppose?' His voice dropped as he began to explain. 'You see all the time I was despising them all. Things were going from bad to worse. I mean the country was going down the drain. I don't need to tell you, Frank, that things are going to get a lot worse yet. I'm one of the lucky ones. I've hit the bottom before the crash. But it was getting bad even then. Politics getting vicious, money getting short, crime getting political, people getting scared. It was getting worse all the time. And what am I doing? I'm watching it happen. They're calling it *The Selzer Interview* now. Week by week I'm interviewing the people who run this bloody country but pretend it's all going to be all right. So gradually I can't stand this and I start telling them that it won't. Or I get them to admit there's a problem and show the viewers how scared they are. You see I wanted to be part of it all. I start making a reputation as an angry leftie. I'm good box. I've got people imitating the show on every station in the country, but I'm in telly too, so I've got to go one better or get out. So now I'm really hating British society, and the viewers are loving it and I'm making money out of it, lots of money, but I'm in telly and that's where we print the stuff. So in the end I'm interviewing the intellectuals and the politicians and the clever bankers, and they're queuing up for the privilege because they don't know any better, and because they want to sell their autobiographies most of them. And now I'm doing to them what I did to the starlets and the lion tamers at the beginning. I flatter and rubbish them. I rubbish them with facts. I'm invincible. I've become TV's first full colour anarchist. A fifty-thousand pound a year top-of-the-ratings crazy crowd-pulling Marxist grand inquisitor, would you believe it? And that's where the Fenton interview comes in.'

Selzer took a long drag on his stubby joint.

'What happened?'

'You know who Fenton is?'

'A Labour MP.'

'Labour? Trotskyite. He calls himself a Tribunite, but the

177

labels don't matter. He's the kind of MP who lives in an urban commune and drives a shit-powered motor-car, uses recycled paper for his letters and also works on the factory floor for the destruction of society as we know it. Okay?'

Strange nodded.

'So I invite him on the programme. He accepts. That's a hell of a coup. He.s never appeared on studio telly before. He reckons it's a cunning burgeois capitalist trick to seduce the masses from the path of revolution. He may be right, but anyway he says he'll come on the programme because I'm an *enragé* and not like the rest of them. And he'll do it so long as there's no audience. Okay?'

Strange said that he was following.

'But the real reason – the only reason – I want him on is because I'd been told – '

'Told? Who by?'

'It was a good source,' he replied non-commitally.

'Who was that?' Strange interrupted. Selzer looked worried.

'Look. I can't reveal it. Okay?' There was anxiety in his voice now. 'Let's leave it at that. I had this tip-off that Fenton has a bank account in Switzerland, laundered investments in the city, and God knows what else. There was also some suggestion he's mixed up in the East-West trade racket. I'm given documentary evidence to prove it. Or at any rate some of it.'

'Letters, bank statements and so on?'

'Yeah. You're sounding like Lister, Frank. Don't.' Selzer paused to stub his joint into the carpet. 'So I bring this out on the programme and we have the usual row. But unlike everyone else he walks out and sues me for slander and defamation and God knows what else. I was wrong for the first time in my life.'

'He won, didn't he?' Strange had a vague memory of the case.

'Why am I here?' Selzer gestured at the squalor. 'He won and the company refused to bail me out. I'd been caught out and they didn't want to know. I was past it anyway. I was no

178

longer news. I'd done it all, screwed everyone, finished. It was a good excuse to dump me.'

'And what happened to Fenton?'

'The case ruined him.'

'Why?'

'It came out in court that he was once involved with terrorists.'

'Fenton?'

'Exactly. The peaceful revolutionary and all that.'

'You must have had good lawyers.'

'Yeah. I could afford it in those days. They were well briefed. It wasn't as bad as it sounds. Fenton had been an ex-officio committee member. When he was involved it was just agitprop. You know, broadsheets in the market-place on a Saturday morning and the occasional demo. It only got violent later.'

'What happened?'

'A handful of extremists took over, inspired by Baader-Meinhof. There were pub bombings and a few shootings. After that revelation Fenton was in all kinds of trouble with his constituents. He's always followed the straight Marxist line that British society would collapse under the weight of its own inner contradictions. I didn't win the case, but he lost all credibility.'

'And that was what Lister was interested in?'

'Yeah. Every detail. To tell you the truth it was painful. It didn't happen very long ago. It was like going through it all over again.' Strange watched the ageing star subside after his narrative. Selzer was sweating and his hands were shaking. He had played back his past like a home movie, but now the lights were up and he was down at the bottom again, waiting for the crash to happen. Strange ran his mind round the story.

'When was the Fenton interview?' he asked.

Selzer gave the date. Nearly three years ago now.

'Was Lister interested in anything else when he discussed it with you on that second occasion?'

'No. He went for a walk to the pub.' Selzer's cool was

179

getting worn down by Strange's persistence. 'Check it with the landlord if you like. It's by the Tube. Then he disappeared.'

Strange leant forward urgently.

'Listen, Lister's dead. He was killed in October.' Selzer stared in horror. Now was the moment. 'Who gave you the information about Fenton?'

'I've told you –'

' – that you won't reveal sources. Not even if they killed Lister?'

'What are you saying, Frank? Are you crazy too?'

'I'm saying that the man who gave you the information about Fenton could have been a man called Cornelius –'

Selzer broke in, 'I didn't say that,' he was almost shouting.

'Well, who was it then? Hoskins?'

Selzer checked. He looked at Strange more calmly. 'Okay, go easy. I know Hoskins. He gave me a lot of stories. Yeah, I've worked with him; but he didn't supply stories. Yeah, I've worked with him, but he didn't supply that bad news. Brian was a good pal. He wouldn't have done that. Dog doesn't eat dog, not even when they live in Whitehall kennels.'

Strange recognized that his guess had come close to something. 'So it was Mayer,' he said conclusively.

Selzer did get angry then. He staggered unevenly to his feet. 'I don't know who you are, or what you want, or why you want it, but don't ask me any more questions, if you know what's good for you. I've been left alone since Fenton and I want to leave it that way.'

'Mayer threatened you, did he?'

'For Christ's sake get out of here. Leave me alone can't you. It's none of your bloody business you nosey sod . . .' Selzer was shaking, and his expression was distorted, with anger, it seemed. Strange stepped backwards and turned in his ungainly way. The grey January air was astonishingly cool after Selzer's flat. As he limped away Strange realized that Selzer wasn't angry but scared.

CHAPTER NINETEEN

Quitman knew that Strange's fears were justified when he heard about Neve's promotion. Turner and the thin man Reeve must have been briefed. He hadn't realized they were part of a subtle vetting process until it was too late. Perhaps that was what Neve had heard Dangerfield discussing at the club.

The sun, shining through the mist on the Thames, promised a day of wintry brilliance. He stood at his solitary window in the Directorate and watched the traffic racing down the Embankment. There was terror in the streets but people were not cowed. When you know you're trapped, he thought, you distance yourself and become fatalistic. He had not even bothered to falsify the surveillance report of Strange's visit to Aldershot. And yet . . . Perhaps Hayter and Preece hadn't made the connection. If they knew his secret why did he still have privileged acess to the case?

He was very busy now, always in the office by eight-thirty. After exchanging the Sibelius tape in Holborn, Strange's latest investigations were dragging the Lister case into the busy interconnections of politics and the beleaguered media. The research work involved in tracking the ramifications for Preece was expanding daily. That, he discovered was the explanation being given for Neve's promotion, for he found with a shock that Neve was on the Strange case as well. Typically, none of this was announed in the Directorate, nor had he been told about it by Hayter. In fact it was his secretary who heard of Neve's success, via Rosie Walford.

Quitman was ashamed to have to grub for information from the typist but he was acutely apprehensive. 'How long has this appointment been effective?' he wanted to know.

'Since the beginning of the week they say,' the girl replied. It was Wednesday. Neve had been working on unspecified

181

aspects of the Strange case for two days and no one had told him, worse, he had not even been aware of it. As usual everything was on a 'need to know' basis. That was how the Directorate liked to work. Quitman decided he would have to be careful not to lose his temper with Preece when he saw him. That would only increase suspicion. Suspicion – it could not be stronger than that. After all, Matthews and Strange were old friends.

He dithered all morning, fiddling with bits of paperwork in distraction, waiting to hear from Preece or even Neve. Surely something would be said. At about eleven-thirty he went down to the coffee machine, slowly, chatting to anyone he met to reassure himself that he was still trusted. Of course it was a delusion. If Hayter did know it would be a guarded secret. He would be transferred and then dismissed hugger-mugger. His colleagues and subordinates would never know of the betrayal. The anger and recrimination would stay behind closed doors. As he dawdled he hoped he might run into Neve and provoke a reference to the new situation, even though, since Liz's party, Neve wasn't talking to him much. The fact that Neve had three years' seniority, and was involved in the same work, effectively meant that Quitman had been demoted. He was surprised how angry this made him. But Neve was nowhere, and in due course he set off upstairs again with a plastic cup of tepid coffee mixture. One or two people were baffled by his behaviour. 'What's he want to drink that stuff for,' said his sallow typist to her friend on the switchboard, 'when he gets it brought fresh to him on a tray with biscuits? The people here, they do make you wonder sometimes, don't they?'

By lunchtime the suspense was too much and he dialled Preece on the internal phone. He had hesitated over this move for nearly an hour, toying with a number of spontaneous openings. In the event his strained gambit was not necessary. An assistant answered the phone. 'I'm sorry, sir. Mr Preece is out to lunch at his club with Charles Neve.'

'Oh. Thank you.'

182

He replaced the phone with a rising sense of panic. So they did know. There was no other way of looking at it. He seized the latest sheaf of surveillance reports, rifling through the typescript yet again to see if he had missed any other clues to his downfall. Quitman's mind ran on in jerks, trying all the alternatives, trying to spot the possible connections. Neve was hostile, but as yet knew little. He'd given nothing away to Rosie Walford. He could trust Liz.

He came back from his lunch hour in such a state of pre-occupation that, swinging through the doors of the Old War Office, he didn't notice Preece and Neve deep in conversation in front of him. When Preece, who had enjoyed his lunch, hailed him genially as he passed, he turned, stared wildly, and nearly bolted. But he managed to recover his nerve.

'Ah, James,' said Preece, waving the stub of his excellent cigar in his fingers, 'how are you? As a matter of fact I wanted to have a word with you if you could spare a moment – '

Even Neve, whose pasty features were for once coloured with a slight flush, gave him a civil nod. The lift had broken down and they all walked up together, deploring the recent bombings.

In his office, Preece's bonhomie was not curtailed. 'Well now, isn't that encouraging?' he began, waving the recent surveillance reports at Quitman, who experienced an almost physical disarming of his fears. 'Strange must be getting desperate if he has to go muck-raking among television journalists. I have no idea what he hopes to gain by that, and though of course the case is not closed yet, I think we have it under control. I congratulate you, James, for your calm performance. Well done.' He crisply shuffled the pages and snapped them together with a bulldog clip.

Quitman managed to say thank you. He wondered privately whether Strange wasn't deluding himself after all.

Preece moved smoothly to his real message. 'I'm particularly grateful to you for this because I'm taking personal control of the information processing part of the department's anti-terrorist operations. I am going to be hard pressed for a week or two. This for your private ear, James.'

'Of course.'

'Thanks to the work of Dr Mayer, the Directorate now has the information resources to play a really strategic role in this field. I am anxious that we should make a decisive contribution to the operation.' A harsh expression came into his face. 'It is time we proved once and for all that the work of the Directorate is too important, too refined, too subtle,' he was becoming unusually animated, 'and too pervasive to be subordinated to the old-fashioned methods of our illustrious controller.' As he spelt out the title there was no disguising his hostility to Dangerfield, and for the first time in his observation of this long-running dispute, Quitman realized what a dogged ally Hayter had in this war with the controller.

Preece was conscious perhaps of the unusual force of his expression because he steered the conversation back to the point he had in mind. 'So,' he continued without pausing, 'I have asked Charles Neve to take over from me as your immediate superior. You can wind up the operation together I hope.' He smiled encouragement. 'Charles will also concentrate on what I should like to call the larger implications of the last few months. That means he will be looking for any sensitive loose ends in the case. Probing for weaknesses.' Quitman was startled by this development and for a moment his own fears surfaced in his thoughts. He half heard Preece working hard to justify Neve's promotion but had already decided that it wasn't in his interests to complain.

'. . . Neve is the obvious choice for this work. As director I cannot overlook the fact that he has been long due for promotion. Besides, seeing the whole picture for the first time, he'll have the fresh perspective of the outsider.'

Quitman had the impression that Preece could go on talking in this vein for several minutes and cut in: 'Have you given Neve a full briefing?' It was a stupid question, he realized, as soon as he'd spoken, a remark that reflected all his private fears. It was none of his business and he made to move with embarrassment.

'Yes, I have.' Preece replied in a tone that did suggest resentment at this interference. He picked up his external phone, a sign that the interview was over, and asked for Hayter's number.

'Thank you,' said Quitman, now at the door.

'Oh,' Preece looked up, as if surprised at his going. 'Thank you, James.'

Quitman walked down the corridor fully absorbed. 'Probing for weaknesses?' Was this the oblique way of saying that they knew what he was up to? But if Strange was right and Lister had found something, then he was justified in helping Strange after all, in the national interest. He could always make that appeal to the higher claim. He returned to his office confused and uncertain. He passed Rosie Walford, in deep preoccupation, and forgot to make the attempt at a greeting with which he had tried to keep up diplomatic relations. When he realized (catching the wake of her perfume) whom it was he'd ignored, he stopped and turned in the corridor, and would have called out. But Rosie was striding confidently away. Quitman's shifty behaviour confirmed all that Neve had told her, in dribs and drabs, over the weeks since the party.

Neve was convinced, he told Rosie, that, given the national importance of his work, Quitman was in touch with some very dangerous people. He explained how he was at a Christmas party at Quitman's flat where there was a most disagreeable investigative journalist called Goldman. The sort of man he couldn't believe hadn't already wormed quite a few secrets out of Quitman. Of course, he said, it was good of James to invite him at all, but really for his own good he ought to be more careful.

Rosie was upset at the thought of missing a party, even if it was given by Quitman's woman. And the bastard said she'd left him for good.

A day or two after these revelations, Neve invited Rosie to lunch. Of course she was only a secretary, he told himself,

185

but the fact was he had few friends and was unable to ignore the flattery of her attention. He took her to a smart French restaurant in Covent Garden where they became quite tipsy over a couple of bottles of Beaujolais. There was white tape across all the windows, but Rosie kept her apprehensions to herself and drank up instead.

'I felt I had to tell Preece,' Neve confirmed as the coffee arrived.

'Tell Preece what, Charlie?' She was finding him pompous as usual.

Neve tried not to feel distressed at her vulgarity. His devious mind preferred to be interpreted not interrogated. 'About Quitman and his friends. They could be a terrible security risk. You never can tell with the press – '

'The press?' Rosie was getting confused.

'People like this man Goldman. He could put lives in jeopardy.' Rosie was not much interested in lives. She said: 'What's she like?'

'Who?'

'James's girl-friend. Liz whatshername.'

Neve was not much interested in Liz. 'I don't really know,' he admitted. Did Rosie find him boring? He signalled for brandy. 'She's rather dressy and sophisticated, not my taste at all,' he said to reassure her, and then realized that he had probably expressed Rosie's aspirations in a nutshell. 'She works for a literary agent or something I think,' he went on hastily. 'The party was full of the sort of flashy people I most dislike from advertising and the media.'

'Was it?' said Rosie with a touch of sadness.

'A most untrustworthy crowd,' he replied, getting back to his theme. 'And this fellow Goldman was the king of the shits. Tricked me completely. I felt I really had to tell Preece about that too. It is all rather delicate. One doesn't like to do the dirty on a colleague. Besides, it could reflect badly on Hayter's appointments – '

'You mean James?'

'Well, yes. But when so much is at stake. I felt I had to do my duty at whatever the cost to me personally.' He shrugged to give force to the sentiment. When the waiter had helped them on with their coats, Neve was holding Rosie by the arm.

A few days later Neve rang Rosie at midday in a state of great excitement. 'You'll never guess,' he said.

'What? I've no idea.' It would have been nice to seem more knowledgeable, but she was flattered at his call.

'Promotion!' Neve crowed. 'Preece has asked me to take over from him as Quitman's superior officer. He says he's very grateful to me for the way in which I have put the Directorate's interests so firmly before my own. You are on your own, aren't you?' Neve sounded nervous.

'Oh yes.'

'So the gamble paid off,' he added.

'What about James?'

'Oh, I expect Quitman will be kept at the same desk. But I'm in charge. Keeping an eye out.'

'Is Mr Preece worried about James?' It was important to know if James was really out of favour.

'Not about Quitman as such. But he is concerned about his friends. I mean, who wouldn't be. I believe he's told Hayter his woman should be positively vetted.'

'Oh! Really!' Rosie couldn't hide her surprise. Lucky for her she wasn't still going out with Quitman.

'Look, Rosie, in a case of this kind it could be vital. That's in confidence of course.'

'Oh yes. Of course.'

'Well, it's certainly a relief to be back on the promotion ladder again,' Neve confided. 'And now I'm in a position to do something about your prospects here.'

'Well, it's not –'

'You're wasted where you are. Everyone thinks that. And I'm going to make sure Preece realizes it. Oh – I am looking forward to seeing how Quitman takes the news.'

Now, as Rosie strode away down the third floor corridor, she could see that Quitman had taken it very badly. He seemed quite broken. Did not even try to say hello. She felt mildly exultant, especially at the thought of promotion.

CHAPTER TWENTY

David Fenton was a hard man to find. Strange visited the address given in *Who's Who,* a terraced house in Battersea. There were railings, a basement yard and a flight of steps leading up to a flaking portico. The front room was deserted. He pressed the bell without optimism. After a minute or two he banged vigorously on the front door. At least that restored the circulation to his hands. A car swished past through the slush in the street behind. He banged again. Then from the basement below there was the sound of a door being scraped back over stone and a woman's voice said 'Who is it?' her question abbreviated by the sound of a baby crying.

Strange limped down the steps and bent over the railing. The woman was in her late thirties probably – Strange was not good at judging ages, especially when it came to women – a large blonde earth mother in a shapeless ankle length Indian dress. She seemed oblivious to the cold, perhaps because she held a small child in her arms.

'I'm looking for David Fenton,' said Strange. 'The MP,' he added.

'Oh – ' the woman put her head inside the door and called out, 'Jan. There's a bloke here wants Dave. Where is he, d'you know?'

The reply was indistinguishable and foreign-sounding, Strange thought. Really somebody ought to clean that child's face.

'He's probably at the club, that's the Ascension Family and Social Club, off Lavender Hill,' said the earth mother.

Strange thanked her and walked on down the street, pulling out his A-Z from his overcoat pocket. Lavender Hill was over half a mile away. He decided to walk.

He passed the Latchmere Baths and the sign to the

mortuary and the coroner's court. The atmosphere, he decided, was late Empire, gone to seed. In the oily gloom under the railway bridge there was a drunk vomiting into a blocked drain. The air smelt of urine and the man was crying. There were tears on his cheeks. Strange climbed the road to Lavender Hill.

The Ascension Family and Social Club was a gaunt Victorian assembly hall abandoned on the edge of a bleak housing estate. As he pushed open the door he could hear piano music and the noise of amateur singing. An elderly man in a toupée and a pair of red corduroy slippers was playing 'Elijah' at the upright. To one side, facing him, stood five elderly ladies with scores, nodding rhythmically and singing. There was another woman through an open hatchway making tea on a gas stove. The door swung back with a loud thump, but the choir hardly faltered and carried on to the last bar which they reached more or less in one voice. Strange wondered whether he should applaud.

The man at the piano put his hands into the pockets of his woolly jumper and stared with silent curiosity at Strange's advancing figure. 'Can I help you?' asked the leader of the choir.

'Yes. I'm looking for David Fenton, the MP. I was told he might be here.' The singers now looked at him with more interest.

'Has anyone seen Mr Fenton?' asked one lady in tones of some disapproval. 'This gentleman wants to speak with him.' The other ladies looked doubtful.

'Is it about tax?' asked one of the contraltos.

'Should it be?' countered Strange with a smile. The choir fluttered together.

'No,' said the first, after a moment's consultation. 'I don't think we can help you. If he comes, can we say who called?'

'Not to worry. I'll find him,' said Strange. 'Any idea where he might be? I've tried his hime.'

'Oh,' said the lady who'd asked about tax. 'It's no good trying his home.'

The pianist now joined the debate in the manner of one who always knew he had the right answer. 'Well, there's always the Bear – that's the pub, you know – on the corner by the sweetie shop – I mean he's always there at dinner time.'

And he was. Strange found him in the Public Bar sitting alone with a pint of Guinness.

'David Fenton?'

He looked up. The discoloured, harassed features of the man spoke of poverty, the heavy muddy boots of canvassing and hard work. His yellow hair was roughly plastered over his balding patch. Strange noticed that his fingernails, pressed against the glass as he hunched forwards over his stout, were bitten to the quick. Fenton was nervous, and his eyes, staring out of the drawn face, were tired and uneasy. When he answered, he spoke harshly, and with an unremitting accent that Strange could not place. He shifted on the elbows of his donkey jacket as Strange pulled up a stool.

'Can I join you?'

'I'm not stopping you, am I?' His uncertain smile showed that this was supposed to be a joke.

'My name is Strange. Frank Strange.'

The eyes betrayed no recognition. 'What do you want?'

'I want to speak to you,' he began, 'about a man called Dick Lister. At least that's his real name, but he may have used another – shabby, worried-looking government scientist with bad breath and an addiction to No. 6.' The description was hardly necessary. Fenton was already disturbed. He looked over his shoulder anxiously. But the bar was deserted, and the transvestite barman by the Appeal for the Blind was busy taking down the Christmas tinsel. 'Who are you?' he asked urgently. 'What do you want?'

'I'm a friend of Dick's. I want to know when you saw him last.'

'Look here, Mr Strange, don't come here putting words into my mouth.' Fenton's lip quivered with anger. 'I never said – '

'But you did, didn't you?' Strange butted in harshly. There wasn't time now to waste on the niceties. 'You did see him.'

Fenton tried to sound off-hand. 'It was months ago now.'

'When?'

'Oh, October sometime.'

'Can you remember the date?'

'I think it was just before the party conference. What does it matter for Christ's sake?'

Strange was unperturbed. 'It matters because Lister was murdered shortly afterwards.'

Fenton looked shocked. 'Who by?'

'That's what I want to know.'

The conversation lapsed. Strange felt that the silence was almost a mute requiem for the dead man. When three youths came into the bar, laughing and swearing, Fenton leaned forward and said: 'Are you a detective?'

'No. But I've got Dick's interests at heart. Why?'

'Well, the newspapers said it was suicide.'

'The papers say what they're told.' He looked sharply at Fenton. 'So you didn't believe them?'

Fenton reacted at once. 'What are you suggesting? How do you know all this?'

'I used to work with Lister. I'm retired now. But I know how the department handles the press.' Strange took a draught of his beer. 'Don't worry Mr Fenton, I've not come here to frighten you. I need your help. It turns out that Lister had found something going on in the department that someone didn't want him to know about. He was killed for what he knew. I want to know who did it and why. As I said at the beginning, I'm a friend.' Strange's voice had hushed as he spoke, he was speaking low as he concluded, 'What he did before he died matters. And you were almost the last to see him.'

There was a seriousness about this statement that made Fenton pause. He drained his glass and called to the barman for another one. He seemed to be sizing Strange up.

'One thing,' added Strange, 'I don't believe in any hammer and sickle nonsense here.'

'Well, thank God for that,' said Fenton, raising his glass to drink, 'Half the country thinks I'm paid by the Kremlin!' he laughed bitterly.

'I'm convinced that this is an internal problem. They're the hardest to recognize of course, and it took me a while to realize –'

'A while.' Fenton glanced at him curiously. 'How long have you been investigating this?'

'Since the day Lister died. I was on the wrong track to start with, you see,' Strange apologized.

'You're right now,' Fenton joined in. He sighed and ran his hand over his head and looked at his watch. 'Lister gave me quite a story – or the beginnings of one – and I did nothing about it. I blame myself, but his death scared me. I'm glad you've come.' He shook his head slowly. 'You've got to understand that my political career has been so totally screwed-up by the Selzer business that nothing seems to have any point any more.' Fenton patterned the table invisibly with his finger. 'When I got elected, of course, I didn't imagine a revolution overnight, but I didn't imagine I'd end up as a Punch-and-Judy figure. They kill be caricature, Mr Strange. It's the most humiliating death. You stop being a real person with ideas, beliefs, integrity even. I'm just Red Fenton, now, the crazy Marxist MP. I'm good for a saying of the week, but no one takes me seriously.'

Strange listened in sadness. He recognized from his own experience the bitterness that a man feels when all that he believes in most deeply is betrayed.

'Didn't you trust Lister?' he asked.

'I don't know. I didn't care then. If the guy was trying to take me for a ride I reckoned I'd been taken so far already by the Selzer business that a bit more wouldn't matter. The only way I'm going to save my seat is if I can come up with something really big that people can't make jokes about. This guy Lister seemed crazy enough and serious enough to do it. It was a gamble. What I'm going to tell you now is a gamble. When I tell you what Lister was on to I'm telling you because, although I don't trust you – no, don't take it personally, I don't trust anyone now – I don't care what you do. Maybe you'll be the billion to one oddity, the man who means what he says.'

Strange recognized of course that Fenton cared very much what happened and tried to moderate his cynical pose. 'I ask you to believe me I will prove that it is so,' he said.

'Shit! Shit! Shit!' Fenton crashed the table three times with his fist. The beer danced. 'You're all the same, you bureaucrats, "I do hope most sincerely that we can achieve our joint endeavours",' he mimicked. '"I want you to believe me that we are right behind you in all your efforts," "you can count on me", "I'm your man", "we must work together". All shit!' he repeated. 'Total shit! Don't give me any more of it.' He glared at Strange, who said, 'I beg your pardon.' Perhaps he was angry, he thought, to feel his defences penetrated.

'Right,' Fenton went on after a few moments as though his outburst had never occurred. 'Getting back to Lister.' So he does care, Strange thought. 'He made an appointment to see me at the House, I remember. I expect you know my views on Defence.' Strange indicated that he did. 'So of course I was interested. He said he worked in a secret section which very few people know about, I forget its title – '

'C Directorate,' Strange supplied.

'That's right. A massive computer section, apparently, a centralized database, linking separate systems, that allows government officials to make a highly advanced correlation of factual data so as to build a complete profile of all the people listed. I'm not just talking about simple census facts, age, sex and so on, but also political behaviour, personal spending patterns, travel, in fact almost a day-by-day, characteristic-by-characteristic record of movements, affiliations and behaviour of all listed individuals. It's what I've suspected for years, but been unable to prove.'

'What's wrong with an efficient filing system?' challenged Strange. 'That's all it is,' he added doubtfully.

'But it's not! Fenton reacted fiercely. 'Information is power they say. The fact is that in your Ministry such information also fuels fear. And fear is at the root of the secret state that lies within the state.'

'What do you mean?'

'You know very well what I mean, but like everyone else you don't care to think about it. I mean the way they manage the news, and blackmail politicians, I'm talking about the way that every time we have one of these "emergencies" more and more civil liberties get curtailed without a single protest, freedoms that were won by generations of agitation. I mean the enlargement of police powers, and the way they spread lies against left-wingers like myself. I'm telling you what you know about, the corruption of the jury system in state trials and the illicit surveillance of so-called subversives. That's what happens in the secret state.'

Strange was silent then. He was for the first time compelled to admit to himself that on his own experience he couldn't deny this.

'We are happy to pretend it isn't going on. We like to believe that our so-called democracy will last forever. Of course it won't. Not of its own accord. We're led of course. It only takes a few tame editors, a handful of TV journalists with political ambitions, some compliant judge, and the usual Tory MPs braying about subversion and everyone accepts an extraordinary paradox.'

'What's that?'

'We're encouraged to believe that it can't happen here, as I've said, but if there's some evidence that it could, then any measures are justified, even those that put the democracy itself in peril.'

'When I was in the department,' commented Strange, almost to himself, 'I was trained to accept a conspiracy theory about the subversive forces in this country. As soon as I get outside I find that the left has its own conspiracy theory about the state. Which is right?'

'Neither of course,' Fenton said dismissively, 'but you can't deny, can you, that Lister's Directorate, C Directorate, now lies at the heart of the system I've described? And it's accumulating and correlating, supplying the security services with more and more comprehensive data about more and more people. It's terrifying, Mr Strange. There's nothing wrong with information, but when you don't know how it's being used, or against whom, or for what reason, the ordinary citizen is not only blind in his own country, it's as though he's lost in a thick fog as well, because he can't rely on anyone else to help him either.'

Strange fell silent, feeling the force of the metaphor. He felt chilled by Fenton's vision, but could not refute it. At length, to get back to details, he asked, 'What else did Lister want to know?'

'He wanted to know all about my assets. He wanted to know what committees I was on, what jobs I'd been offered. He wanted to know everything about me. He was bloody persistent.'

Strange nodded. 'And then?'

'He promised he would do some correlations, that was his word. He was sometimes hard to understand. He spoke his own language.'

'Computer jargon.' Strange looked quizzical. 'Is that all?'

'What d'you mean?' Fenton sounded defensive.

'Didn't he want to know about the terrorist connection?' Strange expected anger at his bluntness, but Fenton looked at him without hostility. 'What do you know about that?' he asked candidly.

Strange smiled. 'I'm not blaming you. It's the sort of risk MPs take all the time. A free society needs parliamentary support for all kinds of pressure groups. I understand that in this case you were on the committee, *ex-officio,* and before you realized it a harmless radical caucus had turned itself into a violent revolutionary cell. Is that right?'

Fenton nodded. 'More or less. It was my mistake, but almost unavoidable it happened so quickly. I resigned at once of course, but by then it was too late. The bombing had started. Selzer could use that against me – and with my record he did.'

'Do you know the source of the information against you?'

'I've already told you that I believe the state spreads

scandal about people, whom it likes to call subversives, it fears.' Fenton was generalizing out of reticence.

'Did you know that you're on file in C Directorate?'

'Lister told me, yes.'

'Did he know about Mayer as well?'

'Mayer?' Fenton looked puzzled. 'Who's that?'

'One of the people we – they employ to collect and process data. It was Mayer who passed the information to Selzer.' Strange was anxious to corroborate his discovery. 'Lister didn't mention a Dutchman?'

'No. But –' Fenton stopped and put his glass down slowly. 'What was he like? Tall? Blond? With a beard? And a lot of gold teeth?'

'So you do know him.'

But Fenton made no reply. He was staring hard at the table.

'Were you followed here?' he asked.

'No,' Strange lied. He'd found people didn't like the idea of surveillance. 'I don't think so,' he added. Fenton was no fool. The MP was suddenly very quiet, very inward. 'By God,' he said at length, 'Lister really did have a story then. He really did.' He seemed stunned. 'No wonder –'

'No wonder what?'

' – that he was murdered.'

Strange was excited. 'Are you saying that someone in the Directorate got rid of him? Mayer perhaps?'

Fenton seemed doubtful. 'No. Not exactly. It's not that crude.'

'But you don't think it was suicide. You knew he was murdered?'

'He was heading for trouble all right. After he saw me, he said he was going to try and investigate the rest of that committee.'

'To see why they turned violent?'

'Oh, he knew all about that. They got taken over by new arrivals fleeing from the continent. The Germans, Dutch and French radicals who know what subversion is really about.'

196

'And then he was dead. Are you suggesting there's a connection?'

Fenton looked at him curiously. He stood up.'Maybe.' He seemed shaken by something he didn't want to talk about. 'Goodbye, Mr Strange.' He put out his hand. Strange took it. Then Fenton said, coming so close Strange could feel his breath on his face. 'There's more than one connection, you know. If I tell you, I don't ever want to see you again.'

'Why?'

'Because I don't want to end up like Lister, thank you.'

Strange looked grave. 'Am I that dangerous?'

Fenton stared deep into his eyes, and for a moment his tiredness was dispelled. He seemed moved. 'You're a very brave man,' he said, 'though you probably don't know it.'

Strange shrugged, disclaimed heroism with a smile. He felt exhilarated by his own sudden fear. 'Well, what is it?' he said.

'Don't you think it's odd,' Fenton said softly, 'that none of the security agencies, armed with all that information you've got, haven't managed to control the bombers?' Fenton pushed out into the cold street, but Strange did not move.

CHAPTER TWENTY-ONE

There was a police guard out at the offices of the *Southern Evening News,* but Strange knew that Brian Hoskins was not the sort of editor to be cowed by the threat of violence. The burly newspaperman seemed pleased to see him and waved him to an empty chair. 'How's the cover-up going, old boy?' he asked with a chuckle.

Strange was startled. However could Hoskins know about that? He decided to play it stuffy.

'I don't know what you mean,' he said.

Hoskins roared with laughter. 'I shouldn't think you do,' he bellowed, banging the table with pleasure. 'That was a good one you pulled – when was it? October? Coming in here, hot from Whitehall I thought, face as long as a barn door, "we are concerned to establish that the case blah-blah-blah". If Preece hadn't rung, I don't suppose I'd ever have realized that you were doing free-lance work, as it were.'

Strange stayed calm. 'Preece rang you, did he?'

'The very next day. He was on the line for twenty minutes I should think. Did I realize that Mr Strange had retired? Was I aware that his behaviour was in breach of the Official Secrets Act? He threw the book at me as a matter of fact.'

'I'm not surprised,' said Strange coolly.

Hoskins's jovial greeting was subsiding. He was now seated behind his desk, leaning forward, peering at Strange across a pile of newspapers, his reading glasses pushed back on his forehead. 'What's going on?'

'I'll come to that in a minute.' At least he could give Hoskins something to chew on. 'But you'll believe me when I say I was followed here. The green van parked just down the street conceals two men from the department whose only job is to watch where I go and who I visit.'

Hoskins was impressed. 'Surveillance,' he murmured.

Strange nodded. 'That's why I need to know first what Preece said to you on the telephone.' Strange reckoned he'd work round to Selzer in due course.

'Oh yes, Preece.' Hoskins cast his mind back to the conversation. 'The usual reasonable stuff of course. "My masters will be very concerned . . . My masters would like to know the nature of the conversation . . ."' He mimicked Preece's smooth delivery.

'Did you tell him?'

'Good God no. You can trust me to protect my sources. Dear old Mr P. referred to "the more formal measures" that "his masters" would have to take if I didn't oblige, but the fact is that he can't do anything unless I print.'

'Did he warn you about talking to me again?'

'He tried. That was bad psychology. He can't stop me of course, and it only whetted my appetite. In fact I thought of sending a chap after you for the story but decided to wait and see. Well, thank God you've called, though I can't say I hadn't been expecting another little chat.' He looked at Strange significantly.

'Good,' said Strange with satisfaction. It was nice to make a visit where one was welcome.

'Now then, Frank, you tell me what you're chasing this story for.'

By way of answer Strange took out his pencil and pulled a scrap of paper off the desk. He spelt out a message and passed it over to Hoskins who stared in amazement and then wrote a quick reply.

Strange opened the door and the clatter of the newsroom invaded the comparative peace of Hoskins's office. But the noise in the composing room was deafening. He and Hoskins stood by the presses and shouted at each other while the headlines NEW BOMB EXPLOSION: MANY DEAD came whizzzing past on the rollers.

'Murdered?' was Hoskins's first word. 'I can't believe it. Why?'

Strange explained about his investigation into the enquiry.

199

'So he was right after all. You'd never have known. I'm delighted. What is the Directorate doing to make amends?'

'Nothing.'

'I see. *Raison d'état* and all that.'

'Perhaps.' Strange paused. 'Did you know that Lister carried on his investigations when he came to London?'

'He wasn't cowed by the enquiry?'

'Apparently not. But he never mentioned his work to you?'

'I told you before. We lost touch. He thought I'd let him down. He had no reason to see me.'

'No reason. Except –'

'Except what?'

' – he did visit Roland Selzer on a couple of occasions.' Strange saw at once that he had done it. Hoskins would talk now.

Hoskins nodded slowly. 'I haven't seen Roland for ages.' He was absorbing all the new information while he spoke. 'How is he?' Hoskins was beginning to see what Strange was up to.

'Down and out,' Strange shouted.

'Fenton finished him. Someone fed him a phoney story.'

'You know that?'

'For sure. Roland told me himself.'

'And you believe him?'

'He's a pal. Besides Hayter tried to get me to play that game too.'

'What game?'

'He tried to get me to plant a false story about the chairman of the National Executive Committee.'

'Did you do much of that sort of thing?' Strange was no longer surprised by these revelations.

'Not as much as they wanted.'

Hoskins bent to his ear to shout. 'It's a fairly obvious idea. Take the Fenton case, for instance. You know how famous he was for his anti-Defence line. The best way to silence him is to get him to tangle with Selzer and ruin him with facts. How do you do that? Give the hottest head in the media a false scandal with a grain of truth. And that's what happened. In that case it was two birds with one stone. I can't prove it, but I assure you it came from the Directorate.'

'Dirty tricks.'

Hoskins nodded.

'When was that case?'

'Just after the Lister business. I was so mad at Hayter for doing that to Selzer that I tried to print the enquiry story. I was looking for a fight. I miscalculated. I didn't realize they could get rid of me so easily.'

'Why didn't you fight back?'

'I got scared, Frank. You know what they're like. We're standing here now because you're scared. I was scared because I saw what they'd done to Selzer. For God's sake! This noise is killing me.'

They walked through the print room. Hoskins stopped to chat to the compositors, praising a lay-out and joking about one or two of the personal ads. They stood watching the proof-readers crouching over their galleys like tailors on a bench. Hoskins, his voice hushed and serious for the first time in Strange's acquaintance, talked on.

'I say I wanted a fight with Hayter. That makes it sound like a mad dog reaction to the row about my job. It was much deeper than that. You need to know about it. I admit I was hired to be, among other things, a one-man propaganda machine for the department. Of course it was my job to defend its interests, but because I have a lot of friends in Fleet Street they wanted me to plant some dud stories there as well. That was Hayter's line. It was the second part of the argument that was indefensible. So we had a clash of politics, of philosophy if you like. Hayter thought, still thinks probably, that all men of goodwill should work together to combat the threat to the state, whenever and wherever that may come.' Hoskins paused in thought, 'How much did you know about his plans for the Directorate?'

'Not as much as I liked to imagine,' Strange admitted.

'I can tell you he had some elaborate plans for what he calls civil defence.'

Strange nodded in recognition. 'Hayter's always been deeply conservative. It's easy to become pessimistic about the future when you have all the intelligence about our enemies at your fingertips. The picture looks a lot blacker from the inside looking out.'

'There's no doubt that he has real fears for the security of the state. When he tried to get me to ruin the chairman of the NEC, he referred to him as a traitor. When I said don't be daft, he said look at what he wants to do to the army. He said the country couldn't afford to have men like that in positions of influence. Hayter really believes he's holding the line against the collapse of British society.'

'Would he betray his country rather than see it sink into bankrupt mediocrity?'

Hoskins looked very surprised. 'Hayter working as an agent? That's a pretty amazing scenario. Is there anything in his behaviour to suggest it?'

'You don't think his belief in saving the country from itself could be totalitarian?'

Hoskins stared at the thundering presses and the print workers hurrying to and fro with ink and type. Strange reflected that the heart of an independent newspaper was a good place to have this kind of discussion. At length Hoskins asked, 'Tell me something, Frank? Where do you get your agents and traitors from?'

'You understand that the Directorate is very embarrassed by Lister,' said Strange. 'Hayter and Preece are trying to pretend he never existed. I mean, why else are they watching me every minute of the day?' Hoskins nodded. 'The question is, Why?'

'Quite.'

'I used to think that Hayter had realized that the Directorate had been penetrated from the outside but didn't dare risk a scandal on account of Dangerfield.'

'I don't follow you.'

'Dangerfield's been looking for an excuse to take over the Directorate for years. Frankly, that was why he put me in there. But Hayter outmanoeuvred him.' Strange resumed the thread of his argument. 'Next I thought that perhaps Hayter himself had been planted. Like you, I can't believe that. It's such an obvious interpretation, it's almost a cliché. Now I'm exploring the idea that the reason for the cover-up lies with some of the Directorate's most secret policies. Policies so secret that not even I knew about them, though I'm ashamed to admit it. The point about the Directorate's powers is that they are largely unaccountable. Everyone accepts that it moves in its own mysterious ways. That's its policy. Not many people ask impertinent questions. Hayter knows that.'

Hoskins looked intrigued. He shook his head sadly. 'Hayter isn't like that. Listen: when I asked to take an active part in the downfall of a public figure I disputed my role with Hayter. I know politics is getting vicious but we aren't at war. I can't accept that sort of behaviour is necessary. Hayter can, though. I had a very interesting session with him. He reckons that peace is just a subtle challenge to countries like Russia to pursue the battle against us by more secret means.'

'Almost everyone in the department believes that. They have to.'

'Hayter is especially old school though.'

'He fought in the war. It's as simple as that. He's never lost the habit.'

'All right. Wait till you hear this. He says that it follows that in the case of propaganda, what he called the battle of words, there is no difference between, for example, an off-the-record briefing and the supplying of false information to the press. Well, you know as well as I do that off-the-record briefings often equal character assassination, but Hayter takes the position a lot further. He claims that the intention is identical in both cases and that, where the national interest is concerned, liberal democratic niceties are irrelevant. Maybe you're right and he is a secret totalitarian. At any rate, as a professional journalist I refused to play ball.'

'Well, thank God for that.'

'Hayter was very much put out. So someone else was responsible for buggering-up Selzer. He didn't even try to get me to do that. But I knew we'd done it. So I counter-attacked with the Lister piece. And that was it. Out I went.'

'I think I know who it was who fooled Selzer,' said Strange proudly. 'Would you be surprised,' he went on, 'if I told you that Mayer did it?'

'Not at all,' Hoskins sounded quite casual. 'Mayer gave me the creeps if you want to know. As soon as he came I wanted to get out. I'd like to know where they got him from. There's more to that chap than just computer wizardry, though God knows what it is.'

'As far as I was concerned,' said Strange inadequately, 'he was just a rather gifted foreign scientist working for Hayter.'

'You may be right.' Hoskins's comment implied his disagreement, but Strange did not press the point. He wasn't interested in Mayer. They began to walk slowly back up to the hallway. 'Of course,' Hoskins went on, 'there's a lot in the Lister case that's not political. His thing with Cooper. I told you about that, didn't I?'

'Yes. I followed it up too.'

'Is he a sleeper?' Hoskins joked.

'No,' Strange admitted. 'But there's something going on between him and Ellison.'

'A lot of politics grow out of some fairly emotional soil, old chap. I'm a married man. Sarah Lister was a lovely lady once. She has a lot to answer for. Before you go rushing off telling everyone that Lister was uncovering a plot in the Directorate, you should talk to her. You say he was innocent after all. I'll bet she'll tell you he was out to get Preece for that. He was only interested in his good name. When he asked me to go ahead with that piece all he wanted was vindication. Not a word about Mayer.'

Strange realized with despair that he hadn't explained the situation adequately. But that didn't matter. He'd found out what he needed. He was content to protest. 'There's more of a pattern than you realize, Brian.'

'That's what I used to think. But I lost the picture. The Directorate isn't keen on patterns. Dangerfield's too cunning to let anyone fit a shape to its activities. That's what the secrecy's for. So you can't see all the bits of the puzzle.'

Strange was not convinced. 'I promise you – I'm on the brink of proof.'

Hoskins shook his head. 'Doesn't matter. Look what's happened to Lister. The organization always wins. It has to – in the national interest!'

They both laughed at that. They reached the marble entrance and shook hands.

'Good luck,' said Hoskins. 'If you do get a story, you'll give us the scoop?'

'Of course.'

The policeman pulled the door back to let him pass. As Strange came out into the deserted shopping precinct, the icy wind caught his open coat and he instinctively backed away to fasten the buttons. So he did not see the three men running at him from the shelter of a doorway. The first thing he knew was a blow, painless on the instant, that sent him sprawling across the paving. For a moment his mind flashed back to the moment the shrapnel burst that day in the Western Desert. The next moment his arm was wrenched fiercely backwards as they grabbed at his briefcase. But it contained many vital documents and he had kept it close to him on all his travels. He gave a cry, but held on. Hoskins ran across and the gang fled. Hoskins bent over him in alarm. 'The bastards. Are you all right? It happens all the time now. You were lucky with your bag. I lost my wallet at knife point only a month back.'

'Did you see them?' was Strange's first question.

'Three men,' said Hoskins. 'Not a hope of catching them.'

'What sort of men?' Strange persisted.

'Oh.' Hoskins was helping him to his feet. 'The usual thugs.' He faltered. 'You don't think . . .?'

Strange looked at him. 'Well, it's crossed your mind, hasn't it?' He sounded almost triumphant.

CHAPTER TWENTY-TWO

Lister's children were cowed by their tragedy. They sat mutely watching Strange in the tatty armchair. Mrs Lister was making tea in the kitchen. Strange regretted that he didn't have an easier way with kids. The dark bruise on his forehead didn't help. He'd tried ages already. Five, said Clarissa; seven, said Joe.

'Where do you go to school, Joe?'

'St Johns.'

'Do you like it?'

'It's all right.'

The little girl seemed lost in her own world. Strange had no idea what to say to her. Whenever she caught him looking at her she giggled and tried to hide behind Joe on the sofa. 'Get away, Cliss,' said Joe.

'No – o!'

Just as an argument seemed to break out, Mrs Lister arrived with the tea. She was pale with bereavement but he could see what Hoskins meant about her looks. She had developed an involuntary way of twitching her neck when asked a question, like a child flinching. Her eyes, weak and red-rimmed, were large with grief and worry. At times Strange had to strain to catch her words, though she spoke firmly enough to the children.

Strange's strong voice and awkward painful movements as he accepted his tea, dominated the subdued atmosphere.

'You're looking much better,' he said. 'Are you working?'

Mrs Lister flinched. 'No. Somehow I don't seem to have the energy. Some days I get up and say to myself, today I'm going to look for a job. But by the time I've got the children to school and done the housework I feel exhausted. There's – there's Richard's pension you see.' Her eyes filled with involuntary tears. Strange bent over his tea.

'The department ought to help you with the job,' he encouraged after a moment.

'Oh, the Welfare people have been very kind. They were very nice to Joe and Clarissa when I was still in hospital.' The children stirred at the mention of their names and the boy said, 'Can I have some more cake, Mum?'

'Yes, dear. Will you offer some to Mr Strange?'

Joe held the plate at Strange who said, 'Thank you, Joe,' with pronounced courtesy.

'Come on, love, put it down,' said Mrs Lister. 'They're still very shocked,' she explained.

'Well, at least you're all together again,' said Strange with inadequate enthusiasm. There were paper-chains sagging across the room. Two or three half-filled balloons wilted over the empty fireplace.

'Yes, it is nice,' she said, inexplicably nervous. 'And tell us what you've been doing since we saw you last, Mr Strange.' She spoke with a sudden energy like a schoolteacher, as though for the children's benefit.

Strange didn't answer at once but looked at Joe and Clarissa. 'I'd like to talk to you in private, if I may, Mrs Lister. Can you send the children out to play?'

'I – well – yes of course.' She twittered with nervousness. 'They could go outside in the garden,' she said doubtfully. It was snowing and there was a bitter wind blowing.

'Don't want to go out,' said the girl, speaking for the first time.

'Well off you go upstairs and play very quietly,' said their mother.

'I don't want to go upstairs,' said the boy, standing at the door. 'Daddy – '

'Don't worry dear – ' Mrs Lister put down her cup with a clatter. Strange noticed that her hand was shaking violently.

'I'm sorry. I'm distressing the children. But I have some things I must – '

'It's all right, Mr Strange. They still haven't got over Richard's death. I try to explain. It's very difficult.'

'Yes,' he said. They sat and listened to the children climbing slowly upstairs, reciting in a rhythmic chant:

> As I was going up the stair,
> I met a man who wasn't there,
> He wasn't there again today,
> I wish, I wish he'd go away.

Mrs Lister smiled. 'Dick taught them that,' she said. 'It was the only way to get them to bed when they hadn't seen him for some days. They loved him so much. He was devoted to them. He calculated that there were as many words as steps, so there's – so there's – ' and she began to cry softly. Strange could hardly restrain his own feelings.

Eventually she was quiet, and Strange began. 'I want to tell you that your husband was a very brave man.' And in a few urgent sentences he told her all about his investigation. She sat quite still, staring at him with her wide-apart eyes, as though she was also attentive to her children moving about overhead.

'You understand,' Strange concluded gravely, 'that if Richard did discover all this and was right about it, then there is one very unpleasant implication?'

Mrs Lister seemed to expect this. She did her best to suppress her sobs. 'Yes – yes – I know what – you're saying – he was – murdered, wasn't he?' She buried her face in her dress. 'They – killed – him – '

Strange was standing over her, proffering a grubby handkerchief. His voice was low. 'Can you help me? You must. Have you any idea what happened at the end?' He could not let go now he was so close to all the final answers. But Mrs Lister's crying seemed to be the release of weeks of bottled-up tension. She sobbed uncontrollably in long painful gasps.

The boy, who had heard the noise, was at the top of the stairs. 'Mum, is anything the matter, Mum?'

When Mrs Lister heard the voice she went to the door, her face red and swollen. Strange calculated that her son would not be surprised at her tears.

'It's all right, Joe. Go and play with Clarissa.'

'What about Daddy?' Strange heard the boy ask. 'Yes, Joe. Go back to your room.' As she came back, she was still flushed. Strange felt embarrassed and ashamed, but there was no other way.

'Do you see,' he said, 'if you want to help vindicate your husband, you must help me.'

She nodded.

'I need to know if Dick left any documents to do with his investigations here. Is there anything here that would help?'

'Yes, yes,' she said without thinking, 'there is something –' She stopped with regret.

'Tell me.' Strange looked at the desk, remembered the little darkroom.

'I can't, I can't,' she cried and ran from the room. This time there was the sound of children crying 'Daddy, Daddy' again. Suddenly with horror, Strange heard a man's voice. He got up from his chair and went to the door.

'Who – ?' he began.

'No – ' shrieked Mrs Lister.

Heavy footsteps were running overhead and thumping down the stairway. Strange gripped his stick.

'Tony! You mustn't!' Sarah Lister screamed, frantic.

Suddenly, there was more shouting – at Strange, at the children, at Mrs Lister – with fear and anger mixed. It was Ellison.

Strange, standing squarely in the hallway, stared at him hard but said nothing. Ellison was wearing incongruous white socks, tee shirt and crumpled trousers, and appeared to have been recently asleep. He was puffing slightly with his running and his heavy figure looked, for all its urgent hostility, out of condition. His eyes were ringed with fatigue. As Strange took all this in he realized that it had to be Ellison for there was a recent scar running down the side of his neck like a surreal smile. He was clenching his fists nervously, Strange noticed, his alarm subsiding, but not doing anything with them.

Mrs Lister was distraught but lucid. 'Mr Strange, you must go away. This is nothing to do with your story.'

'What story?' snapped Ellison, turning on the woman with ferocity. He seemed every bit as disagreeable as Cooper had said. Mrs Lister ran to him. He pushed her away as she spoke. 'It's all right, dear,' she was saying. 'It's nothing to do with you.' Strange marvelled at the lie, and stood there between them, sizing up the situation. Tony Ellison was glaring at him. Mrs Lister was in the kitchen doorway, weak from crying, but commanding in her desperation. And now the children were peering, frightened, round the foot of the stairs. Mrs Lister was speaking again. 'Go away please, Mr Strange,' she said looking at him quite sweetly, 'I don't want to know about Dick any more.'

Ellison started. 'You lying bitch. What have you –'

'Darling, it's nothing, I promise –' she began, but Ellison shouted her down.

'Bullshit,' he was savage with fear. 'You don't have to tell me why he's here. He's raking over the shit, and when he's got enough he'll throw it at the fan.'

That made Strange angry, especially the language; he was also determined to be provocative. He said: 'Is that how you normally talk in front of kids,' adding insultingly, 'or your – I mean Mrs Lister. It might make her think she was living with a gangster.'

Ellison was fighting hard to control himself. Strange went on quite calmly. 'No, you're not going to call the police, or go for me. There's a limit to the number of deaths even the Directorate can cover-up in one household.'

Ellison fell into the trap. He turned on his mistress. 'What have you told him?'

Mrs Lister flinched and implored him: 'I haven't said anything, darling. But you've never told me . . . He wanted to talk about . . . But . . . but . . .' and she began to cry again.

'Well if you've got any questions you can ask me,' said Ellison pointing dramatically with his finger.

'Oh, it's all right,' said Strange lightly. 'It's only the odd detail I need now. And I just thought I'd look in here before I went back to London. I don't want Dangerfield worrying her unexpectedly,'

Ellison started, 'Dangerfield? What's Dangerfield got to do with it?'

'I haven't spent the last few months living out of a suitcase for the hell of it,' said Strange sharply. 'After all, Dangerfield is the controller.'

The man ignored the sarcasm. 'Dangerfield won't believe you. There are things you don't know.'

'That's what I've discovered recently. It makes me curious.'

'You haven't a chance. He'll see at once what you're up to.'

Strange knew he was bluffing. 'And what's that?'

Ellison fell silent, not even bothering to reply. Strange started to walk to the front door. Ellison barred his way. Strange took another step, his good leg hurting from his fall.

'Don't –' pleaded Mrs Lister, fearing violence.

But her lover was already in a state of acute anxiety. His face contorted in an attempt at a smile, an expression that had once had great charm. 'Don't get me wrong, Mr Strange. I was going to suggest you had another cup of tea before going back to london. Sarah, love, put the kettle on. There are things,' he went on, ushering Strange back into the living-room, 'that you ought to know if you're going to talk to Dangerfield.'

They sat down. Ellison took the hard chair by the table.

'You're going to tell Dangerfield why Lister was murdered, aren't you?' he said as they settled themselves. He spoke straight out like a criminal who, having made the decision to go to the police, tells the whole story in the first sentence. But Strange wanted more than that. He wanted to get back to the roots of the story that he knew were buried here in Cheltenham. He looked at him in the late afternoon shadows and saw the haunted, drawn look of the man with death on his mind. He realized that Ellison had lived alone with his secrets, unable to confide. So he ignored this question and asked, with a sympathy that also hinted at a full knowledge of the case. 'It's been a long time, hasn't it?'

Ellison knew what he meant. 'Frankly, Strange, there were some days when I prayed I wouldn't wake up. Those were always the worst. Never sleeping. Just turning the whole thing round in my mind.' He lowered his voice, 'Frankly, if it wasn't for his wife – for Sarah – I wouldn't be talking to you now. She got me through. Odd, isn't it? Dick's wife. But she loves me, you see. You can't believe that, can you?'

Strange protested. He had learnt, in his retirement, in the course of his investigations, that the springs of loyalty and attachment are many and various. 'What about Lister?' he asked.

'She loved him too. That was the tragedy. There never was a real breakdown, just the inevitable separation when he was moved to London. She's a lot younger than him.' Ellison was speaking with a greater objectivity now.

Silence hung between them like shame.

Mrs Lister came in very quietly, filled the teapot, kissed Ellison and withdrew.

'How much does she know?' Strange asked at length.

'Not very much.' He seemed defeated. 'She's given everything for nothing.'

'But she suspects . . .'

'I know. That's the hardest part, not saying anything when I know she . . .' he gestured the end of the sentence.

'And all this time they've told you nothing?' Strange hazarded.

'I'm a bad security risk,' admitted Ellison savagely. 'Of course they tell me nothing. They never did much. Now it's even less.'

Strange realized that Ellison was like Cooper. A desperate man at the end of a line waiting for news that never comes. He realized he would have to try another opening if he was to persuade Ellison to develop his game. 'They pay attention to some,' he said. 'You know I was followed here?' It was a natural gambit.

Ellison looked horrified. 'No,' he said. 'Where – what – ?' He became inarticulate with fear.

'If you ask me to get out,' Strange went on relentlessly, 'they'll still want to know what you told me, and they won't believe you if you say, "Nothing", because they know I've been on this trail too long to take No for an answer.'

'I don't believe you,' said Ellison without conviction.

'All you have to do is look out of the window,' said Strange.

Ellison got up and walked to the bay. He peered past the lace.

'Across the street,' said Strange. 'You see how bold they are.'

Ellison sat down again and rested his elbows on his knees, leaning forward, sucking air through his teeth nervously. He obviously didn't know what to say next.

'The best thing you can do now is tell me all you can so that we can get this thing out into the open. You aren't safe if it stays secret. If you keep the game to your chest you will suffer like Lister.'

Ellison looked distantly into the corner. He began to speak, in abbreviated sentences, that jerked the story forward like the jolts of a computer tape. 'It all started so long ago. In the Sixties. As you know Preece was in the Cheltenham office then. Here. The rising star. Feared and respected for his intelligence. He also gave us some self-respect. We were badly paid. A joke. They called us the boffins. Computers were quite new. People distrusted them. So they made it a joke. Typical British attitude. It was humiliating. We knew what we had.' His pride flared. 'We knew the power of our office. In time. Preece expressed our feelings. He made us feel wanted. Lister was there too. He and Preece were friends then. That's often forgotten. They fell out much later on. The next thing that happened was that ordinary people in other departments began to get access to our secrets. They got to know what we stored. They wanted the information. We were a government agency. We couldn't stop them. Wanted to, though. Surprising how possessive you get about data. Then we discovered that people were making money out of our secrets. Money out of "our" work.

213

That's how we thought of it. The Directorate is not run by ordinary civil servants. It's got academics, engineers, mathematicians. People who enjoy solving problems, playing games. The people produced by our universities. They treat people like binary statistics. That's important. Anyway we saw other departments making money out of our database. But obviously we knew far more than them. They knew about their bit. We, some of us, knew it all. Preece gave us pride you see. He was the boss. He encouraged us. Just a few of us. He let us do freelance work. Processing things for people, friends usually. Selling information. For cash. Remember that inflation was just starting. Money was getting cheap. Preece said it was just a perk. It wasn't exactly criminal, just not terribly ethical. Especially when we started dealing with non-government personnel. Yes, it was a kind of consultancy if you like. Just in Cheltenham. That limited us. It wasn't the big time you understand. Small money, small deals. It didn't bother me. We were quite scrupulous about office materials and office time. At first. But gradually it took up too many evenings. So we started to use the office. Used our secretaries for occasional letters. Odd jobs. You see no one understands computers. That's what made us so mad. And daring. We never kept copies of the letters and the secretaries never stayed long enough to find out what was happening. Preece wouldn't let them.'

'Did Lister do this?' Strange broke the flow quietly, with reluctance.

'That was why he and Preece quarrelled. Long before the enquiry. Lister knew what was going on. You can't fool a computer log surreptitiously. At least we couldn't then.' He smiled to himself. 'But he kept quiet to start with. A conspiracy of silence. Hell, it *was* a perk. But he wouldn't have anything to do with it and later he accused Preece of manipulating the database. There was a row. Nothing was done. Lister was a real boffin. Brilliant. He didn't care about anything, except his beloved computers and their programmes. And Sarah. Before he met her he was married to computers, and afterwards she was the only other thing in his life. I'll come to that. As far as the database went he didn't mind Preece using its facilities on the quiet, what bugged him was when it was made to carry secret material that was dubious. But that wasn't till later.'

'When?'

'I'm coming to that. So the Cheltenham network was established. There was me and Preece and Cooper. There was also another man who has retired and who will die if this ever got out, so let's leave him out of it, shall we? That's a secret between me and myself. And we were all doing very nicely, thank you. Then we got risky. That was when we started to hide things from Lister. You see before he caught me he'd been suspicious for some time.'

'What sort of risks?'

'In the way we made the money. One example. You know how we keep lists of terrorists in Britain and Northern Ireland. Well, as part of the department we also had access to the lists we keep of arms dealers in this country, and in Europe and America too. Cooper and I made a lot of money selling the names of bombers and gunmen to the dealers.'

Strange was stunned at Ellison's matter-of-factness, but he managed to ask: 'Did Preece know about this?'

'Sure. As you know, presumably, he'd initiated a more systematic procedure for accumulating details about terrorists. We were just turning the list to profit for him.'

Strange reflected on the stark contrast between the routine work of the Directorate's narks who collected names and addresses, visited bookshops, pored over interminable tracts, and sat through intolerably dull radical meetings; and, on the other hand, its consequences: splintered glass in shopping centres, wrecked cars, broken bodies in casualty wards.

'Yes,' he said distantly. 'Didn't it worry you, this?' Ellison shrugged: 'Not really. I don't care frankly. The country's finished. I want to make some money while there's still some around.' His eyes ducked Strange's concentrated stare.

'Then Lister made his accusations?'

'Not quite. First the inevitable happened. Preece was promoted. Sent to London. He was better for us than we knew. Kept us in control. Back here things went wrong. We were getting too ambitious. Just before Lister caught me, we were starting the same system with the criminal underworld. It's easy now we're linked to the police computer. But there were rumours we were up to something. A lot of bad feeling. We also started accumulating classified material from other databases on our own frame In case it was useful in future. Preece didn't object. He was too busy in London. He was also planning to put one of his most sensitive projects into our database for security. He wanted to hide it, do you see. That was what Lister caught me with. Part of the index to it.'

'That was Mayer's detailed index to the interconnections of international terror?'

'You know about that, do you?'

'Yes,' said Strange. 'I do.'

'As I say,' commented Ellison, 'we got careless.'

'Why did Lister start getting aggressive?' Strange asked.

Ellison looked evasive. 'Lots of reasons. But this,' he pointed at himself again, 'was the main one. I've told you how he loved Sarah. Well, I've had this affair with Sarah, on and off, for several years. I've never admitted it before but I did it partly out of spite. Lister was the cleverest programmer of the lot. We could have used him. But he wouldn't play. So he was always a threat. We relied on his silence. So I went for his wife to get back at him. To start with. Then it got serious. Then Lister got me. Cooper was still a friend of his. Cooper's a rat though. He tried to make me face Lister alone. Probably wanted to build up his own empire. I soon fixed that. I dragged him in as well. Things got very hot. It's amazing everything didn't come out then. But you see by a stroke of luck Preece got himself the job of handling the enquiry. So he was asked to hush it up. So London would never know. He did, didn't he? Preece is clever. He even managed to get the rumour about Lister to stick. You know, the one that Lister was covering up his own dirty tricks. People will believe really big lies, won't they?'

'Yes,' said Strange, 'they will.'

'It was different after that. Cooper had a row with Preece for not standing by him when I dragged him into the enquiry. He left. He got scared. Preece was getting very big for his boots. The fourth man retired. He was scared too. Lister was moved to London. And I was left alone here.'

'Why do you think Lister was moved?'

'That was a mistake. I think Preece thought he could keep an eye on him there. He also thought he was cleverer than Lister. But the real reason was that he wanted to ruin him. And he did. Lister soon had trouble with his house, his wife, his kids, me – the lot. And that of course drove him wilder. That was why he picked the fight with Preece.'

'Why was it different here after Preece went to London.'

'Well, for one thing, Preece moved away from the straight processing of data. He started to want to accumulate it. He got very interested in correlated personnel data. CPD as it's called. I expect you to know about it.'

'Yes,' said Strange, 'you mean building up individual profiles on disc.'

'That's it. When I asked him about it, he said it was another perk. Lister said it was much more political than that. He said Preece was in with some big fish.' Strange was about to interrupt but Ellison was in full swing. He let him talk. 'The fact is that once Preece had people in his pocket he used them. He's got me for instance. I depend on him. There must be others. In the last two or three years, since the enquiry in fact, I've had very little idea what the work I've done for Preece is all about. I just do it. I don't complain. I'm getting a rake-off. I'm a very wealthy man, you know, Mr Strange,' he confided with some pride. 'I know I don't look it, but I am. It's the same old story, wealth does not equal happiness, QED. I'm saving to leave, but each year the money gets bigger and my savings are worth less. I can't afford to spend it of course. Preece won't allow that. That would draw attention. I want to emigrate, take Sarah away, put all this behind us, forget all about this shitty little country and start afresh. I wish I could tear myself away.'

Strange used the pause to clear up a slight mystery. 'You say that Lister said that Preece was involved in political work?'

'Yes.'

'When did he confide that tit-bit?'

Ellison was not bothered by that. 'Oh, that happened at the end – on the night he attacked me.'

'Ah, I see,' Strange breathed out like a diver coming to the surface. It was too good to be true the way the conversation was turning.

Ellison went on without prompting. 'He arrived here and accused me of all kinds of things, mostly to do with Sarah and shouted about how Preece was mixed up in a political racket. Then he went for me. He was drunk I think.'

'And you defended yourself?'

'It was harder than I realized. He looked very unco-ordinated and a bit weedy, but he was strong. There was something about his behaviour, as though this was what the aggieved husband ought to do. You know, draw a knife and shout a bit. But I actually chased him away after he'd made his gesture.' He pointed to the scar.

'And you never saw him again?'

'I never *saw* him again. No.' Ellison paused to light a cigarette. The family atmosphere of tea and cakes was becoming weary with smoke. He looked at Strange. 'He rang you see. From a phone box. Ten minutes, perhaps a quarter of an hour later. The ambulance was here. I was lying, here as a matter of fact. On blankets. Bleeding. I'd been sick as well. Shock I think. One of the ambulance men answered. Said it was Mr Lister. Wanted to speak to his wife. Sarah was hysterical. The doctor was trying to sedate her. But she got her way. Went to the phone with him. The line was dead.' Ellison gave a bitter laugh. 'Twelve hours late, so was Lister. I feel guilty. It's been hell. But at least I've told someone.' He seemed incredibly relieved. 'It was never suicide. He was murdered because he knew too much.' He looked queerly at Strange. 'He knew as much as you do now.'

Strange felt his fears creep back again. 'Who do you think carried out the operation?'

'Preece wouldn't have had any trouble there. You know the sort of people the Directorate monitors. Hit men. Terrorists of course. It's easy to divert the flow if you have the right contacts. There's an odd affinity sometimes.'

'Was Mayer involved?'

Ellison looked blank. 'In what? Lister's death? God knows. Why?'

Strange ignored Ellison's question. 'Did Preece ever mention Michael Hayter?' he pursued.

'Not much. He said Michael Hayter was very interested in our expertise here. Yes, I think he once said that he and Hayter had a lot to offer each other. Of course they're very different types of people. Hayter's very much of the old school I believe.'

'Yes, I suppose he is,' agreed Strange, thinking that probably made him old school as well. 'What did Preece say about me then?' he added.

Ellison was embarrassed. He was obviously liking Strange.

'Go on, don't mind my feelings. I wasn't in the job for popularity.' He'd have been better off as a schoolteacher, he thought, like his father.

'He said you thought you knew it all, but were really years out of date,' said Ellison abruptly. 'He reckoned you didn't understand the Directorate despite your years in it,' he added with an effort.

'Thank you,' said Strange, 'I respect your honesty.'

'That's why he thought you'd never find out.' Ellison smiled grimly. 'He was wrong.' Ellison looked exhausted. His mine was ragged and his restless eyes strayed towards the window.

It was time to go. He thanked Ellison again, rose and went towards the kitchen. He looked at his watch. Six o'clock. Mrs Lister was at the kitchen table finishing a simple jig-saw with her children. She gave a start as the door opened. Strange thanked her and said good-bye to the children as well. Hoping to break the ice, he bent over the puzzle and fitted a piece in place.

'See, Joe,' he said. 'It's just a question of seeing the pieces in the right way.'

The children stared blankly and Tony Ellison and Sarah stood in the hallway at the bottom of the stairs, pale and pathetic-looking, linking fingers in love for courage.

'God bless,' he said unexpectedly and to his own surprise, and fled out of the house. The slamming of the door echoed down the empty street. The van was still there. He couldn't see anyone in it, but you never knew. He wondered what would happen to Ellison and hoped the house wasn't bugged. And then his own fear caught up with him and he became egocentric again.

He had to get his report to Dangerfield. But for the moment he was alone with his secrets. Lister had died alone. But Lister hadn't known all that he knew. If he stayed on the move he'd be all right. He could drive through the night. Record the tape at the same time. If he kept moving he'd be okay. It was too risky to go direct to Dangerfield. They'd get him if he tried that. All he had to do was alert Quitman. They didn't know about James: Quitman was the trump card. This time he did laugh. He was still warm from the happiness it gave him as he walked into the Post Office to send his last telegram.

CHAPTER TWENTY-THREE

Quitman had gone to work when Liz answered the door of the flat. There were two men in open raincoats and slightly rumpled dark suits standing outside at the top of the stairs. In another setting they might have been a headmaster and his deputy from a minor public school. It was this that made Liz voluble in her apologies for her bathrobe, the absence of make-up and so on. And when she learnt that they were from Jamie's department and wanted 'to have a chat' with her, she became embarrassed and ashamed and tried to make amends with a pot of freshly-ground breakfast coffee.

Now the two men were sipping it appreciatively and admiring the pink décor of the sitting-room like undertakers in a boudoir. Mr Hollingsworth, the elder man, spoke first.

'I will come straight to the point,' he said, and then spent several minutes establishing, with painful circumspection, that Quitman lived with her, that they were not married, not even, noted Mr Gibben, his assistant, engaged.

Hollingsworth went on, 'Mr Quitman has been doing very well in the department, and as you know, men and women who work hard and conscientiously in the Civil Service are always considered for promotion.' He spoke like a recruiting officer. 'However, as I expect you are aware, Mr Quitman,' – Liz found it odd to hear her lover described in this way – 'is in one of the more "political" sections of the department, dealing with highly classified, that is to say, secret, information.' Liz nodded in silence. Words, she felt, would only complicate matters. 'It is longstanding departmental practice,' he continued 'before certain promotions into the higher grades to undertake what we call the positive vetting of the candidate's immediate circle, his family, closest friends and relatives, to establish to our satisfaction that he or she is "sound", if you understand my meaning.'

'Not a spy,' said Liz.

Mr Hollingsworth looked rather pained at the bluntness. 'Or vulnerable for one reason or another to some form of personal pressure –'

'You mean blackmail,' said Liz, wishing now that she'd answered the door in the nude. Poor old Holly, thought Mr Gibben, you've met your match here.

But Mr Hollingsworth did not ruffle easily. He made a note on his clipboard and Liz began to realize, after her first pleasure at her insolence had worn off, that if Jamie was going to get the job, she'd have to co-operate.

'More coffee?' she asked with h. winning smile. Mr Hollingsworth and Mr Gibben accepted with much gratitude, and when the former resumed his questioning he was pleased to note a change of attitude.

'You say you have known Mr Quitman for seven years?'

'Yes,' she became as composed as her dressing-gown would let her.

'So I may take it that you know a good deal about his past?'

'Yes, I do.'

'Has he ever taken part in any political activity?'

'Not that I know of. He's rather unpolitical.'

'How does he vote?'

'Secretly.' She said it quite politely and the issue was not pursued.

'And as far as you know Mr Quitman has never committed any criminal offence?'

'No.' Liz smiled 'Do you know Jamie? He's not like that.'

'So, since you've known him,' Hollingsworth summarized with magisterial solemnity, 'he has been involved in no court action of political radicalism or contentious work of any kind.'

'Jamie's great passion is medieval chivalry,' said Liz, a remark which provoked an unworthy thought in Mr Gibben. 'He's writing a book.'

'Splendid,' said Mr Hollingsworth, as though congratulating a favourite pupil. 'And what are his relationships with his colleagues, would you judge?'

'I believe he gets on very well with them.'

'Does he see them at all in out-of-office hours?'

'Sometimes.'

'Who does he see?'

'Oh. I've no idea really. They're not my friends.'

'Does the name Rose Walford mean anything to you?'

'No – who's she?' asked Liz sharply.

'A colleague,' he noted her reaction. 'Or Charles Neve?'

'I know him. He came to my party. He quarrelled with James recently.'

Hollingsworth made another jotting. 'His best ally,' Liz volunteered, anxious to sound more positive, 'was quite a senior man called Strange.'

'Frank Strange?' asked Mr Gibben, speaking for the first time.

'Do you know who I mean? You should speak to him about Jamie. He'd reassure you. But I expect you've already got a reference from him. I know he was very impressed with James.'

Mr Hollingsworth wrote with great deliberation on his pad. 'Would you say Mr Quitman knows Mr Strange well?'

'Oh yes. He treats Jamie like a son. It's very comic.'

'When was the last occasion they met, to your knowledge?'

'Well, of course he's retired now, but they still keep in touch. Now I think of it Jamie did say something about seeing Strange the other day. I forget what. But Mr Strange could tell you much better than I how discreet and reliable James is. Why, he doesn't even tell me what he's up to when he comes to the office!' And she laughed winningly, while Mr Hollingsworth marshalled a dozen supplementary questions in his mind.

Quitman was quite relaxed again. The work was not heavy now and as there had been no more mention of Aldershot his fears of discovery had receded. When Preece came into his office that same morning he was stretched back in his chair reading *The Times*.

'Good morning, James,' it was assured and friendly, the greeting of colleague to respected colleague. 'I'm glad,' he added without irony, 'that you and Charles have got everything under control. You've done well together. Michael Hayter is pleased.'

Quitman made the usual disclaimer. 'It was worrying when he went back to Hoskins,' he said.

'He knows he's beaten. It won't be long before he retires to Devon. I wish I could say the same about the bombers. It's getting worse every day.'

He did look tired, thought Quitman. The smooth tanned skin was slightly grey with exhaustion and his normally poised expression bore the strain of long nights of worry. Even his normally immaculate suit was creased and baggy. 'In fact,' Preece continued. 'I've had a long talk with Michael about you' – Quitman's old fears rushed back – 'and we both feel that it's time you widened your experience outside the Directorate in another part of the department.' Quitman stared. 'I want you to go and see a very dear friend of mine, Gordon Robertson, next week. He's got some very interesting assignments lined up for you.' Preece's tone changed. 'This is, of course, another rapid move with increased salary and commensurate regrading. I hope you will understand the need to be discreet about it within the office. If I was you I'd keep it to yourself until the transfer has actually been made. There's no point making enemies for yourself.' He sounded so immensely confidential that all Quitman could find to say was 'Certainly, Guy.'

Preece moved carefully on to a new topic. 'I was dining with your old tutor over the week-end, by the way. He was most pressing to hear about you. He said something about research.' He smiled indulgently. 'What's this, James? Do we have another G. M. Young in our midst?'

'Oh, it's just something I started at college. On medieval chivalry. I'd like to write a book about it one day but there's so much to read, and so few hours to do it in.'

'Well, perhaps Gordon will give you time off to follow that bent, we could do with one or two really first-class historians in the department. Rosie will tell you about the appointment with Robertson. You will excuse me, won't you?' The door closed.

With the privacy Quitman realized how paranoid he had become about his double role. Suddenly, in a sentence, Preece had released him. The promotion was by the way; what mattered was that he was free from anxiety. Once he was out of the Directorate he could be of no more use to Strange. He experienced a profound relief. The work had begun to affect his relationship with Liz, forcing him to distrust her. He wanted to ring her there and then and tell all. Instead he went off to find Rosie Walford to confirm the good news.

'Good morning!' His bonhomie sounded false, but he managed to conceal his awkwardness that way.

'Hello, James,' she said, pausing icily between the words. She was celebrating her affair with the newly successful Neve with a new wardrobe, and was today perched on her swivel chair, the pleats of her skirt flowing like a fan from her waist.

'Preece said you had all the details about my appointment with Gordon Robertson next week.'

'Oh yes, of course. A little bird told me you're leaving the Directorate, aren't you?' She could never resist to stir, but there was little animation in her voice.

'Secondment. It's confidential.'

'Of course,' she snapped. The reconstructed Rosie Walford didn't gossip in the office, though later, in bed with Neve, she did say: 'You won't believe this, love, but Preece has sacked Quitman.'

'No! – good God – when?'

'Promise you won't tell a soul till it's announced. It's supposed to be a secret. He's being moved across to Robertson in Supply.'

'How boring.'

'That's what I said to Maisie. Now you've got the Strange case all to yourself.'

'That's a fag end. Strange is more or less finished.'

'But after that – ' she kissed him.

'No Quitman, no rivals!' he laughed. 'How did Quitman seem?'

'He was trying to pretend he didn't mind, the arrogant so-and-so. But he left the office early.' Rosie considered that to be an infallible sign of job fulfilment.

'Good old Guy. He knows how to wrap things up. He probably told him it was promotion.'

Rosie was wrong. Quitman left the office early to tell Liz about his news. He paced the pavements of Whitehall almost skittishly. When he reached the Westminster Underground he thought, No, I'll walk. The air was nipping; it cleared his head. He loped off towards St James and Constitution Hill. But as he crossed in front of Buckingham Palace, darkened and shuttered by austerity, he had an indefinable sense that he was being followed and looked round. There were two men, in conversation, also carrying briefcases, about a hundred yards behind. Unremarkable at this time of the afternoon, he thought, but when he discovered that they were still there as he trudged into Knightsbridge, he made a detour into McDonald's for a hamburger. The security guard at the door stood back to let him in. It was crowded as usual. A fire-engine barged impatiently through the rush-hour in the street outside.

The familiar lines of the unemployed in overcoats and grubby denim shuffled towards the cash registers, a dark grumbling tide beneath the blazing white neon. Crunching over discarded polystyrene, Quitman carried his micro-heated hamburger to the window and stood munching. The two men were standing by a bus-stop. As he came out, the one shook the other by the hand and vanished with an attenuated farewell into the crowds. Quitman decided he was getting jumpy. He walked on. Outside Barkers there were three wrecked cars and a crashed squad car on its side. The ambulances had gone. It must have been quite a small bomb. The shattered glass glittered hard and cold under police arc lamps. He strode through the crowds. It was getting worse, as Preece had said.

He stood on the steps leading to Liz's flat, grating the key in the front door. A man with a briefcase swung round the corner. Quitman couldn't make him out in the darkness but pushed the door open in a hurry with some apprehension.

'Hello, love,' said Liz as he came in. She was waiting for him. 'You look worried. Cheer up! I've got good news for you.'

'Snap!'

'Tell me.'

'No. You first.'

They laughed and kissed and Liz poured out drinks. 'You've found the novelist of the decade?' he teased.

'Don't be mean, darling. No, it's about you.'

'About me? You're not pregnant?'

Liz gave a peal of laughter. 'No, no, wrong track completely. I'll tell you. Today – this morning – I had a visitation. Why do you look so scared? What's the matter?'

'Who was it?'

'Two men. Most mysterious, isn't it? They said they were special investigating officers.'

Quitman seemed pleased. 'So it *is* promotion. That's my good news as well. Preece came in today to say I was being moved to another part of the department. Hayter is pleased with my work. The Strange case – ' he stopped.

What strange case – ?'

'Nothing. They're very happy with me and it'll mean more money, another grade up and perhaps even time off to work on my knights.'

'Really.'

'Well, you know how they like you to be good at your hobbies in Whitehall. The English amateur and all that. I'm hoping I can wangle a day a month in the Bodleian. But tell me about the special investigators?'

'It was terribly funny. Two quite seedy, middle-aged men, they looked like prep-school masters, knocked on the door. I was in the middle of my yoga and in my dressing-gown but they didn't mind. They wanted to know all about your friends and relations. Well, there wasn't much to say about the family of course, though I mentioned your dear old guardian. They'd seen him. They wanted to hear all about our relationship. I was horribly frank to shock them. Not that they seemed shockable. And then I told them about your friends. They asked about someone called Rose Walford. Who's she, darling?'

'Just a girl at work. We have lunch occasionally.'

'And that boring Charles fellow.'

'Neve?'

'Yes. And then I thought I'd give a real boost to your chances – '

'What did you say?'

'I told them how much you were respected by senior civil servants like Mr Strange. Wasn't that clever? I thought it was the least I could do after all you've done for me lately. Oh, darling I'm so happy!'

Quitman stared at her bravely, without a word. Then he said, 'You told them about Strange?'

'They were very impressed. They wanted to know all about him, when you last saw him, what you thought of him, etc, etc. I told them as much as I knew.'

'Yes, of course you did,' said Quitman, quite calm. He wasn't angry with her. It was his own fault. He'd been too secret. Then suddenly he was scared, perhaps more frightened than he had ever been before.

'What's the matter, darling?'

'It's – it's hard to take it all in,' he managed to say. 'It's all so sudden. You did very well.' He kissed her. then the bell rang. 'I'll go,' he said quickly. He shut the sitting-room door behind him. The hall was in shadow, but the glass door on to the landing cast some light. There was a dark figure outside. The bell rang again.

'Who is it?' he challenged, in a low voice, hoping that Liz wouldn't hear.

'Telegram, sir. Name of Quitman.'

He pulled the door open. The helmeted courier thrust the envelope into his hand. The message was simple. He hadn't finished with Strange after all. He looked carefully at the boy.

'There's no answer. Thank you.'

He went back into the sitting-room to Liz. 'Jehovah's Witnesses again,' he lied, stuffing the telegram into his pocket. She seemed not to notice his sudden nervousness. 'Well,' he went on, 'I think this calls for a celebration. I'll just pop out for some champagne. How about that?'

Liz was delighted. She kissed him fondly. 'Don't be long,' she said, slamming the door after him.

There was no time to think about the correct moves now, his only course was to hide. He found himself acting unconsciously, prompted only by the urgency of his own fear. He hurried down the stairs, buttoning his coat as he went. In the hallway he paused and checked the corridor that ran behind the stairs. There was no one about. He went to the front door and looked out cautiously. There were no pedestrians in the street that he could see, but plenty of parked cars and a pair of tail lights, moving away slowly, glowed in the darkness. Whatever he did was a risk. He ran down the steps and set out at a brisk walk towards the Fulham Road not daring to look behind.

CHAPTER TWENTY-FOUR

Guy Preece was speaking urgently on the telephone. His head was throbbing with the beginnings of a heavy cold. Time was running short. He had a lot on his mind that morning. He had to move fast, despite his exhaustion.

'An old grey Volvo.' He gave the registration number. 'Yes.' He looked at his watch. Eight-twenty. 'On the M4. Travelling east. Yes, to London. Must be. Exit 17. You can't miss him. No, they won't obstruct. Thank you, Cornelius. Good luck.'

All he could do now was wait. That was exhausting, and he was already so tired. But his anxiety kept him painfully alert and there was some relief in knowing that whatever happened it would all be over by the end of the day.

He'd got the news about Strange's visit to Ellison last night, just as he was leaving the office. It meant putting off a promising dinner with Jenny Ashworth, 'resting' between shows, and he had driven like a madman to Cheltenham. As he told Hayter, just before he left, there was no one else he could trust.

'All right, old boy,' Hayter had said, rather distantly. 'You've made your bed, you've got to lie in it, what?'

That made Preece very angry. Hayter was part of this as much as he, even if he didn't know the Cheltenham end. By the time he reached Lister's house at ten-thirty his temper had not improved.

Ellison didn't help matters. Preece remembered him as a lightweight provincial on the make, anxious to please, easily coerced and venal; but the man had acquired a surprisingly stubborn streak. Ellison plainly resented the way in which he had been abandoned after Lister's death, and once he saw that Preece was alone, refused to co-

operate, insisting that Strange knew very little and had gone
away empty-handed.

'But I don't believe you,' repeated Preece with exasperation. 'Strange can't be going on nothing. He's been making
life hell for us for months now, since Lister died in fact.'

'Since Lister died . . .' Ellison sneered. It was a poor
revenge for his bad conscience, but it made Preece shake with
rage.

'He won't be the only one,' he muttered.

Ellison said nothing, merely lit another cigarette. It was
after midnight. There was nothing more to be said. The
threats had failed.

After Preece had slammed the door and revved his
Mercedes down the street, Ellison went upstairs to pack.
Sarah could follow. The main thing was to get out of the
way.

It was still dark when Preece coasted into the underground
car-park in the department, past the saluting duty officer. He
didn't want to go home. After his divorce it was cold and
cheerless and haunted with bad memories. He could sleep in
one of the armchairs in his office for a couple of hours, get
breakfast at the club and still be back in time to get an early
start to the day. It didn't matter about Ellison. There were
other ways of dealing with Strange. Hayter would approve.
He'd have no choice by the time he was at his desk. Lazy
bugger.

Quitman did not sleep until it was light. Then, as the hotel
began to wake up, and doors banged and bath-water
thundered down the ancient piping, he dozed. Someone was
hoovering overhead. For some reason the noise reminded
him of being ill at school. He slept. Then he became aware of
hammering through his dreams. He jerked awake. Someone
was knocking on the door.

'Who is it?'

'Eleven o'clock,' replied the maid. 'All guests out by
midday please. Do you want another day?'

'No – thank you,' he shouted back.

The footsteps retreated down the creaky corridor. While he shaved and dressed he thought about his next move. All that mattered was the 4.30 rendezvous.

The Hotel Zanzibar, which bore a greater interior resemblance to its previous incarnation as the Claremont, did not offer breakfast to its residents after 9.30. Lunch was not served until 12.30, and if that had any similarity to the previous night's dinner, Quitman reckoned he was better off in a pub. The foyer/reception reeked of cheap scent, scrambled eggs and floor polish. He paid his bill, and stepped out into the daylight, unsure how to preserve his anonymity. You have to keep moving, he told himself. Keep alert. There was a bus at the bus stop as he passed. He climbed aboard.

'Where do you go?' he replied when the conductor asked for his fare.

'High Street Ken. Albert Hall. Knightsbridge. Park Lane. Marble Arch. Oxford Street – ' Quitman settled for Marble Arch, well away from Whitehall. The bus juddered and stalled uncertainly down the street.

The fear of discovery did not relent with daylight, just became more diffused. He chose the back of the upper deck and tried not to look out of the window in case he recognized a face in the crowd. He'd been so frightened last night that he just found the hotel, snatched a meal and bolted for the narrow room. He was still frightened now. What did Strange want? He thought he'd told him all he could. Anyway he couldn't do any more for him. Not now. What if Strange was wrong after all . . .? He didn't know about Strange any more. He'd answered his questions, provided him with information from the Directorate's files, watched him, of course, as he was tracked round the countryside, but he didn't know what he'd found. No one knew that. He had exchanged information with Strange on a number of occasions in the last few weeks, but it had become a one-way transaction. Strange had stopped talking about his progress on the tapes. He just listed names, asked for details, without comment. For security perhaps, but possibly the reason was more ominous. Was he going to admit defeat at last?

'Marble Arch,' shouted the conductor.

He clattered down the stairs and was out on the pavement in a rush. He bought a newspaper and headed for the nearest pub. The paper was full of the ceaseless government battle with shortage, disruption, violence and poverty. Even the journalists seemed cowed by events. The reports were lifeless, as though language itself was deteriorating. Quitman wondered if the pub was a target, but read that 'government personnel and installations' were at risk. He ordered a second pint.

Strange was still driving, as he had done throughout the night, stopping only for petrol at motorway service stations, standing where the artificial light was brightest and making eager conversation with other night drivers to dull his loneliness.

When the dead of night came and he had ceased to care where he was or where he was going, he switched on the tape recorder on the seat beside him and, slowly to stop the old car's vibrations, recorded what he had to say with what seemed to him extraordinary lucidity, considering his exhaustion.

Later, a grubby dawn, wet and smudgy, merged into the more vulnerable daylight, and now the motorway was opening up eastwards across the south of England and he was keeping the green van in his mirror like a marksman. He wanted a shave.

But despite the discomfort of the last twelve hours, he felt peaceful, The throbbing of his bruised leg did not distract the flow of his thoughts as he drove. He had made the last moves. The telegram had gone. He had a rendezvous. The last tape was in his pocket. That was almost the easiest part, and making it had drained his fear and anger at the story he had to tell. Now he had to trust that James would be there for it to make a good endgame. Motorway driving is too much like waiting.

Strange decelerated to let an articulated lorry past, its

trailer swinging dangerously in a rush of wind. The green van slowed too, like a shadow.

He was planning in his mind a route to the rendezvous that would not encounter delay. A stop in London would be fatal. But he had surprise on his side, unlike Lister. He would come in down the Cromwell Road and then cut down to the Embankment where the traffic would be flowing quickly and then follow the road through to the Strand. They would be expecting him to go straight to the department. He could park in Covent Garden and be inside the Civil Service Stores before they realized. It would have to be a quick dash, but once inside the building he'd feel safe. Then it was up to James.

He thought of Quitman then, hard at work at the Directorate. Telephoning perhaps, or drafting one of his inimitable memos. He smiled at the thought and made a mental note to have him down to Devon for a week-end in the spring once all the fuss was over.

Preece was wrong about Hayter that Friday. He was alert to the crisis early, and had Hollingsworth's report on his desk when he called his colleague in for a hasty conference before lunch.

'Quitman is working for Strange,' was his first comment. It sounded like an accusation. The country geniality of the old soldier had become the glacial stare of the local magistrate. Hayter had abandoned his customary tweeds for a conservative dark suit; a single glass of scotch and water on the desk tempered the formal atmosphere. Preece was speechless. 'I thought we were all getting a bit cocky about things,' Hayter continued, giving him a chance to digest the news, 'so I had Hollingsworth vet him. Dammit, Guy, he hadn't been with the chap's floosie, a lady by the name of,' he focussed his glasses over the page, 'Liz Sayer, for ten minutes, when she came up with the rather alarming intelligence that Quitman is in regular contact with Strange. Considering you're supposed to have turned Quitman round, it is a rather surprising discovery, hm?' Preece saw Hayter's natural choler surfacing and kept quiet. Hayter came round the desk and faced him. He was very cold. 'You're running one of the most secret government Directorates, God help you, using unorthodox methods of political control, which if they were made known would make Watergate look like a committee room caper, and you can't see that one of your chief assistants has ratted on you.'

Preece was rallying. 'Are you sure he was passing secrets?'

Hayter's anger was explosive. 'Well, it wasn't the time of day, was it? Quitman's supposed to be completely disillusioned with Strange. But here,' he waved the report, 'we have a little bit of fluff in Kensington telling us quite freely that Quitman sees Strange, I'm quoting do you understand, "quite often". You don't know about it, so it was in secret. Secrecy means secrets. I suppose you think we can weather this?'

Preece tried to speak but Hayter talked him down. 'Of course, what we do is justifiable. It's legitimate in a crisis, and this is a crisis, though no one seems to take any notice of it. But you try telling that to the liberal toadies in Fleet Street,' he glared at Preece. 'Where is Strange now?'

'On his way to London.'

'What's he doing?'

'All we know is that he talked to Ellison yesterday.'

'You've seen Ellison – what did they discuss?'

'Ellison says Strange knows nothing.' Preece knew that was no good.

'Balls,' said Hayter. 'Absolute balls. Strange hasn't been a thorn in our flesh for however long it is with nothing to go on. And now we know he did have things to go on. From Quitman, dammit. Do you mean to tell me you flogged all the way to Cheltenham to get that sort of answer? Where is Quitman?'

Preece admitted that he hadn't seen him that day.

'Well, find him for God's sake. And you've got to stop Strange of course – '

Preece was able to interrupt more confidently. 'That's already in hand, Michael. Mayer is making sure that he won't have a chance to reach Dangerfield.'

'Well, I haven't got time to ask questions. I can only assume, though God knows why I do, that you are in control. We're both ruined if you fail. Dangerfield's very soft on liberal democratic nonsense like open government. That's why he wants to take us over.'

Quitman killed the afternoon, when the pub closed, in Hyde Park. It was too cold and desolate to sit still and read. He walked slowly up and down the bald grass. A man with a dog came and threw sticks for it. The dog barked and bounced up and down, its breath foggy in the cold. Quitman continued to pace. As the winter day faded he walked back towards Speaker's Corner, where an old man with a sandwich board was urging 'Ecological Government'. Nearby, a shabby evangelical in a blue raincoat, holding a Bible, was making a monotonous speech about Christianity. Four or five fellow disciples stood listening in a shifty circle, sheafs of apocalyptic leaflets clasped in their nervous fingers. They cast surreptitious guilty looks at passers-by, but no one was listening much. A man said, 'What about the Pope?' but the speaker ignored the question and carried on with the Father's Loving Kindness.

Quitman took the tube to Embankment. A couple of drunks were having a fight on the platform as he got out. The other passengers drew away but made no move to stop them. The station guards stood by the steps and watched the fight. One of the men made a joke in his own language and his colleague laughed.

There was rubbish piled high up Villiers Street, smouldering harmlessly, and on the wind rancid frying from the station hotel. The air in the Strand was fresher. Quitman walked along quickly until he was opposite the Civil Service Stores. It was 4.15. He swung through the doors without difficulty and located the right floor. He stood and browsed through a collection of boxed operas and wondered if *The*

Magic Flute would appease Liz. It was 4.30 now by his watch. He knew Strange swore by an old Timex that had to be adjusted each morning. He could be anything up to five minutes late and still be on time by his own calculations. And then there were the delays. Quitman kept his eye on the flight of stairs that ran up from Soft Furnishings and went on to Glassware and Crockery expectant for the familiar figure to arrive.

At 4.37 he thought he heard heavy footsteps and looked up. The only person on the stairway was an elderly woman with two carrier bags. But Strange had already arrived. He came from another part of the Stores and walked past breathing heavily. Quitman stared at the broad back moving away from him. Strange had reached the tape section. There was a pause. Now he was leaving. Quitman looked up. It would do no harm now to make a brief greeting. He began to manoeuvre. Strange was to the side, only three or four yards away. It was not as if . . . Now was his chance.

'Hello, Frank – ' he began, but stopped short in shock. It was Strange, it had to be with the stick, but it was Strange altered in appearance and expression almost beyond recognition. Quitman saw the face of an old man, a staring, haggard look, bruised and unshaven. His hair, now almost white, was dishevelled and matted. Strange did not speak or indicate any recognition, but strode past with a haunted, lonely air about him, eyes red-rimmed like a tramp's.

'I beg your pardon, My mistake . . .' Quitman's voice trailed away. Other shoppers stared.

He watched him disappear, this time down the stairwell. As soon as he was out of sight he collected the tape in the usual way and rushed over to the cash desk. The girl was interminably slow calculating the cost and surrendering the change. Quitman hurried away to the front exit. He came out of the swing doors and looked hastily up and down the Strand. No sign of Strange. Then he realized he wouldn't park his car at the front. There was a back entrance. He hustled impatiently through the shop, oblivious to the complaints of the other customers. Across a vast hall of lingerie he glimpsed Strange striding unevenly through the exit. Then he ran. The doors were still revolving. He pushed.

The shock waves and the dry wall of heat hurled him backwards. He thought he was going to be sick. It was incredibly quiet. For about ten seconds he felt muffled by the sudden stillness. He wanted to shout but, as in a nightmare the sleeper cannot cry, his shouting choked in his throat. Gradually the noise returned. There were screams breaking in through the silence, very distant to start with, and then immediate, painful. He became aware of blood on the floor and dust blowing in from the street through the shattered doorway. He put his hand to his head involuntarily. He was not injured. Just as the sound of sirens could be heard over the hubbub and Quitman, realizing he was only shocked, was staggering to his feet, he found himself being helped from the carnage by friendly hands. It occurred to him that the ambulances were getting very quickly until, focusing on one of his rescuers, he recognized the melancholy expression of Alec Reeve.

The news of the explosion so close to Whitehall confirmed the department's views about the danger it faced and sent the sirens racing up past Nelson's Column. The Bomb Squad roped off the Civil Service Stores and Chandos Place with white tape. Shoppers and survivors were quizzed for clues. One or two mentioned an odd-looking down-and-out with a stick; several spoke of a young man running. The officer-in-charge wasn't hopeful but radioed through for the Identikit people to come over. Forensic experts moved in from specially-equipped vans to sift and collect the gruesome debris of terrorism: bone, skin, shrapnel, teeth, hair, glass. The first news that came back to the office was that a car had been blown up. Everyone in the immediate vicinity was dead and there were a number of other serious casualties. No one was quite sure of numbers. It was a terrible mess. Preece knew then that he had run his quarry to death. He had been half expecting it in Whitehall. You could never tell how reliable Mayer's connections were. Sometimes they'd play

238

up to embarrass you, like they had with Lister. But although it was a relief to know that Strange had taken his secrets with him there was still the pressure of his search for Quitman The man had vanished. The case wasn't closed till he was found.

He had already vented his exasperation on Neve after lunch.

'Why didn't you report his absence?'

'I didn't –'

'It's a Directorate rule that during a red alert all absent personnel are to be reported to me personally. You know that. Find him.'

The bomb was now making that search more difficult. Too many useful people were anxious to start processing the latest data. They couldn't see why Neve and Preece were flapping about Quitman. It wasn't as if he was terribly important now that he was moving. They all knew that. Preece didn't give up easily, but at six o'clock, after another row with Neve, he rang Hayter to admit temporary defeat.

But when he got through to Hayter's office the secretary said that her boss had already left, without saying where he was going.

CHAPTER TWENTY-FIVE

'Brandy?'

Sir Gerald Dangerfield's office, Quitman assumed, had everything. Its efficient modern furnishings conveyed a sense of secret power. If he had a cardiac arrest he felt sure that the appropriate technology would be wheeled in at a word from the controller on the scrambler telephone. The office, a suite of rooms really, was incredibly neat, astonishingly quiet and decorated in subtle shades of grey that found colour here and there in an exquisite miniature Fragonard or a porcelain vase of winter roses, but above all from the changing light of the London sky, for Dangerfield's study had a spectacular view – of Westminster, of Horseguards and Nelson's Column and away down the fair sweep of the Thames to St Paul's and the City. It was hard to believe that this sanctuary was in the same world as the Directorate. Yet as soon as the car plunged abruptly underground after its short dash from the Strand, Quitman knew that he was going back to the department.

Dangerfield was a tall but heavy man with an impassive brown expression. craggy but surprisingly approachable, until you saw the eyes, deep set, ringed with the shadows of many late working nights, glinting beneath snowy eyebrows. Dangerfield's hair was similarly a shocking white, as though it had turned quite suddenly overnight. As a younger man, Quitman thought, he must have been overpowering. It was natural that such an impressive figure should have a tone of voice that commanded attention, but its grating, almost hoarse expression was both surprising and hypnotic. Dangerfield spoke slowly, articulating deliberately, with a slightly calculating logic. There was nothing yielding about the controller.

240

He spoke now, handing Quitman an exquisite balloon glass and settling himself in an adjoining armchair.

'Cheers,' he said gravely. 'I want you to understand that this operation was for your protection.'

'I suppose it must be,' commented Quitman, feeling a warmth returning. 'I've never been offered brandy before here.'

Dangerfield's laugh was a well-practised, clubland chuckle. The grey eyes did not smile. 'I don't imagine you know what's been happening today?' he said, implying extraordinary complexity.

Quitman shook his head

'How much do you know about Frank Strange's career?' Dangerfield tilted his brandy. There was something about his manner that suggested there was always much more to things than one realized.

'As much as he's told me since I joined. That's not much. He's very discreet, even with – ' he broke off.

'He's a close friend, I'm told.'

'It sounds immodest, but I think he's fond of me. I admire him more than – ' He stopped. For a moment the habit of discretion choked his candour, and then he realized that there was nothing to lose any more. 'He was a true Englishman,' he said definitively, and was surprised at his overstatement, adding, 'I mean, he was sort of heroic, wasn't he?'

'I agree with you,' said Dangerfield, falling in with the elegiac mood. 'He was a complete patriot. A man of the highest honour.' He paused to study Quitman. 'I promoted him, d'you see, because I recognized he had qualities I could – ' he paused to choose his words, 'depend on. He had a ruthless persistence when it came to good administration,' he continued, sounding like an obituary. 'That's surprisingly rare. Many of my colleagues are anxious to get promotion, make money, win power, influence people and so on. They'll always put themselves and their empires first. Not consciously perhaps, but it happens. Fortunately we demand such a high standard of achievement that we are able to call their success good government. But Strange was different. He was not ambitious like that. He would sacrifice anything in the national interest.'

Quitman recognized the truth of that assessment. Dangerfield moved into an historical key. 'Some years ago when the micro-processing revolution was just starting – very few people recognized it at the time – I became convinced about the potential power of the Directorate. I felt it ought to be given, as it were, a springclean before it was too late. Secrecy can be very corrosive you know.' A ghost of a smile hovered on his features. 'Strange was my new broom. I'd watched his work in other sections and I felt I could appoint him in the sure knowledge that if there was anything nasty in the woodshed he would find it. I was wrong.' His expression became suddenly harsh. 'The vested interests proved too strong for him and he was driven out.'

'Is it naïve to wonder why you didn't protect him, if he was your man?'

This time the eyes glowed with an intensity that Quitman had not noticed before. 'In this secret state in which we have to work, things rarely seem as they are. I see I must go back a bit.'

He recharged their glasses and sat still.

'I never told Strange of my fears about the Directorate. I was anxious to avoid a hasty response. A crusader like Strange would have carried the Dangerfield banner too conspicuously into the enemy camp. My intention would have been thoroughly confounded.' He looked sharply at Quitman. 'You're going to say that it was anyway?'

Quitman protested.

'Don't apologize. It's a logical point of view. In fact Michael Hayter put pressure on Strange to resign with my authorization. Indeed,' he added, quite calm about this revelation, 'he could not have done it without my approval. There are still some limits to a deputy's power. In fact I let him execute that manoeuvre so that he would over-reach himself – as indeed he has done.'

Quitman held his brandy in both hands, and stared into its golden reflections. 'Did you know who Lister was referring to in his memo?'

'No – but I was quite willing to let Hayter believe that I accepted his claim that it was Strange.'

'I don't follow.'

'You see, Quitman, in the secret world the rules of behaviour are different. If Lister didn't dare name names he was obviously on the trail of something big – assuming he was *bona fide*. Strange himself was no longer effective enough in the Directorate to make the investigation. He'd reached the limits of his career. He was not enough of a computer expert, for instance. He needed to see the problem from another angle. So when Lister came up with that memorandum, and Hayter, who's so ambitious for his section, panicked, it was the perfect opportunity for me to give Strange a fresh perspective from the outside.'

'Did he – did he know you were doing this?'

Dangerfield was quite shocked. 'Of course not,' he said with asperity. 'Have you no respect for a man's self-esteem?' He put his glass down and became almost soothing. 'I knew Strange. I knew how he would take things. I knew he would be furious. And I knew what I had to do to make sure that he would not let go of the Lister case if it was – ' Dangerfield's enjoyment of psychological insights betrayed him. He stopped short.

'And it was the last thing he did,' retorted Quitman. 'Thanks to your devious method he's been murdered.'

Dangerfield was not flustered by this accusation. He was experienced with the effects of shock. 'On the contrary, as your presence proves, we have made very serious efforts to preserve you both from catastrophe.'

Quitman pondered the implications of this conversation. 'Did you tell Hayter you knew I was working for Strange?'

'You're wondering, I take it, who authorized the vetting of Miss Sayer?'

'Yes. Partly.'

'That was Hayter's own idea I was not consulted – though

I was informed about it from another source. Hayter was getting worried about Strange. Naturally, he suspected you. As far as I was concerned that interview confirmed what had already been established.'

'You're referring to Aldershot?' queried Quitman, as another piece of the jigsaw fitted into place.

'You were very careless, if I may say so,' parried Dangerfield. 'That was one indication.'

'And one which,' Quitman riposted, 'you were happy to discuss with Alan Jenks at your club shortly before Christmas.'

Dangerfield looked at him narrowly. 'This is not a game, Quitman. Do not flatter yourself that I had you watched out of any intrinsic regard for your safety.' His expression hardened with pent-up feeling. 'If I was interested in the personal welfare of anyone it was Frank Strange – a remarkable man.'

'But he's dead,' Quitman reiterated bitterly. 'Your surveillance wasn't good enough it seems. Why didn't you intercept earlier?'

'And give away the entire operation? Strange himself would have been furious. He was willing to take the risk. Witness the desperate chances he took at the end. The telegram to you, for instance. He must have known it would be monitored.'

'By you?'

Dangerfield inclined his head imperceptibly. 'Well, luckily, at that stage the surveillance operation that HQ Security thought they were running for Preece was being completely overridden by another agency. Preece had no idea how ineffectual his source had become.'

Quitman looked startled. In the Directorate there was always the sense of being part of a self-contained maze that one had to learn to navigate. Talking to Dangerfield, he realized that the Directorate was only a corner of a much larger labyrinth. He said, 'Nonetheless Strange gave up everything for the department. I saw him today. He looked twenty years older. And you still let him die.'

'We underestimated the risks of his coming to London.' Dangerfield was defensive.

'So there are some secrets that even you don't know!'

Dangerfield was angry at last. 'Look, young man. The secret war we fight in peacetime is getting vicious. That means that something is at stake.' There was a harsh passion in his voice as he spoke. 'We don't cut much of a figure in the world any more, but this country has some standards and the department exists to uphold them. Most of our budget is spent – since the public demands it – on military preparations for a war we cannot, none of us, win. But there is another war that people don't know about, a lonely, insular struggle that keeps its battle cry in secret. It is as vile as any other war and it has its casualties. Strange was one of them. He died defending values he and I believe in, and he knew what he was doing.'

He looked at Quitman with candour, 'I am telling you this because you have a tape-recording of some information that I very badly want to hear, and I don't believe in getting something for nothing.' Dangerfield held out his hand. 'You have it with you, I believe?' He had traded enough confidences for the exchange.

Quitman pulled the cassette out of his pocket and passed it over. There was of course a smart pocket tape recorder at the ready on the desk. For a moment Quitman wondered whether their own meeting was recorded, but the anticipation of Strange's last tape drove away the consideration.

Dangerfield pressed the button. Suddenly the room was filled with music. Dangerfield checked abruptly. 'What?'

'No, it's all right,' explained Quitman. It was part of our arrangement. He borrowed my tapes. That's only the leader. It lasts for about a minute.

'Good precaution,' said Dangerfield with approval. The music broke off. There was a hum, and then Strange's voice invaded the calm atmosphere of the room.

'There isn't much time left.' It was when the words began that Quitman caught the tension of those last hours. There was a background of noise, like the revving of a car engine, and Strange was almost shouting. 'You've got to get this to Dangerfield as soon as possible. I'd do it myself but it's too risky. Get it to Dangerfield, but listen to it first and see how sick everything is.

'It's about four o'clock in the morning here and I can't see a thing except the road in front of me. I'm literally dictating this on the run, driving non-stop. Otherwise they'll get me, like Lister. It's amazing how close I feel to him now. So you'll have to put up with the poor reception. It doesn't help that the weather is bad. You've put up with a lot lately. I know I haven't told you what I was up to, just bullied you for details, but the more I found out, the more risky it got, and I wanted to protect you. The truth is so much worse than I suspected, sordid and corrupt beyond my worst fears. I feel now that my work at the Directorate was irrelevant, but that's by the by ' Quitman glanced sideways at Dangerfield but the controller was impassive with concentration.

'The last time I told you about my suspicions I said I thought that Hayter was covering up enemy infiltration. I think I said that it might be connected to Cooper. That turns out to be absurd. I've had to shed a lot more prejudices to see the true picture. There are no agents. The system was never penetrated from the outside. I'm forced to the conclusion that no one cares about us enough to bother with that any more. No, the answer is sadder and more disgraceful. We are corrupting ourselves from within. That's where the enemy is, burrowing from the inside, almost invisibly.'

There was a noisy pause. Quitman heard the odd little whistle with which Strange sometimes prefaced his opinions and realized that he was marshalling his thoughts.

'There are several strands to the story, and they're all related to what I have to recognize as our absurd mystique of secrecy. First of all there's Hayter who believes that the country is in danger of falling apart. So, like the good soldier he is, he wants to mobilize all his forces. He'll do anything to preserve a way of life, what he'll call democracy. I know the Directorate is bristling with safeguards against mavericks, but when it comes to someone whose heart is so obviously in the right place, these all go to pieces. There's the code of the club for you. There's another thing about Hayter. He's an apocalyptic Tory – that's your phrase, James, I've remembered it tonight – so no one takes him seriously. Not completely. They can't believe he means what he says. It's too frightening, and no one in the department ever takes anything at face value. They pay him the compliment of interpreting his remarks and so lose their true meaning. But he does believe what he says, every word, and so he's dangerous.' Dangerfield seemed to be about to speak, but waved silence with his glass and leaned forward intently. 'Then you've got Preece. As you might expect, this is much nastier. Quite independently, he's been making money for years out of the secrets of our databases. He started on a small scale in Cheltenham in the Sixties and has gradually expanded. That's what Lister came across. It's a full-scale racket. You see, what the secrecy we live by can never do – and this is where Preece is so clever – is to stop someone exploiting the restrictions to his own advantage. Security can cut both ways if you're Preece. Secrecy can make you invulnerable – from the inside. In fact he's made a great deal of money out of our obsession with confidentiality. You see, if you break the system into tiny self-contained units operating on the "need to know" principle, then no one knows what anyone else is up to, and there's no room for the whole picture. That's considered a virtue by Dangerfield – '

'And the rest of my colleagues,' Dangerfield interpolated quietly.

The voice ran on implacably. '. . . but it means if you're as cunning as Preece you can process work through the system, and in an area that no one understands like computers no one knows enough to challenge him. Worse than that is the fact that many of our personnel that Preece has exploited have not been aware what they were doing. That's the nature of computer work.

'I blame myself, of course, for much of this. I recognize now that it was a mistake to insist on playing everything by the rule book. I was educated to believe in rules, but it was the rules in fact that gave Preece his big opportunities. All the files on this case, by the way, will be with me in the cottage when Dangerfield wants them. I have them in the boot now for reference.'

Dangerfield leant forward and stopped the machine. 'Was the car destroyed completely?'

'I don't know. I never saw. It must have been.' Dangerfield looked grim and switched the machine on again. Strange's urgent speech continued unbroken.

'The facts are that Preece and his associates, among them Tony Ellison, Mrs Lister's lover, have exploited classified information for cash. Information is a sort of currency like anything else, it just happens that Preece has had free access to rather a lot of it. Preece has supplied trading banks, large companies and multi-nationals with confidential data. He has sold personal information about prominent people without their knowledge. He has also worked as an agent for other private data-accumulating organizations, which, as you know, are not restrained by law.' Quitman recognized, with a grim frown, Strange grinding one of his most recent axes. But the tape was still running.

'The most appalling example of Preece's operation in action happened while Lister was still at Cheltenham. You'll remember that about four years ago the growth of terrorist violence led the Army to undertake a massive intelligence gathering exercise. With the aid of the Directorate's facilities they were able to store, for almost immediate retrieval, detailed information about the homes and fellow-residents of suspect citizens throughout the country. Well, Preece and Ellison used this operation to draw up what amounts to mail-order lists of criminals and terrorists. They then sold these to British and European arms dealers. Dammit, James,' Strange's anger overflowed suddenly, 'they were manipulating the Directorate to promote the supply of arms to the underworld right under my nose.'

Dangerfield stopped the tape momentarily. 'Who did Strange visit to corroborate this story?'

'It all fits into place,' Quitman replied. 'He made trips to an arms depot in Birmingham, and another in Manchester, and to several independent data-processing organizations in the Home Counties. He must be right.'

'Oh, he must be right,' murmured Dangerfield, starting the tape again. 'Strange was always right in the end.'

'The point is, James,' the disembodied voice continued, relentless, 'That there is potentially no limit to Preece's activities in this area. People are simply not aware yet of the extent to which damaging personal information can be gathered and how easily. Preece is exploiting what we like to think of as an open society against itself, and that's how it will disintegrate – when people with influence no longer care to defend it.'

'True,' said Dangerfield involuntarily.

'So Preece is simply a crook in pinstripe. What makes him interesting is that to survive in Whitehall he's had to evolve a philosophy, a front, if you like. As it happens, he's discovered that Michael Hayter's radical conservatism gives him the most scope. It is, after all, the philosophy that is most cynical about the means it employs to achieve a given political objective. Preece has undoubtedly exploited Hayter's fears.

'Hayter, on his side, wants to put the Directorate's computer power at the heart of the department as a whole. With Mayer and Preece he wants to control all the department's data and to initiate all its data-gathering programmes. That's typical civil service empire building. It wouldn't be so serious if Hayter wasn't willing to let Preece teach the Directorate some very dirty tricks. This is what is happening and Dangerfield is going to have to deal with it at once. I believe he'll be only too glad to have the chance to stop Hayter in his tracks, but it may take some cunning. When Hayter has the bit between his teeth he's not to be underestimated – as I know to my cost.' He was speaking now in a matter-of-fact tone, Quitman noticed, that seemed quite purged of his earlier bitterness.

'Hayter is so set on what he sees as a defence of our society that he will do anything, however dark and secret, to achieve his aim. Not to put too fine a point on it,' Strange could be heard to chuckle in the dark, 'and no one's ever accused me of that, have they, Hayter has now embarked on a programme designed to discredit, and in some cases ruin, people he sees as the enemies of the state. It's very discreet. But it's getting more and more extensive, and more and more unscrupulous. Lately I've discovered they're bugging a nuclear scientist with some allegedly suspect friends in radical organizations. He's doing vital government work, but that won't stop them exploiting any damaging inform-ation against him, and you can be sure that Preece will be making money out of any secrets he can pick up.'

'Who's that?' Quitman asked involuntarily looking at Dangerfield.

'It could be any one of a dozen people,' the controller replied wearily. For the first time he seemed defeated by these revelations.

'Needless to say,' continued Strange, 'the operation is very well camouflaged. What makes it all the harder to spot is that there are already plenty of our colleagues in the department as a whole who will manipulate newspaper editors, discredit statistics, prune vulnerable civil liberties in a crisis and wink at the growth of non-statutory police powers.

'But there is one case study, just one clue. Lister's notes from the VDU. What he saw was, in simple terms – Davenport can give you the details – part of a secret index. What Lister read was data referring to a number of so-called "subversives", among others, David Fenton, one of the most striking victims of this campaign. The plain fact is that the collapse of Fenton's reputation is the result of Preece's work, approved by Hayter. This is only one example. There are many more, less dramatic. The more the crisis of British society grows, the greater will be the temptation to enlarge the programme. The problem is that Hayter is not an elected politician, but a bureaucrat whose powers and behaviour are accountable to no one but Dangerfield.'

Quitman was intrigued to recognize the repeated assump

tions that Strange was making about Dangerfield's controlling influence. Had he, he wondered, realized at the end the extent to which he himself had been manipulated?

'. . . the picture is much blacker yet.' Strange seemed almost to be relishing his dramatic unfolding. 'Don't forget that Preece is basically a highly civilized gangster who's got his claws into Hayter. This is the vilest element of all. In order to provoke Hayter's worst fears, and thus to inject fresh urgency and vigour into the campaign against subversives, Preece is infiltrating the terrorist organizations that the department is supposed to be at war with. This is perfectly legitimate. The Special Branch and security people do it all the time. After all, the Directorate was partly formed to co-ordinate the information about such groups. But the purpose was to break them down this way. Preece, however, is using his contacts to incite these factions to further violence. This is an old Nazi trick. It justifies the emergency measures the department is taking these days, and, as it were, it proves the claims made by people like Preece and Hayter about the threat to our society. Oh, and by the way, Preece has also used such connections in a more conventional gangster way to get rid of people like Lister, for instance.'

Dangerfield let the tape run.

'As the violence increases, Hayter will develop the siege mentality of the old soldier. He'd rather drive his enemies into the open and have a full-scale offensive than attempt the less glamorous, undramatic low-key work of monitoring and surveillance. It's becoming a crusade if you like.'

For a moment, as he listened, the pedantic thought came to Quitman that all this had little to do with the chivalry of his studies, and then he felt ashamed at the irrelevance of this notion beside Strange's final sacrifice.

'None of these connections made any sense until I could see why Preece should want to adopt such a course. I mean, when did it start and why has it got worse with him? The answer lies with the state of the country today. I never saw that until I started to travel. We live a very sheltered life in Whitehall. It's clear to me, thanks to Tony Ellison, that

Preece thinks the country has no future. He sees with horror the rise in violence, the growth of crime, the erosion if status, the threat of living standards – you see all these things if you travel, James. All he wants to do now is pillage what he can from the ruins and run for it when the final collapse comes. Hayter who sees the same picture wants to make a stand and is being exploited by Preece. It's hard to know who's the more contemptible, but both will destroy us in the end.

'There it is, James. There are lights coming round the corner in my mirror, so they're still there, the watchers.' There was a faint grim chuckle. 'Shadows in the dark. God knows what's to be done. What's the Latin? – you'll remember – about those that the gods destroy they first make mad. The main thing is to admit that it is happening and that we've made it happen. I can do this now, though it's taken all this time on the road to do it. Look after yourself, James. You made this investigation possible. It was a brave thing to do. I'll leave the rest to Dangerfield. God bless.'

There was a click. Dangerfield was sunk in silence. Quitman thought of Strange alone in the darkness, and as he did so, the music on the tape came back again, a slow mournful solo horn that Quitman recognized as the dying cadences of the Elegy in Britten's *Serenade*.

He roused himself. 'What will happen now?' he asked lamely.

Dangerfield began to speak slowly, formulating his reply with caution. The hoarse, powerful voice was quite steady, without a trace of bitterness, as he filled in the past. 'Before Strange, the issue between Hayter and myself was not of strategy but of tactics. Michael has always wanted to fight a hot war, on the principle that the ends justify the means. I, and other senior colleagues, have disagreed with him. His conservatism has always seemed too radical for us. I believe that when we abandon our traditional methods we cease to be civilized. He claims that we shall cease to be civilized unless we abandon them. But now . . .' He shrugged with a defeated air. 'We are confronted with a political problem far more complex than mere radical conservatism. Strange is right. Hayter plainly represents an important body of opinion within the department. He couldn't have done what he has without the tacit approval of colleagues.' He paused, refilled Quitman's glass, and considered the question.

'Hayter himself is not a problem. He happens to be a coward. He will retire at once, of his own accord. He is also an old-fashioned patriot. He may even take his own life. He knows all about the gun in the library.' Dangerfield was very matter-of-fact. 'Preece is more difficult. He's what we used to call a cad. He won't resign, become indignant with self-justification, I imagine, and blame it all on Michael and his subordinates. He will have to be moved.'

Quitman was outraged by this answer. Despite the pain in his back, he made to get up to face Dangerfield. 'But that's impossible. You can't let it rest. Won't there be a trial? Justice?' He was speechless.

'And expose the department, worse, the secrets of C Directorate to public scrutiny?' Dangerfield queried. 'I'm all in favour of open government, Quitman, but I will not have Preece *sub poena* every file in the building.' He waved Quitman back to his chair. 'I can assure you that Preece will end his days at the Ministry of Agriculture administering the butter mountain. He will have to live with his disgrace. That's far worse. And C Directorate will be properly reconstituted under my complete control.' There was a tremor of satisfaction in his voice.

'So there's nothing to be done.'

'On the contrary, there's a great deal – in secret.'

'But! But – !' Quitman was angry. 'You've heard what Strange has said! Can't you learn even now? Secrecy has been your undoing and you still can't break the habit.'

'It's not a habit, it's a necessity – whatever the risks. You forget that we can build safeguards into a reformed system. Occasionally, Quitman,' Dangerfield concluded, with measured imperturbability, 'we have to tell lies for the greater good. Equally, we sometimes have to live with crimes for the greater good. Strange will not have a public vengeance. He wouldn't have wanted it anyway – a remarkable man.'

There were no more arguments, apart from the useless moral ones. As he and Dangerfield sat staring into the shadows of the ebbing day, Quitman felt the cynicism of power envelope him like a fog.

Eric Ambler

A world of espionage and counter-espionage, of sudden violence and treacherous calm; of blackmailers, murderers, gun-runners—and none too virtuous heroes. This is the world of Eric Ambler. 'Unquestionably our best thriller writer.' *Graham Greene*. 'He is incapable of writing a dull paragraph.' *Sunday Times* 'Eric Ambler is a master of his craft.' *Sunday Telegraph*

SEND NO MORE ROSES 95p
THE DARK FRONTIER 80p
DOCTOR FRIGO 80p
JOURNEY INTO FEAR 80p
JUDGMENT ON DELTCHEV 80p
THE LEVANTER 85p
THE LIGHT OF DAY 85p
THE MASK OF DIMITRIOS 85p
THE NIGHT-COMERS 80p
PASSAGE OF ARMS 80p

Fontana Paperbacks

Fontana Paperbacks

Fontana is a leading paperback publisher of fiction and non-fiction, with authors ranging from Alistair MacLean, Agatha Christie and Desmond Bagley to Solzhenitsyn and Pasternak, from Gerald Durrell and Joy Adamson to the famous Modern Masters series.

In addition to a wide-ranging collection of internationally popular writers of fiction, Fontana also has an outstanding reputation for history, natural history, military history, psychology, psychiatry, politics, economics, religion and the social sciences.

All Fontana books are available at your bookshop or newsagent; or can be ordered direct. Just fill in the form and list the titles you want.

FONTANA BOOKS, Cash Sales Department, G.P.O. Box 29, Douglas, Isle of Man, British Isles. Please send purchase price, plus 8p per book. Customers outside the U.K. send purchase price, plus 10p per book. Cheque, postal or money order. No currency.

NAME (Block letters) _____

ADDRESS _____

_____

_____